THE NEIGHBOURS

DANIEL HURST

www.danielhurstbooks.com

D1087069

1

PROLOGUE

There are lots of good things to be enjoyed when you receive the keys to your new home and finally set foot inside it as the official occupier for the first time. Having your own space. Being able to get creative with the decorating. And best of all, knowing that you now have somewhere to call your own. Then there are the things that aren't quite as exciting as those initial joys but are still benefits of the house purchasing process, like inviting your family around for Sunday dinner or hosting a housewarming party for all your friends. Or maybe, even making new friends by meeting your new neighbours and getting to know them a little better.

When a person buys a house, they have a pretty good idea about the building they are moving into, and they might even know about the other buildings in the area too. The best schools for any future children. The most popular restaurant that just has to be experienced. And the nearest supermarket where you can go to buy your essentials on a weekly basis. But what about the other buildings on your new street, or rather, what about the people already living inside them?

There is a saying that you can choose your friends, but you can't choose your family.

That might be true, but it can also be extended to include neighbours because you can't choose them either. You just move in and get what you're given. Usually, that isn't a problem. Most neighbours are polite, respectful and cheery enough, even if your relationship with them only ever extends to a quick wave or a ten-second chat on your driveway as you leave or enter your house. But sometimes, you can get unlucky with your neighbours. Sometimes, they aren't the kind of people that you want to live close to at all.

Sometimes, they can turn out to be the neighbours from hell…

1

KATIE

Staring at the mountain of boxes in front of me isn't going to get them unpacked any quicker, but right now, it's all I can do. I'm overwhelmed by the size of the task ahead of me, and my only response to that is to stand here and keep looking at the various cardboard cubes and wonder how I ever came to own this much stuff in my lifetime. Of course, the answer to that is quite a simple one. I have this much stuff because I bought this much stuff. Sales, shopping sprees and spontaneous spending have all led to this situation here, with me standing in the spare bedroom of my new home scratching my head and wondering just how I am supposed to fit all of this stuff into the one wardrobe we have in here. I could call my husband, Sean, into the room to help with the dilemma, but I'm not going to do that because I have a pretty good idea what his first words would be if I did.

'I told you that you had too much stuff!'

That would be closely followed by the questions *'Do you really need all these extra coats?'* and *'Can't you just get rid of some of these shoes,'* neither of which deserve an answer because that answer is obviously a big fat *'No.'* Then all there will be left for him to do is huff and puff and walk back out of the bedroom while shaking his head and leaving me to it.

It's not often that I am envious of my partner, but I am right now because I know that he has already unpacked all of his things, and that means he is free to enjoy some of his evening while I am stuck up here trying to figure out where to put all of the items that I haven't been able to unpack yet. It's not that Sean is unhelpful or doesn't pull his weight. It's just that he owns so much less than me that it didn't take him long at all to get his stuff in the wardrobe and chuck the empty suitcases in the attic. I, on the other hand, could probably spend the next week unpacking my belongings and still have a few boxes left over to look through at a later date.

Fortunately, I do have a lot more time on my hands than my husband does, so I don't have to get everything done in one go. He will have to go to his office on Monday and spend all day sitting at his desk, whereas I work from home so I could always do some more unpacking then. Technically, I should be using that time to work too, but I'm a freelance artist, and that means I can pick and choose my own hours. At least that's the glamorous description of it anyway. The unglamorous version is that I don't have many customers at the moment, so

I'm not exactly overwhelmed with the urgency to get my paintbrushes out and create some new art.

Painting is my passion, and I'm thrilled that I get to do it full-time, but that's only because Sean is paid so well in his job that it doesn't really matter if I have a lean month or two on the art front. But that doesn't mean I slack off. Far from it. I love nothing more than sitting down in front of a blank canvas and creating a new painting, but it would be nice if I was actually able to sell more than the occasional painting to somebody outside of my family or friends. But I'm getting off track. I'm supposed to be thinking about unpacking, not painting.

I guess that's my biggest problem.

Overthinking.

Coming to the grim realisation that these boxes aren't going to magically unpack themselves, I drop to my knees, not in prayer, but because this position will make it easier for me to go through my possessions. As I scour through the first box, which is full of more dresses that I'm not even sure I'll ever wear again, but I can't be too careful, I find myself smiling at the fact that I'm even in this house at all. Sean and I first viewed this property three months ago and we were instantly charmed by its current state as well as its potential. It's a two-bedroom, detached house on a small cul-de-sac, so small that there are only three other houses alongside this one.

This house was the last one on the street to be built and is only five years old as opposed to the three other homes here, all of which have stood since the sixties. It seems some clever architect was able to squeeze one more property in and make himself a lot of money, at least if the prices around here are anything to go by. It's also the reason why our house number is Two A, while the house next door to our right is just Number Two. I don't know why they couldn't just make us Number Four and be done with it but never mind. But I'm sure the postman gets confused every now and again.

It was the relatively new build of the house, coupled with the quiet setting, that made it very appealing to Sean and I when we were house-hunting. Not only does a cul-de-sac mean no extra cars driving down the street, but fewer houses means fewer neighbours, and fewer neighbours means fewer cars taking up all the parking spots and leaving us struggling to get our vehicle on and off the driveway every day. Our previous house was a great property, but it was on a very busy street, and we lost track of the number of times we had our driveway blocked or almost got run over by a speeding motorist using our street as a shortcut to get somewhere else. This cul-de-sac certainly appealed to us, and the quietness of it made it seem like the perfect place for Sean and I to start the family we have always dreamed about.

But before we can get to the fun part of trying for our first child, we need to get this house in order. We only moved in this morning with the help of family members and a couple of burly removals men, and that means there is a lot to do around here to get it how we want it. But we have a plan. I will tackle the inside of the house while Sean will deal with the outside. Some of the upstairs rooms need redecorating, while the back garden is a mess of weeds and dead grass, but together, we will work hard and transform the parts of this property that aren't quite to our tastes yet. But thankfully, there isn't as much to do as there could be. The downstairs is immaculate, and the main selling point is the brand new kitchen that the previous homeowners had installed. With marble surfaces, a large breakfast bar and beautifully styled cupboards, it's every cook's dream kitchen, and I certainly love to cook. It's a stunning room, and I can't wait to get the full use out of it. I'm also very grateful to the previous owners for having the vision, and the money, to decorate in such a way, and while I do love it, I can't help feeling a little sad about the fact that neither of them will ever get to enjoy it again.

The former owners of this house were a couple called James and Sarah, and they were in their mid-thirties, just like Sean and I are now, but sadly, that's where the similarities end. While we are in love and happily married, it seems they are the exact opposite these days. Their reason for selling this place was because they were separating and needed the money from the sale to divide up in their divorce, and that was also the reason why they were in such a rush to get out. We were just as keen to move in and were thrilled when we had our offer accepted, especially because it was a little under the asking price, and we got here in the end, though it took longer than it should have thanks to the usual array of slimy solicitors and errant estate agents getting involved too. I am glad we are here now, but I do feel sad for the previous owners because they looked like they had made a lovely couple once, although those days were obviously in the past.

I don't know the reason for their separation, and I was hardly going to ask, but from picking up subtle hints and clues during our viewings, I think one of them cheated on the other. If I had to guess, I'd say it was the man because it's usually the man, isn't it? But maybe I'm doing the poor guy a disservice, and it might have been her fault instead. Who knows? Either way, they are out and we are in, and I wish them all the best, but that's as far as my sympathies can go. That's because as lovely as they made this home, it's not perfect and it's going to take time to get it how we want it. Neither of them were obviously green-fingered if the state of the garden is anything to go by, and there is certainly plenty of space here that could have been utilised better. It's all space that I am definitely going to need if I am going to have any chance of fitting all my clothes and shoes into this place.

But with one box already unpacked and only fifteen more to go, I'm feeling optimistic. I'm happy, Sean is happy, and soon, this home will be happy too, possibly even filled with the sounds of a baby's laughter in the not-too-distant future.

One thing at a time, though.

Let's move on to box number two.

2

SEAN

Our first night in the house was fun. Katie and I got a takeaway, had a couple of drinks and watched a movie before finally reaching our hastily-constructed bed, exhausted after a day of unpacking but excited about the future ahead. But the second day hasn't been quite as fun. That's because I've spent most of it trying to dig out all of the weeds in the garden and give some TLC to the lawn, which certainly needs it. I'm not the best gardener in the world, but I'm pretty confident that I can't be any worse than the last owners were. This grass looks like it's been burnt, which is strange because North-West England is hardly known for its scorching weather, which leads me to think it's more to do with the poor groundskeeping of the last person to look after this lawn rather than the searing sun overhead. I've definitely got my work cut out here, but I'm in no rush. We're going to be in this house for a long time, potentially even for the rest of our lives, so I'm sure that's enough opportunity for me to turn this bedraggled patch of grass into a luscious lawn.

But it seems like I'm not going to have much more time to work on it today because no sooner have I headed inside for a quick cup of tea then I am met by the sight of my wife, and she has a suggestion for what we should do next.

'We need to go and introduce ourselves to the neighbours,' Katie tells me before I've even had a chance to put the kettle on.

'Sure, but there's no rush. We've only just moved in.'

'But this is such a secluded street. We really need to make an effort.'

'I know that, and we will. But it doesn't have to be today, does it?'

'I'd prefer it if it was. Let's just break the ice with them so that it's not awkward if we see them on the driveway later.'

I could potentially get away with trying to have my cup of tea first, and maybe I could even get the opportunity to get changed into more presentable clothing, but one thing I definitely won't be able to do is put off going around to the neighbours today. That's because when my wife has her mind set to something, then it has to happen. There is simply no other alternative, and I learnt that the hard way when we first started dating.

After quenching my thirst with a glass of water from the tap and after swapping my scruffy gardening clothes for a smarter looking t-shirt and jeans, I have joined my wife out on our street where we are making our way towards the first house on our list. Thankfully, there's only three other houses on this cul-de-sac besides our own, but Katie is right. It's so secluded that it would be very awkward if we were to live here without getting to know the other people around us.

So that brings us to house number one.

This property is to the left of ours if you were looking at it from the front, and it's also on the end of the street. There is no car in the driveway as we approach the front door, so it's hardly a surprise when there is no answer a few seconds later. I knock twice so that Katie can't accuse me of not trying, but all I can do after that is shrug my shoulders and lead her back onto the road and over to house number two. This is the house to the right of ours, and while it looks the same from the front, I've already noticed that the back garden is immaculate, having spied it from one of our upstairs rooms yesterday. Whoever lives here is obviously a keen gardener, and I suspect they are mortified at the state of our garden at the moment, but I don't get a chance to find out because nobody is home at this house either.

'This is going well,' I say sarcastically as Katie and I make our way back down the driveway and head towards the third and final house we plan to call at today. But unlike the first two, there is a car on this drive, and I suspect our next knock on a door will get answered now.

Sure enough, I see movement on the other side of the frosted glass of the front door, and when the door is eventually opened, my wife and I come face to face with a man who looks like he has just stepped right off the page of a male modelling magazine. He has piercing blue eyes, a chiselled jawline and a set of teeth so straight and white that they put my yellowish pegs to shame. I'm struck by the fact that I've noticed all that about this man in a split second, but if I have noticed then I can be sure that my wife has noticed it too. Sure enough, it only takes a quick glance at her beside me to see that she is just as surprised at the unexpectedly handsome appearance of one of our new neighbours.

'Hey, how's it going?' the man asks with such casual confidence that it's almost as if we aren't strangers but people whom he has known all of his life.

But we are strangers, and we are standing on his doorstep, so I better introduce ourselves quickly so as not to make this awkward, even if this guy looks anything but awkward.

'So sorry to bother you, but my wife and I have just moved into Number Two A, and we thought we'd just pop round to say hi,' I say, doing my best to keep my lips closed as much as

I can so that I don't offend this man with great teeth with my own inferior gnashers. 'I'm Sean, and this is Katie.'

'Oh, of course. I saw the removal truck yesterday and wanted to come over and help, but I was a little tied up here,' the man replies, beaming widely. 'I'm Chris. Pleasure to meet you.'

He extends a hand out towards Katie first because he's obviously a gentleman, and they greet each other with a light shake. Then he offers his hand to me, and we engage in a firm handshake, although my vigour is all down to me trying to give off a good impression while I suspect his is just because he is the kind of man that always gives a strong handshake.

'How are you finding the new place? Are you settling in?'

'Yeah, it's great,' Katie replies enthusiastically. 'This is such a lovely street.'

'It's quiet but cosy. You're going to love it here.'

Chris is still smiling at both of us, but I'm not a fan of small talk on strangers' doorsteps, so I'm just about to wrap this little meet-and-greet up when I see movement behind him. There's somebody else in the house, and after quickly clocking the wedding ring on Chris' left hand, I realise who it must be.

We're about to meet his wife.

Chris must sense her presence behind him because he turns around and steps to the side, and that allows us to get a first look at the woman who snared this ridiculously good-looking man. But if Chris's appearance is noteworthy then the woman he lives with is off the charts.

Brunette. Brown eyes. And a smile so show-stopping that I wonder if I haven't stepped off my street and onto the set of a Hollywood movie.

'This is Abi,' Chris says as his wife joins us. 'Abi, these are our new neighbours.'

The woman in the doorway doesn't stop smiling as she greets us both and shakes our hands, and even though I know it's silly, I definitely feel a shiver down my spine when I get my chance to touch her skin. Unlike her husband's handshake, this one is as light as a feather, and I get a glimpse of her red nail varnish before she whisks her hand away and returns it to her slender side.

'It's so exciting to have new neighbours. You're going to love it here,' Abi says to us, looking at both Katie and I in equal measure.

'That's what I just said,' Chris cuts in. 'This really is a great place to live.'

They both sure do seem convinced that this is the place to be, and that is good to hear, not that it would have made too much difference for us if not. We liked the house, and we like the street, so we're not sure that anything could have put us off buying here. But it is always good to get an endorsement from the neighbours, and we certainly seem to have got that.

'Well, it was lovely to meet you, but we better get back,' I say, trying to make my voice sound as casual and as confident as Chris's does when he speaks. 'There's lots to do. I'm sure you understand,'

'Of course. Do you need a hand with anything?' Chris asks because that's seemingly the kind of guy that he is.

'I think we're okay, thanks,' I reply quickly, but Katie doesn't seem so sure.

'Are you any good in the garden?' she asks Chris. 'Sean's got his work cut out getting ours back under control.'

I'm just about to laugh off her comment and say that I have it covered, not just for our new neighbours' benefit but for my own as well, when Chris flashes that pristine smile of his again and tells me that he would be happy to give me a hand in the garden if I want it.

I do my best to downplay how much I could use the extra help, but Chris is not having any of it and tells me that he will go and get some scruffy clothes on before coming round to assist me shortly. Looking at him now in his smart attire, I can scarcely believe that a man like him owns scruffy clothes, but he disappears back into the house to get changed before Abi tells us both that he will be around in a minute.

I thank her and turn to leave, feeling strangely pleased that I wasn't wearing my own scruffy clothes for the first time I met her today even though I have no idea why I would need to impress her before leading my wife up the driveway back to our house.

Katie waits until Abi has closed her front door before speaking so that she is presumably out of earshot, but when she does, I can see that my wife is very impressed with our new neighbours.

'Aren't they a good-looking couple,' she tells me as if I hadn't been able to notice it for myself. 'I wonder how they met.'

'Probably on a fashion shoot,' I mutter back as we reach our driveway and head around the side of the house to where my beleaguered back garden awaits.

'It's nice that he's going to help you,' Katie muses as we reach our patio and I look out across our pitiful lawn. 'He's lovely. They both are.'

If I was a little insecure then I might think that my wife added that last sentence to hide the fact that she was enamoured with Chris, but I'm doing my best not to be. But I'm not stupid. I know she will be attracted to Chris, just like I'm a little attracted to Abi. But that doesn't mean anything. They're just our neighbours, and

21

we'll probably hardly see them again. I'm sure they have lots of good-looking friends who they spend their spare time with, doing whatever good-looking people do.

Then again, Chris is already at our front door, and he has a spade in his hand, ready to get to work in my garden.

Maybe we'll be seeing much more of him.

Maybe we'll be seeing a lot more of his wife too.

3

KATIE

Our first weekend in the house is almost over, and it's been a productive one. Despite my initial laziness, as well as my husband's scepticism, I was able to unpack all of the boxes of my belongings and fit them all into our new home, even if it meant hoarding some things away in the attic where they're likely to just end up getting covered in cobwebs and thrown away in the future. Sean has also done his part, making a solid start on the garden, but he did have help. Our neighbour, Chris, gave up a couple of hours of his time to assist my husband, and we were both grateful for that. It seems like we might have a new friend, or rather, a couple of new friends. Chris and his wife, Abi, are lovely, and I presume we will be seeing a lot more of them in the future and not just because we live so close to each other now. It's also because they have told us they sometimes liked to organise social events on the street. That sounds fun, and I'm glad we are already being warmly welcomed into our new place of residence. All that and we still haven't even met the people who live in the other two houses on our cul-de-sac.

The other driveways are still empty, so I'm guessing the homeowners are still out, and according to Chris, it might not be as easy to meet them as we first thought. The house to our left, Number One, is apparently occupied by a forty-year-old man who works away a lot on oil rigs in the North Sea, and when he is home, he is busy spending time with his fifteen-year-old son, who he lost custody of to his estranged wife. On the other side of us is Number Two and Chris tells us that an elderly couple live there. We're told they are in their early seventies and both retired, and when they're not pottering around in their garden, they're usually out spending their pension money on trips to the seaside or on new items for their home, which they obviously take great pride in if the appearance from the outside of it can be any indicator. They really have given great care to their garden, which might be why Sean feels so motivated to get ours up to scratch too, and I presume the inside of their home is just as well-kept. Maybe I'll get to see it one day, but first, we have to actually meet and greet them. But that can be a job for another day now. It's Sunday night, and it's time for a little relaxation before another week of work begins.

I'm currently in the kitchen preparing a chicken pesto pasta dish for our evening meal while Sean is upstairs ironing the last of his shirts for the upcoming days in the office. I'm all ready myself for Monday morning and the blank canvas currently sitting on an easel in the spare bedroom is proof of that. Tomorrow morning, just after Sean has left the house and started his commute, I will make my own much shorter one into the bedroom where I will take out my paintbrushes and palettes and begin work on my next piece of art, and this one will definitely sell.

At least that is what I'm telling myself anyway.

It takes me a little longer than usual to get the food cooked and served up into two bowls, simply because I'm still finding my way around this new kitchen as well as still remembering which cupboard I put all the bowls into when I unpacked them earlier. But finally, the food is on the table and our hunger can be satisfied, as well as our need for a strong drink after all the upheaval and stress of the last few days.

'Cheers,' I say to my husband as I raise my glass of red wine towards him across the table. 'Here's to the new house.'

'To the new house,' he replies as he clinks his glass against mine and takes a sip before letting out a deep exhale that he sometimes does after his first alcoholic drink in a while.

We eat quickly and drink just as fast, a consequence of a day spent on our feet doing menial chores, but we still find the time to chat about a few of the first jobs we plan to do on the house, like redecorating the main bedroom and painting over that awful wallpaper in the hallway. We also talk about Chris and Abi and speculate as to what some of the social events could be that they like to organise every now and again. Barbecues, perhaps. Maybe a wine and cheese night. And who knows, there might even be the odd street party to attend. I guess we'll find out in due course.

By the time our pasta bowls are empty and our wine glasses have been topped up again, Sean and I are feeling full and very satisfied with our current life situation. We're feeling so relaxed that we decide the washing-up can wait for the morning and choose instead to go into the living room and put on a movie on our widescreen TV that was one of the first things to be unpacked. As we settle onto the sofa and use the remote control to scroll through the channels for something to watch, I am feeling very contented. With this evening. With this house. And with my partner.

Everything is just right.

And then we heard somebody tapping on our front door.

Sean and I glance at each other as we both hear the knock at the same time, and both of our expressions tell the other one that we have no idea who it could be. But of course, one of us has to say it to reinforce our surprise.

'Who do you think that could be?' I ask my husband as I reach over and carefully place my half-full wine glass onto the top of an empty plastic container that I had been hoping Sean was going to put in the garage earlier.

'I've no idea. Your parents?'

'No, they're coming round later in the week. What about yours?'

'It can't be. They wouldn't just turn up without checking we were in first.'

Then we hear the knocking again. It's not a hard knocking, but it's not a soft knocking either. It's a polite, respectful knock but the fact it has happened twice now suggests it does need to be answered rather than ignored.

'Could it be Chris again?' Sean suggests, and I shrug my shoulders.

'Maybe.'

'God, I hope he's not going to be one of those needy neighbours who calls round every day.'

'I'm sure he's not. Just go and answer it.'

Sean lets out a sigh as he puts his glass down before getting up and heading out of the room, leaving me curled up on the sofa with the volume on the TV turned down so that I can hear exactly who is out there when my husband opens the door.

When he does, I detect a male voice, but it's not one I recognise so it can't be Chris. Then I hear an unfamiliar female voice too, and now I'm really intrigued as to who it could be out there. Then I hear some more talking, but I can't make out the words. Did I hear a name then? Are they making introductions? I want to know what is going on, but I'm not going to go hovering in the hallway as that could be awkward. But it sounds like I won't need to do that anyway. That's because I hear the man ask if he and his wife can come in, and to my surprise, Sean agrees that they can.

I hear the front door close and the shuffling of several feet on the hallway carpet, so I sit up quickly on the sofa and try to make myself look a little more presentable than I currently am for our mystery guests. I've just managed to get my scraggly hair into a ponytail when Sean re-enters the room with a slightly awkward look on his face. But before I can ask him what's going on, two more people walk into the room behind him.

An elderly man and an elderly woman, grey-haired, slightly hunched and smiling.

'Hello dear,' the woman says to me as if I am a cherished relative of hers and not just some person she is meeting for the first time.

'This living room looks just like ours,' the man says as he looks around. 'Except everything is on the opposite side.'

And then it's finally time for Sean to speak, and he is the one who I was really waiting on because he is the one who can presumably tell me who these two strangers are.

'This is Albert and Eileen,' my husband tells me as I continue to inspect the old couple standing beside him. 'They're our next-door neighbours.'

4

What started out as a very quiet night in involving just me and my wife has now turned into the pair of us hosting our next-door neighbours, and that's why I'm currently rummaging around in one of the boxes in the kitchen for an old bottle of Scotch that I'm sure is in here somewhere. If whiskey seems like a strong drink for a Sunday night then I would be in agreement, but it's not for me, nor is it for my wife. It's not even for Albert, the charming old man who just knocked on my door and introduced himself and the woman standing beside him before asking if they could come in for a quick chat. It's for Eileen, Albert's wife, and a woman who obviously has a penchant for a stiff drink to close out her weekend.

I finally lay my hands on the bottle I am looking for and remove it from the box before unscrewing the lid and going in search of a suitable glass to pour a measure into. I'm sure it doesn't really matter which glass I find in the cupboard, but I feel like I want to make a good first impression on our new neighbours, so I take the time to find a proper whiskey glass instead of just any old receptacle. Fortunately, I do have one whiskey glass in my kitchen, so I pour the drink and put the lid back on the bottle, sealing it up for a future date when it will be opened again. But I'm not much of a whiskey drinker. In fact, I'm not much of a drinker at all these days. I tend to limit myself to a couple of glasses of wine every now and again, and that's because I'm starting to be more conscious about my health as I get older. I'm only in my mid-thirties, so I'd like to think that I have plenty of years ahead of me yet, but that doesn't mean I can't plan ahead and try to avoid any health issues that might crop up down the line thanks to an unhealthy diet and binge drinking. That reminds me, I must look for a new gym in the area this week, so I can get back into my fitness routine. I cancelled my last gym membership before we moved here as it would have been too far to drive now, but that's no excuse for not finding one a little closer to my new home.

'Are you okay?'

I spin around and see Katie entering the room, presumably coming to check on me to see why it's taking me so long to get Eileen's drink ready.

'Yeah, I just had to look for the bottle. But I found it now,' I reply, holding up the glass with the single measure of whiskey in it to prove that I have actually been doing something in the kitchen and not just hiding in here to avoid any awkward conversations in the living room.

'Well, hurry up. I need some help in there,' Katie tells me in a low whisper. 'You know I'm not good at making small talk with strangers.'

I smile at my wife's anxious ways and let her know that she no longer has to entertain our neighbours by herself by walking out of the kitchen and into the living room where Albert and Eileen are sitting a little rigidly on one of our two sofas.

'Here you go,' I say as I hand the glass to Eileen. 'It's all I've got in. I hope you like it.'

'I'm sure it will be fine,' Eileen tells me with a warm smile before putting the glass to her lips and taking a small sip. If she doesn't like it then she does a very good job of not letting it show because her expression remains the same either way.

'Are you sure I can't get you anything, Albert?' I ask the old man next to her.

'No, I'm fine, thank you,' he replies, repeating the answer he gave to me when I made the offer a few moments ago. 'I had a cup of tea just before I came over and I better not have anything else now, or I'll be up and down to the toilet all night.'

I laugh at his joke, although I'm aware that it might not actually be a joke, before taking a seat on the sofa opposite them besides Katie who has already curled up again with her glass of wine to hand.

'Aren't you having a drink?' Eileen asks me when she notices that I haven't got anything in my hand.

'No, I've already had enough myself this evening,' I tell her, aware that I am speaking more eloquently than usual, and my posture is much stiffer than it would be if I was just relaxing without guests. 'I don't tend to drink much these days.'

'Sean likes going to the gym,' Katie cuts in there, seizing an opportunity to enter the conversation herself, which I know she would have been waiting for to make herself feel a little less awkward in front of our visitors.

'Ahh, a fitness fanatic,' Albert muses with a wry smile.

'I wouldn't say I'm a fanatic, but I do try and stay in shape,' I reply with a dismissive wave of my left hand.

'Are you a member of a gym?' Eileen asks me in her slightly meek voice before raising a trembling hand back to her lips and having another sip of her drink.

'I used to be, but I cancelled my membership when we moved. I need to find a new one.'

'There's a good gym on Westgate Road,' Albert helpfully points out. 'Not too far from here at all.'

'Great, I'll look into it,' I tell him, grateful for the suggestion.

I'm then expecting the conversation to move away from me and my health habits and onto the more traditional topics of conversation when two sets of neighbours meet each other for the first time.

Are you settling in? How long have you lived on this street? What day do the bins get collected?

But to my surprise, that's not what happens at all. Instead, Albert puts a hand on his wife's leg and sits forward a little in his seat before clearing his raspy throat and appearing like he has something important to say.

'Now, I know you two are still finding your feet here and will need a little more time to settle in, but we thought it best to call around and give you some pointers about what it will be like for you living here,' the old man says very seriously.

I glance at my wife who looks just as puzzled as I am before asking Albert what he means.

'I'm talking about the other neighbours,' he replies, and I notice that while his eyes looked weary when he arrived here, they are now looking much more alert as they stare at me from behind his pair of spectacles.

'What about the other neighbours?' Katie asks slightly hesitantly.

Albert looks to Eileen to take over from there, and she seems happy to do so.

'Have you met Chris and Abi yet?' she asks us, and we tell her that we have so she goes on. 'What did you think of them?'

'They seem lovely,' Katie replies, and I back that summation up.

'Attractive?' Albert asks.

'Well, yeah, I suppose so,' my wife answers the question. 'They are a good looking couple.'

But that response seems to be concerning to Albert because he looks back to his wife again.

'Chris and Abi are very friendly and very good looking,' Eileen tells us. 'But that's the problem. They can be too friendly and too good looking for their own good, and for the good of others too.'

What the hell is that supposed to mean?

My face must express how confused I am at what I have just heard because Eileen quickly adds to her surprising statement with another one.

'Don't let them get too close to you. They will try and seduce you. It depends what you're into, of course. Not every couple is as traditional as we are. But if you value the sanctity of your marriage, and I presume you do, then just be careful around them. We've seen other marriages destroyed by them, and we'd hate for that same thing to happen to you.'

I don't need to look in a mirror to know that my jaw is hanging open and my eyes are wide. To say I'm stunned by what I have just heard would be an understatement. Has this dear old woman really just said what I think she said? That our attractive neighbours are going to try and seduce us and potentially break up our marriage? Is she for real?

'I know it sounds a little strange, but it's true,' Albert adds at this point. 'We have seen it happen before, including to the last couple who lived here before you. Did you know they were getting divorced?'

Katie and I look at each other before nodding our heads.

'We suspected that was the reason for them selling the house,' I say, and Albert takes his turn to nod at us.

'It was such a shame. They were a lovely couple when they moved in here. Very much in love. But then they met Chris and Abi, and things were never the same again.'

I know Albert turned down my offer of a drink when he got here earlier, but I can't help wondering if he hasn't been drinking something strong all day before coming around here to tell us this story. That might explain where he is getting all these ideas from. Yet just from looking at him allows me to see that he is stone-cold sober, and that is perhaps the most troubling part about this whole thing. He's not drunk, and neither is his wife, even though she has a glass of whiskey in her hand. They both seem very sane and very sensible, and that makes all of this even more disconcerting.

That's because it makes it feel like they are telling us the truth.

5

This evening has got very weird. I need more wine. The problem with that is the bottle is in the kitchen and it would require either me or Sean to get up off the sofa to fetch it, and neither of us wants to do that because we are too transfixed by what we are being told by our elderly neighbours.

Albert and Eileen have just finished telling us about Chris and Abi, or rather, the problem with Chris and Abi. Apparently, they are not just an attractive couple who are looking to make friends. They are an attractive couple who are looking to make friends who they might then be able to turn into lovers. Of course, both my husband and I are stunned at this revelation, and that's backed up by the fact that all we have done since hearing it is ask questions in return.

'What do you mean?'

'Are they swingers?'

And the question I have just asked, which is 'How are they still together if they keep cheating on each other too?'

Albert fields that question and tells us that Chris and Abi obviously have an open relationship, whereby they aren't put off by either one of them being intimate with somebody else. That is shocking for me to hear because from where I come from and how I was raised, I never knew marriage could be like that. I thought you picked your partner, made your vows and then stayed loyal to each other for the rest of your days. Or maybe I'm just as old fashioned as the clothes that Albert and Eileen are wearing right now. Maybe there is another way for married couples to behave, and by the sounds of it, Chris and Abi are having a great time exploring it. But it doesn't seem like everybody else is. Albert and Eileen have told us that they have seen other couples broken up by our neighbour's seductive powers, including the last couple to live here before us, James and Sarah. That is ominous, and it also explains why they have come around to give us a word of warning. We are to be careful around Chris and Abi if we value our marriage, which of course, we both do. But surely this is a bit much. Surely we don't need a literal warning. This is like something out of a TV show, not real-life suburbia. I'm sure Sean and I could have restrained ourselves around Chris and Abi without needing our elderly neighbours to give us a heads-up beforehand. But according to Albert and Eileen, we are to be on our guard now because no matter how strong we think our marriage is, it will apparently be tested to its absolute limits if we let Chris and Abi get any closer to us.

I could be forgiven for thinking that the shocks and surprises are over for the night after this, but I'm wrong again because no sooner have Albert and Eileen finished warning us about the people who live at Number Three then they move on to warning us about the people who live at Number One.

'You won't have met Ian yet,' Eileen says as if she is some wise old sage, which perhaps she is. 'He works away on the rigs a lot. But he'll be back soon. Sometime this week, I expect. And he'll have his son with him when he arrives. He's called Jackson, and he's a very spirited young soul.'

'That's the polite way of putting it,' Albert cuts in, and he shakes his head to show an obvious disdain for the fifteen-year-old son of our next-door neighbour. 'Another way would be to call him a nuisance.'

It's not really fair to talk about somebody's personality before we have met them, and it's certainly not fair to judge them, but I can't help asking for them to elaborate.

'He's trouble,' Albert says, still shaking his head. 'He has no regard for other people's privacy or property. I've seen him in our garden before, and I've even caught him trying to steal something from my garage before after I left it open by mistake.'

'Have you spoken to his dad?' Sean asks because that would seem like the obvious thing to do.

'Ian? He's just as useless as his son is,' Albert scoffs before Eileen puts a hand on her husband's arm, presumably as a sign for him to calm down in the presence of others.

Albert heeds his wife's gentle warning and stops talking, leaving it up to her to carry on explaining the situation for him.

'Ian doesn't tend to get too involved in what his son gets up to when he's staying with him. He mainly just sits in his armchair and drinks lager when he's home from the rigs, leaving Jackson free to roam around and cause trouble where he sees fit. It's a waste of time trying to get him to tell his son to behave. Believe me, we've more than tried over the years.'

'But surely he can't be that bad or you could just call the police,' I say because that's what I would do if a parent failed to control their child and it was causing undue stress and hassle in my home life. 'Especially if he was trespassing and stealing?'

Albert rolls his eyes, which lets me know that my idea is a bad one, and Eileen confirms as much by telling us that they tried that once, but the police did nothing, and it only made things worse. 'Ian got angry with us after that. Told us to stay away from him and his son, so that's what we've done. We're civil with them now but no more. We don't want any trouble. We just want to enjoy our retirement.'

'That's the best bit of advice we could give you there,' Albert chimes in again. 'Try not to let Jackson bother you. He wants to get a rise out of you, but don't give it to him. He'll just get bored and find something else to do then. But lock your doors. That kid will steal anything that isn't fixed down.'

Just like the warning about Chris and Abi, this one is ominous too. But unlike that first one where trouble seems quite easy to avoid as long as we don't allow ourselves to be seduced by our attractive neighbours, this information about Ian and Jackson feels more concerning. I can handle living nearby to an adventurous couple, but I'm not so sure I can handle living so close to a lazy parent who lets their thieving child run wild. And it sounds like my husband is feeling the same way.

'There won't be any stealing around here,' Sean says firmly. 'I'll make sure I get through to his father if the son tries taking anything of ours that doesn't belong to him.'

That seems pretty final, but Albert rolls his eyes again and obviously has something else to add.

'You're not the first person to live here who thought like that,' the old man says before looking to his wife. 'Remember Greg?'

Eileen nods solemnly, but that doesn't help me or my husband.

'Who's Greg?' I ask.

'He was the first person to live in this house. He sold the house to the couple you just bought it off. Just like them, he had a good reason to leave this street behind.'

'And what was that?' I ask, slightly dreading the answer because the longer this conversation goes on, the less satisfied I am feeling about choosing this seemingly perfect place to live.

'He ended up being given a restraining order from the police,' Albert tells us. 'He wasn't allowed within ten metres of Ian or his son, which made it quite difficult considering he was living right next door to them.'

That doesn't sound good, and I'd almost like to leave it there, but Sean quite rightly wants to know more.

'Why was he given a restraining order?' he asks.

'Because he assaulted Ian. Punched him right in the face on his own doorstep after he had got sick of things going missing in his garden and Jackson getting away with it. But the police took Ian's side. They charged Greg with assault and harassment because it wasn't the first time he had gone round to his house and got angry. In the end, he was lucky just to get the restraining

43

order. We were convinced he'd have to serve some time, weren't we?'

Albert looks to Eileen who nods her confirmation, and after a few more seconds pass without them speaking again, it seems like they are finally finished with the warnings.

I stare at the elderly couple sitting opposite us while trying to wrap my head around what they have just said. But I can't really do that while they are still here. I need some space to think. These two are lovely, but I really need them to think about leaving now. Fortunately, they seem aware of that because they both get up off the sofa and thank us for our hospitality before heading for the door. Eileen compliments Sean on his choice of whiskey, while Albert offers a few tips on how to get our lawn looking better than it does right now but thankfully, it's only a few more seconds until they are out of our house and on their way back to their own.

By the time Sean closes the front door behind them, I am already pouring myself another glass of wine in the kitchen. So much for a quiet Sunday night before a week of work. It seems like the two of us are going to be up late and kept busy after all. That's because we have plenty to discuss.

We have to talk about our new neighbours.

6

SEAN

'They must be winding us up,' I say when I've had a little more time to think about things and come to a sensible conclusion. 'There's no way they are being serious with us.'

I glance across the bedroom to see what the response will be from my wife, but she doesn't seem so sure.

'Why would they do that? What could they possibly have to gain?'

'I don't know. Maybe that's how they have fun in their retirement.'

'I don't think so.'

It's obvious that Katie is taking the warnings much more seriously than I am, and I can appreciate her concern, but I'm not exactly worried about what I just heard. If Ian's son, Jackson, is as unruly as we were told then I will handle it in a safe and sensible manner, and if Chris and Abi are really adulterers who love nothing more than getting their claws into other couples, then that will be quite easy to avoid too. I'll just say no thank you and leave them to it. I'm sure Katie will do the same. So as far as I'm concerned, there is nothing to worry about even if it is true, which I seriously doubt it is anyway.

'Maybe they're just confused,' I suggest as I strip down to just my boxer shorts and climb under the duvet. 'Maybe they think things are worse than they are. They are quite old.'

'They didn't seem confused to me,' Katie replies as she removes her makeup in the mirror where she has set up a makeshift dressing table until she can order a proper one for our new room.

'Who knows what they are really like? We've only just met them, just like we've only just met Chris and Abi too. And we haven't even met Ian and Jackson, so we can hardly judge them yet, can we?'

'I just don't see why they would come around to warn us if there wasn't something to be worried about.'

I sigh as my wife continues to get ready for bed and try to distract myself by staring up at the ceiling and counting how many cracks in the plaster I can see that will need to be fixed when it comes to redecorating this room. But it's no good. Just like Katie, I can't stop thinking about what just happened.

'I can't wait to tell the lads at work about this tomorrow,' I say with a chuckle. 'They'll have a right laugh.'

'Don't you dare tell anybody about this!' Katie suddenly snaps, spinning around and fixing me with a steely glare. 'I don't want people thinking we have moved onto a street with a bunch of weirdos!'

'But we haven't. This is just a normal street!'

'It doesn't sound like it!'

I don't fancy having an argument this late at night and this close to another Monday morning, so I decide it's best to stay quiet and wait for Katie to turn off the one lightbulb in here and join me under the duvet. When she does, I decide to try and take her mind off things by kissing her neck and seeing if she is in the mood for a little romance. But I get my answer pretty quickly when she moves her head away from me and gets up out of bed to go over to the window.

'What are you doing?' I ask her as I see her peering out through the scraggly curtains that the previous homeowners left behind for us. They definitely need replacing, but at least we have them because without them, we'd end up being woken up at dawn with the sunlight streaming in.

'I'm looking,' Katie replies.

'Looking at what?'

'The neighbours.'

'What for?'

'Just to see.'

'See what?'

'What they're doing.'

48

'What do you think they're doing? They're probably all in bed, just like we are.'

'No, they're not. I can see some lights on.'

'So what? Come away from the window. They might see you.'

'They won't.'

I realise that Katie isn't going to get back into bed anytime soon, so I have a choice between either rolling over and going to sleep or getting up to go and join her at the window. I am tired, but I am also intrigued as to what it might be that my wife thinks she will be able to see by peeping out, so I pull back the duvet and go and stand beside her at the gap in the curtains.

'See, they're still up,' Katie says as she gestures towards both Albert and Eileen's house and Chris and Abi's.

She's right, they are both still up because I can see lights on, but I'm not sure what it's supposed to signify. The only dark house is Ian's, and that is to be expected because apparently neither him or his son are back home until later in the week.

'So they don't go to bed as early as we do? What does that tell us?'

'I don't know. But we need to find out more about these people so that we know if any of it is true.'

'And we're going to do that by staring out of our bedroom window every night?'

49

'Just get back into bed.'

'Not without you.'

I try to tickle my wife and get her to see how silly she is being by hovering at the window to spy on our neighbours when she suddenly lets out a yelp and ducks down below the windowpane.

'What are you doing?' I ask her as I look down at her crouching by my feet.

'Somebody just looked out at us!' she replies, obviously worried that her snooping has been rumbled.

'Who?' I ask as I look back out of the window.

'I think it's Chris!'

I squint my eyes as I try to get a good look at his upstairs window where the light is on, and even though my eyesight has deteriorated somewhat thanks to all my computer use in the office, I can make out the dark figure standing in the window across the street.

'What are you doing? Get down! He'll see you.'

'I think he already has,' I reply with a chuckle. 'He's waving right at me.'

'What?'

'He's waving,' I repeat before lifting up my right hand and returning the gesture to him.

'Stop it!'

'Why?'

'Because Albert and Eileen said we were to stay away from them!'

'And we are doing that. We're all the way across the street.'

'They said not to be friendly.'

'I'm only waving, and I'm only doing it because they have caught us spying on them. Or rather, they caught you spying on them.'

Katie isn't happy with me, but I've had enough drama for one night, so I pull the curtains closed and return to my cosy spot under the duvet. Thankfully, my wife does the same thing a short time later, and now we can finally try and get some sleep.

It's no surprise to me that I feel myself drifting off quickly after the busy few days I have had sorting the house move out and digging up weeds in the garden. I'm going to be just as busy tomorrow when I get back to the office, but for now, I am going to savour every single minute I get to lie here in the dark and drift off to sleep.

I'm not sure what time it was when I woke up again because it was still dark, and Katie was still fast asleep beside me. But I am sure about what it was that woke me. I was having a dream, and while it can't be called a nightmare because it was far too enjoyable for that, it's certainly not perfect enough to have prevented me from waking up with a jolt.

As I lie there and stare up at the dark ceiling, I think about what it was that I just experienced in my slumber, and I'm glad only I am witness to what it was. If Katie knew then she would most likely be mad at me, and I could hardly blame her. That's because I just dreamt about myself with another woman, and I'm not sure that any wife wants to hear about that. But this wasn't just any woman. This was someone we both know.

It was Abi.

I know Albert and Eileen just told us to stay away from her and Chris, and I know Katie seems keen to heed that warning, which means I better heed it too, but I'm not sure what I'm supposed to do if I see them in my dreams. More worryingly is why I am seeing Abi in my dreams. Does it mean I like her? Hardly, I barely know her after all. It was just a dream. It's silly and it doesn't mean anything. Just like what Albert and Eileen told us doesn't mean anything either. At least that's what I tell myself as I close my eyes and try to go back to sleep.

But this time it isn't as easy to drift off. This time I find myself starting to feel as anxious as my wife felt when she was standing at the window looking out at our neighbours.

This time I start to worry that there might be some truth in what our elderly neighbours told us.

7

KATIE

I didn't get the best night's sleep after the events of yesterday, which explains why I'm feeling so tired now as I sit on my stool in front of a blank canvas with a paintbrush in my hand and an idea in my head of what it is that I want to create. But the tricky part is getting the idea out of my head and onto the canvas, and so far, that hasn't happened for me today. I could blame it on painter's block, which is exactly like writer's block, except substitute pen and paper for paintbrushes and palettes. But I have a feeling that's not what it is at all. Rather, it's because I'm still distracted about what our elderly neighbours told us when they called around to visit yesterday.

Albert and Eileen's 'housewarming' present to us was a word of warning about the people we share this cul-de-sac with, and all I can say is that I would have preferred a more traditional gift like a bottle of wine or a small potted plant for the kitchen windowsill. Instead, Sean and I got the full rundown on what we can expect from our other neighbours, and it doesn't sound good. Is it enough to make us reconsider where we are living? Of course not, we both love this house, and we have only just got here. But it is certainly enough to make us worry about what might happen in the future, or at least it's enough to make me worry anyway.

Sean doesn't seem too bothered about it at all, and he left for work this morning without so much as a word about what happened last night. But then again, he's always been less of a worrier than me. We balance each other out, which is a good thing, but it can also lead to arguments, which is a bad thing. But thinking about all of this isn't going to get me any closer to starting this painting, so I reach over and turn the radio on, filling the room with music that will help clear my mind and give me a better chance of being creative.

Eventually, my paintbrush is moving across the canvas, and I'm feeling a lot better about things now, as I usually do when I'm lost in my work and not thinking about anything else but art. But that blissful state is interrupted by a knock at the front door downstairs.

My paintbrush hovers inches away from the canvas as I stop what I am doing and wonder who it could be that has just come to my house. I haven't ordered anything, so it can't be a delivery driver. Maybe it's a door to door salesman trying his luck after realising some new people have moved in on his patch. That could be it.

Or maybe it's one of my neighbours, and I'm about to get another surprise to go with the one I got yesterday, which was the last time there was a knock on our door.

I hear the knock a second time, and that forces me up off my stool and out of the spare bedroom towards the top of the stairs, where I look down and try to get a better idea of who might be out there. We have a small sliver of glass beside our front door, and it gives us the opportunity of seeing who might be out there before we open the door. But in this case, whoever it is is not standing near the glass, so I can't see them.

Or at least I can't until they move their head right in front of it and look inside, catching sight of me loitering at the top of the stairs.

It's Chris, and he has seen me, which means I have to answer the door now or I'll look rude. I wonder what he wants as I head down the stairs, trying to remind myself that he is just a friendly neighbour but also aware of Albert and Eileen's warning to me yesterday in which they instructed Sean and I to not get too close to this attractive couple. But there's not much I can do about that when one of them is stood at my front door, so I turn the handle and find myself face to face with Chris again.

'Hey! Sorry to bother you,' Chris says with a trademark flash of his pearly whites. 'I was just dropping off this hedge trimmer for Sean. I told him he could borrow it.'

I look down at the hedge trimmer leaning against the wall and feel myself relaxing instantly because he is here to do a kind neighbourly duty, not to try and seduce me like Albert and Eileen warned. I feel ridiculous for even thinking that might be what was about to happen, and I let out a nervous laugh, which is a bit silly because Chris will have no idea what I find funny about this situation.

'Thanks, that's great. I'll let him know you dropped it round, and we'll get it back to you as soon as we can,' I say as I accept the trimmer and prop it up in the hallway behind the door.

'So are you one of the work from home brigade as well?' Chris asks me with a smile.

'Er, yeah, kind of.'

'Me too. Some people hate it, but I love it. I definitely don't miss commuting, that's for sure.'

'What is it you do for work?' I ask, genuinely curious, although also aware that I'm not exactly heeding my neighbours' warning about staying distant from the couple at Number Three.

'I'm an I.T. technician, which basically means I fix other people's computers remotely.'

'Cool,' I reply, but Chris just laughs.

'The wage is nice, but the work isn't. Do you have any idea how many times a day I have to ask somebody if they have tried turning it off and on again?'

Now it's my turn to laugh.

'I imagine it's a lot.'

'You'd be amazed. So, what is it you do from home?'

I pause before answering, not because I'm embarrassed about my job but because painting is such a personal thing to me. I don't talk about it with too many people, and that's mainly because I haven't met many people who know a lot about it, but also because I worry they will ask me how many paintings I have sold and I'll have to lie to make myself look better. People tend not to be impressed if I'm honest and say I barely sell anything because I'm not very good at the whole marketing thing. But Chris has asked me, and I should be honest with him because there's little reason not to be, so I go for it, conscious that I am slightly intrigued about what his reaction will be.

'I'm an artist,' I say, hating how that sounds out loud because I don't really feel like one on the inside. I'm more of a person who is trying to be an artist but is actually just lucky I have a supportive partner who is funding me while I try.

'Seriously? That's amazing!' Chris replies with genuine surprise and enthusiasm. 'What kind of art?'

'Paintings mainly.'

'Wow, I can't believe I live on the same street as a famous artist!'

'I'm hardly famous,' I tell him with another laugh.

'I'm sure you're super talented. You must be to be able to do it full time. So what kind of things do you paint?'

'All sorts, really. Landscapes. Objects. Sometimes other people.'

'That's so cool. I'm envious. I always wanted to do something creative, but I ended up in I.T. instead.'

'I'm sure it's not that bad.'

'Yeah, but it's not painting, is it? Seriously, I'm super impressed. Well done for following your dream.'

I'm flattered that Chris is so enthused about what I do for a living, or at least what I try to do anyway. I'm also intrigued by what he said about him wanting to do something creative with his life.

'So do you like art?' I ask him, doubtful that he does but chancing my arm anyway.

'I love all forms of creative expression,' he replies excitedly. 'Painting. Writing. Music. You name it. I just love being in the presence of somebody's inner thoughts and feelings expressed in those ways.'

That's exactly how I feel about things, but I decide not to say that, although I'm not exactly sure why. Maybe it's because I don't just want it to seem like we have so much in common, and that is probably because I'm still conscious about what Albert and Eileen said to me last night.

"Don't let them get too close to you. They will try and seduce you. We've seen other marriages destroyed by them and we'd hate for the same thing to happen to you."

'Are you painting something right now?' Chris asks me after I have failed to say something at my turn in the conversation.

'Yeah, kind of,' I reply, thinking about the blank canvas upstairs.

'When will it be finished? I'd love to see it. In fact, I'd love to see anything you've done if you have any around the house now?'

I can see that he genuinely means that, and he is obviously telling the truth about being a keen art lover because I can tell when people are feigning interest in what I do, but I'm not sure letting him inside to see what I am doing would be the best idea and certainly not when Sean isn't here with me.

'Most of my paintings are still in boxes,' I lie, figuring that is a good excuse considering we have just moved in. 'And the one I've just started is in its very early stages, so I wouldn't want to show that to anybody yet.'

'Of course, I understand. But you'll have to let me know when I can have a look. I'd really love to see your work.'

I smile at this pleasant and eager man on my doorstep and tell him that I will show him some of my paintings at some point, although I make sure not to put a definite date on it. Then I tell him that I better get back to work, and he agrees that he should do the same, so he bids me goodbye and walks away down my driveway and back in the direction of his house.

Watching him leave, I feel a strange mixture of relief and disappointment. Relief because he's going and that's what Albert and Eileen would want but disappointment because I was enjoying our interaction together. By the time I have closed the front door and returned to my stool in front of the canvas upstairs, I am not thinking about painting anymore. I'm thinking about my neighbour who seems genuinely fascinated by what I do. I'm thinking about how his face lit up when he found out I was an artist. And I'm also thinking about how Albert and Eileen told me he would probably try to seduce me at some point.

Is that what that was? Has it started already?

No, I'm sure he was just being honest and actually has an interest in all things creative.

But the fact that I'm unable to concentrate enough to get back to work tells me that I'm not sure at all.

Maybe he was just saying what he thought I wanted to hear. Maybe he is already working on me just like he worked on the last woman who lived here, and look how that ended up. She got divorced and moved out.

But that won't happen to me. I'm too smart to do anything stupid that might risk my relationship with Sean, and I know he is the same. So why do I feel so uneasy? Why can't I go back to painting? And why do I now find myself staring out of the window in the direction of Number Three?

8

SEAN

After a busy Monday in the office, I'd like nothing more than to just go home, put my feet up and while away the remainder of the evening in front of the television. But I know that's not going to be how it goes because there is a lot that needs doing around the house, and I'm going to have to do some of it because otherwise, it just simply won't get done.

Katie called me earlier and told me that Chris had been around with the hedge trimmer for me to borrow, so I better get some use out of that so I can return it to him quickly. I don't want to be one of those people who borrows something and then holds on to it for too long, leaving the person who lent it feeling awkward about when they will ever see their possession again. But trimming some hedges in my garden is hardly the most exciting thing to look forward to doing as I turn my car onto my street before parking up on my driveway and turning off the engine.

I grab my suit jacket and my briefcase from the passenger seat before climbing out of my vehicle, and I'm just about to go and unlock my front door when I hear a female voice calling out to me from behind. Turning around, I see that it belongs to Abi, and she is waving at me from her garage, which is wide open and filled with all sorts of fancy looking gym equipment. She has obviously been using that equipment too because she is wearing a sports bra and Lycra shorts and looks to be a little out of breath.

'Good day at work?' she asks me as she steps out of her garage before taking a swig from the water bottle in her left hand.

'Er, yeah, it was alright for a Monday,' I reply, trotting out the same weary line I always do whenever anybody asks me how my first day of the week went.

'You look like you could use a good workout. Blow off some steam,' she tells me, and I would have to agree with her if I wasn't now feeling a little self-conscious about the fact that she has just observed that I'm looking a little jaded after a day in the office.

'I'll get plenty of exercise in my garden this evening,' I tell her, rolling my eyes and gesturing towards my overgrown hedges. 'Thanks for the hedge trimmer. I'll get it back to Chris as soon as I can.'

'No problem, have it as long as you like.'

She gives me a smile, and even though she was presumably working out just a few seconds ago, she doesn't look at all sweaty, and there's not a hair out of place on her head, although maybe that's because most of her long locks are scrunched back into a ponytail.

'That's quite the set-up you have there,' I tell her, looking past her at the exercise bench, dumbbells and medicine balls that fill up most of the space in the garage.

'Yeah, I used to go to a gym, but I decided to bring the gym to me. It gives me less of an excuse not to exercise now when I only have to walk a few yards to get here.'

I laugh. 'Fair enough. Well, it certainly looks like you have everything you need.'

'Everything but a pool, but I can get a day pass to the local gym for that,' she tells me, and I nod my head, impressed at her apparent appetite for fitness. Then she says something that would be a compliment if only it didn't make me instantly think back to Albert and Eileen's strange warning last night. She tells me that she can tell I'm no stranger to a gym and she does while glancing down at my torso, which is completely covered by my work shirt but must be just tight enough for her to see some of my muscles beneath it.

I am flattered that she has noticed my reasonably decent body, but according to Albert and Eileen, I should be on my guard because she might not just be being friendly. She might be after something more, and it's something that I definitely can't give her.

'Yeah, I go to the gym every now and again,' I say, batting a dismissive hand in her direction to downplay how much I actually do like to work out. 'But not as much as I should do.'

'Well, you're welcome to use some of this equipment anytime you'd like,' she tells me, turning back to her garage and waving a hand at all of her fitness furniture. 'Although the dumbbells are probably a little too light for you. I imagine you lift much heavier weights than these.'

I'm hardly Mr Universe, and I definitely won't be entering any Strong Man competitions anytime soon, but I do lift reasonably heavy weights, and Abi is right in assuming that there isn't likely to be much I can use in her gym. But it's a kind offer all the same, and I thank her for it whilst also making sure to politely dismiss the suggestion because I know I better not get into the habit of using my neighbour's home gym and particularly when I've been advised to stay away from that neighbour if I value the sanctity of my marriage.

'Well, if you change your mind, I keep a spare key for the garage under this plant pot right here,' Abi tells me, and she nudges her foot up against a small red plant pot that sits on the edge of her neatly trimmed lawn. 'You're welcome to use it anytime. I'd hate for you to not get to the gym as much as you would like. I'm sure you have a very busy job.'

I do have a very busy job, but it's not that exciting, so I don't want to talk about it and ruin whatever picture she has of me as some high-flying businessman, even though I'm not sure why that is so important to me. That's why I just thank her again before telling her that I have to get inside and grab something to eat before a fun evening of hedge trimming.

'Have a good night, and don't work too hard,' she tells me before giving me a wink. With that she spins around and heads back into her garage, her gait light and bouncy and her ponytail bobbing about against the back of her bare shoulders.

I turn around myself and head for my front door, my movements much stiffer and more ponderous than hers, and I have the eight hours I just spent sitting in an office chair to thank for that.

As I unlock the door and step inside, I take a look back over my shoulder at the garage of Number Three and see Abi already lying on her back on the exercise bench, and lifting a couple of light dumbbells up and down above her torso. Her arms are slender and toned, and her ample chest is rising and falling in time with her movements as she breathes in and out and maintains good form. But just before I can turn away and close the door, Abi stops her exercise and looks in my direction, and she definitely catches me looking at her.

I feel my face blushing as I worry she might think that I was ogling her, and I close the door before there can be any more awkward seconds to endure. Then I drop my briefcase at the foot of the stairs, hang my jacket on the coat hook and head into my home, calling out for my wife who could be doing all sorts of things right now, but one of them definitely won't be exercising because she finds it tedious and dull.

Katie is very different to Abi. There's no way my wife would ever walk around in a sports bra and Lycra shorts for a start, nor would she even know how to perform a chest exercise correctly. But that's why I love her. She has her own interests and hobbies, and she doesn't try to pretend to be anything that she is not. I did try getting Katie to join a gym with me once, but she just laughed at the idea and told me that she would rather die. I think she was joking, but I can't be sure. But I guess it's a good thing we have our differences, and they do say opposites attract. I guess that's why I ended up with her and not someone like Abi. And I guess that's why I still think Albert and Eileen's warning is silly because even if Abi might be flirty and up for a little mischief, just like her husband apparently is too, that doesn't mean I have to be. I'll just keep to myself, which means I definitely won't be going around to Abi's to use her gym

68

equipment. The only time I will go over there will be to drop the hedge trimmer off. Then I'll come back to my own house and my own wife because that's just the normal thing to do.

So why do I feel like I need to remind myself of that?

9

KATIE

I feel like I'm starting to find my way around the new kitchen now, and to prove it, I have cooked up a feast of Italian food for my husband after his first day back in the office following our house move. Sean is extremely grateful for that too as he tears off another slice of the homemade garlic bread and drops it onto his plate beside the meatballs that he has been enjoying ever since I served them up ten minutes ago.

'This is amazing,' he tells me with a mouth full of food, and I smile at him while also feeling pleased that it doesn't take much to get in his good graces. Like most men in life, the key to keeping my partner happy lies in his stomach.

'This is just what I need before tackling those hedges,' he adds before taking a sip of his water, and that comment makes me think again about telling him about my brief interaction with Chris when he dropped the garden appliance off earlier.

'Chris was chatty when he called round,' I say as I twirl a meatball around on the end of my fork. 'Apparently, he's an I.T. technician and works from home.'

'Really? I wouldn't have had him down as an I.T. worker.'

'What did you think he did?'

'Besides male modelling, you mean?'

I laugh. 'Not every good looking person has to be a model.'

'So you think he is good looking?'

'No. Well, I mean, I guess,' I reply, finding myself fumbling over my answer.

'It's okay. I'm not jealous. I know you prefer more rugged men anyway,' Sean says, giving me a wink, and I laugh because my husband likes to think that not shaving for a couple of days and being very casual with his hairstyle makes him look rugged, whereas some could argue it just makes him seem scruffy. But not me. He's right, I do like my men rugged.

'He asked me what I do for work too.'

'Did you tell him?'

'Yeah, I had to. It would have been awkward if I didn't.'

'So what did he say?'

'He seemed like he was actually interested in it. Said he always wanted to be creative himself.'

'Really? Did he then ask you if you wanted to go to bed with him like Albert and Eileen said he would?'

I shake my head and try not to show that my husband's sarcastic comment has amused me.

'Don't be silly. He was just being friendly.'

'Because he wants you.'

'Stop it,' I say, making out like I'm going to flick my meatball sauce at him if he carries on being silly.

Sean laughs and says he is only joking before telling me that he had an encounter with Chris' other half today as well.

'She said I could use her home gym whenever I fancied it,' he says as he chews another slice of garlic bread. 'She even told me where her spare key is kept.'

Unlike my story, this is a little concerning.

'She did what?' I say, stunned that Abi would apparently tell my husband where the spare key to her home was. Never mind the fact that she barely knows him, giving out information about the location of a spare key to anybody who doesn't live in that home is usually a massive no-no.

'Don't worry, I made sure to politely decline the offer.'

'Well, good. You can't be letting yourself into someone else's house. That's ridiculous.'

'It would have only been the garage.'

'That's not the point. Don't you think that's very forward of her?'

'I don't know. I think she was just being nice. You know, like Chris was.'

'Or she wants you in her home where she can try and seduce you.'

'Now who's the one being silly?'

I put down my knife and fork and sit back in my chair, processing the information that Sean has just given me. I was perturbed by what Albert and Eileen said to us last night, and I was still worrying about it when I woke up this morning, but as the day has gone on, I had told myself not to be silly and that Chris and Abi weren't really some adventurous couple who liked to prey on the new neighbours to spice up their sex lives. I had just started to put the whole thing down to an overreaction on the part of our elderly neighbours, who are most likely a little old fashioned and reading far too much into things that aren't really there. Maybe one or both of James and Sarah did have an affair with Chris or Abi, and maybe that's why they separated and sold the house, but I highly doubt that happened via some weird strategy that the couple at Number Three employ to any newcomers who arrive on their street. But hearing Sean tell me how Abi told him that he could use her spare key to access her home gym has made me a little rattled. Sean might not think it's much of a big deal, but how would he like it if Chris offered me the chance to go around whenever I wanted to? I bet he wouldn't be making jokes then.

'What's the matter?' Sean asks me when he notices that I have stopped eating.

'I'm just confused about all of this. Maybe we should go round to Albert and Eileen's and ask them some more questions.'

'Like what?'

'I don't know. Maybe see if they were joking last night. Or if this is something we should actually be worried about.'

'What's there to be worried about?'

Now Sean has put down his knife and fork too, and he sits back in his chair waiting for me to answer him. But I don't want to come out and say what is on my mind, so I just try to avoid it instead.

'I don't know.'

'No, come on. If you are serious about this then it must mean you are worried about us falling foul of Chris and Abi. So what does that mean? You think I would cheat on you with her?'

'No, of course not!'

'Then what? You might be tempted by Chris?'

'No!'

74

'Then what is there to worry about?'

I get my husband's point. Even if Chris and Abi are as dangerous to our marriage as Albert and Eileen suggested they were, it doesn't change the fact that neither of us are going to stray outside of our relationship anyway. So what if Abi wants Sean to come around and use her gym so she can get closer to him, and so what if Chris might be pretending to be interested in what I do for a living just so he can get closer to me? None of that matters as long as neither me or my husband do anything we shouldn't do. So why do I have this weird feeling in the pit of my stomach that that isn't enough? Why do I feel like I need to go and have another word with the old couple next door to try and put my mind at ease again?

'Come on then, let's go round to Albert and Eileen's now and talk about this some more with them,' Sean says, standing up from his seat and stepping away from the table to show that he is serious about doing it if I am.

'Wait,' I tell him before he can get any further. He has called my bluff, and he has won. I don't really want to go next door and ask our elderly neighbours to elaborate on what they told us last night. It's silly. The best thing to do would be to try and forget about all of this and just get on with enjoying our lives in our new home. Who cares what the neighbours may or may not be up to? We'll be friendly whenever we see them out on the street, but other than that, they don't have to be a factor in our day to day existence. They're only neighbours. Most people don't even bother with their neighbours, and we could just be the same. Smile, wave, make polite chit-chat and just get on with living separate lives. That's what we'll do. All this nonsense about warnings will just end up being some funny story we end up sharing with our friends one night after a few bottles of wine. They will laugh about it, and we will laugh too.

So what if we have quirky neighbours?

They can't bother us if we don't let them.

10

SEAN

The hedge trimmer that I was lent by my neighbour, who may or may not want to sleep with my wife, came in very handy, and I was able to get the job done much quicker than if I had been left to use my rusty old pair of hedge clippers that were handed down to me by my father several years ago. I'm so ahead on the odd-job front that I have even had time to get my ladder out and make a start on clearing out the gutters on the roof of the house, which is obviously a job that has been neglected for years because it's now almost completely blocked.

Reaching my gloved hand back into the gutter, I scoop out another clump of dead leaves and drop them to the floor below while thinking about how good that bottle of beer in the fridge is going to taste when I'm done here in about ten minutes' time or so. But before I can finish my job, I hear the sound of a car arriving on the street, and I look up to see a small black hatchback parking on the drive at Number One. I can see two people inside the vehicle and based on what Albert and Eileen told me, I have an idea of who they are. That must be Ian behind the steering wheel, and that teenager in the passenger seat must be his son, Jackson. But because of what Albert and Eileen told me, I am a little wary about meeting them for the first time because, according to them, Jackson is trouble, and Ian does very little about it. I briefly consider not saying anything and pretending to be busy with the guttering, but there's no way they will have failed to have seen me up this ladder, and they'll know that I will have seen them too. That means I'll seem rude if I don't say hello, and I don't want to get off on the wrong foot with them. That's why I climb down the ladders as the two of them get out of their car, and by the time that they have, I'm back on the ground and making my way over to them to introduce myself.

'Hi. We haven't met yet. I'm Sean. My wife and I have just moved into Two A.'

I make sure to put a warm and friendly smile on my face and keep my body language open as I walk across my lawn in anticipation of shaking Ian's hand in a moment's time. He looks at me as I get closer, but Jackson is already on his way into the house, seemingly not bothered about making a new friend today.

'Ian,' the father mumbles as I reach him and he shakes my hand, although it's not at all like the handshake I received from Chris when I first met him. This one is very limp, and there's not much enthusiasm behind it. Is Ian as rude as

Albert and Eileen told me he was? I'd have to say that he's not got off to the best start. But maybe he's just shy. Let's find out.

'I hear you work on the oil rigs. That must be an interesting job,' I say, hoping that I came across as sincere and not as if I am being sarcastic because I'm not meaning to be.

'Who told you that?' Ian asks me, and I suddenly worry if I was too forward in letting on that I already knew some things about him. Why didn't I just pretend like I knew nothing about him and let him divulge the information as and when he wanted to? Instead, I have made it seem like I've been talking about him behind his back, which of course I have, or rather, the old couple at Number Two have.

'Oh, I heard from one of the neighbours,' I say, being deliberately vague. 'They were just telling us a little about who else lives on this cul-de-sac.'

'That's the problem with this place,' Ian replies while shaking his head. 'People are too bothered about other people's business instead of keeping to themselves.'

Ian didn't say that in a cold manner, rather in one that suggests he is tired of having to have these types of conversations with people like me. I guess this isn't going as well as I hoped it might when I climbed down off my ladder. Maybe I should have stayed up there and kept clearing out the gutter. It was a boring and menial task, but it was better than this awkward chat right here.

'Is that your son?' I ask Ian, gesturing to the teenager who has already disappeared into the house. Of course, I already know that it is, but I've already made the mistake of sounding like I know too much, so I won't be doing that again. Now I'm just going to play dumb and pretend as if Albert and Eileen haven't already told me plenty about this man and his offspring.

'Yeah. That's Jackson. I have him whenever I'm back from the rigs. I've got shared custody with my ex-wife.'

'I see,' I reply, nodding my head and trying to be respectful of his difficult situation with his former partner. I can't imagine what it must be like to not only go through a marriage breakdown and subsequent divorce but also have to split caring duties for a child and make do with only seeing them on specific dates.

'He's a bit grumpy today,' Ian goes on, and I presume he has said that to explain why Jackson made no attempt to hang around and meet me.

'Typical teenager,' I say with a laugh, but Ian doesn't exactly reciprocate it. He just looks tired and grumpy, just like his son.

'Well, it was nice to meet you,' he says as he locks his car and turns for the door. 'Enjoy your new house.'

'Thanks, you too,' I reply. 'Er, I mean it was nice to meet you. Not enjoy your new house. It's obviously not your new house, is it?'

I'm rambling on and making things worse, and Ian looks at me almost as if he feels sorry for me and my lame attempts at conversation. Then he just gives me a nod and heads into his house, closing the door behind himself and leaving me standing on his driveway feeling like I've not exactly made the best first impression in the world.

As I plod back over my front lawn and return to the foot of the ladders, I shake my head at my feeble social skills. Surely I could have made a better job of that. I'm not usually that awkward when I meet new people. But as I climb back up the ladder, I know exactly what the problem was. I was feeling awkward before I even met the guy, and that was because I had already been told some things about him that made me go into the interaction with a different edge to me. I almost wish Albert and Eileen hadn't said anything about Ian now and left me to make my own mind up about them, just like they should have done with Chris and Abi too. Maybe they were trying to do us a favour, or maybe they are losing their marbles, but either way, Katie and I are old enough to make our own minds up about people without having some preconceived notions clouding everything we do from here on out.

Back at the top of the ladder, I return to my tedious task, scooping out more dead leaves and dropping them to the ground below. While I work, I glance over at Number One and wonder what Ian and Jackson are thinking now. Jackson barely noticed me, so I'm sure he's not thinking much, but Ian will definitely have got an idea about me, and I'm not sure it's the one I wanted him to get. He's most likely now thinking that I'm somebody he will have to tolerate living besides rather than someone he might enjoy a beer with every now and again, and to be fair to him, I was thinking the same thing, but that was before I had even met him. And that was thanks to Albert and Eileen.

The more I think about it, the more I really wish they hadn't said anything. From now on, I'm just going to take people as I see them without letting their warnings cloud my judgement. As far as I can tell, Chris and Abi are nothing but polite and friendly, and Ian seems okay too. Jackson was hardly a font of conversation, but then again, he's fifteen and what fifteen-year-old is? So far, everything seems okay, and I'm sure it's going to stay that way too. This is just everyday England, not an episode of EastEnders. Life is boring in the real world, and that's perfectly fine by me. I'll just clean out this gutter, have a shower and then have a beer. And I won't bother giving my neighbours a second thought because I sincerely doubt they will be thinking about me either.

11

KATIE

It's almost been a week now since we moved into this house, and slowly but surely, we are putting our stamp on it. I have got most of the things inside the house where I want them, and Sean has done a great job of sprucing up the outside areas to make them look more presentable. There will be some redecorating to do at a later date, but for now, we're just going to enjoy living here and figuring out what works and doesn't work with the house as it currently is. But despite things going well on the home front, things haven't quite been going so well on the job one. Despite having all week to come up with a new painting, I haven't been able to finish anything, starting several but giving up at various stages with them all because none of them were anywhere near the level that I know I am capable of producing. That's troubling to me because I've never gone this long without finishing something, yet here I am now, sitting in front of another blank canvas and worst of all, it's Friday lunchtime. The working week will be over soon, and I can hardly say I've worked, unlike my husband who has been slaving away at his office, actually producing some work of merit. I need to get something on this canvas before the weekend comes, just to make myself feel a little better before next Monday rolls around and I'm back here again. But what? Like so many creative souls who have come before me, I turn to the last resort.

I stare out of the window and hope for inspiration to strike.

It's pathetic. I should be more professional than this, but I'm desperate, although I'm not expecting to see much out on the cul-de-sac to get my creative juices flowing. But I'm wrong. I see something almost immediately, and it gives me an idea of what to paint.

Chris is on his driveway, and he's working beneath the bonnet of his car, a strong display of domestic masculinity if ever there was one. As someone who likes to paint both landscapes and people, I have the idea of combining both those things. I could paint the landscape of Chris' house as it appears to me from this vantage point, and I could also put Chris himself in the painting. It might not be the best idea, but for someone who has been starved of an idea for a long time, I have to take the inspiration where I can get it. And besides, I've never painted a car before so it will be a new challenge.

I dab the tip of my paintbrush in the palette beside me before touching it on the canvas and beginning to make some broad strokes that will lay the foundation of what I hope this picture will eventually turn out to be. As I do, I make sure to keep looking out of the window at my muse outside, taking in all the details of the view so that I can apply them to this painting and make it look as realistic as possible. The car is dark blue, just like the jeans Chris is wearing, while his t-shirt is white, matching the colour of the clean pair of trainers on his feet. The car is stylish, as is the fashion sense of the man currently tinkering with it and add to that the immaculate garden surrounding them both and I have plenty of ways to make this picture pretty.

I have no idea what Chris is doing under the bonnet of his car, but I'm happy for him to stay out there for as long as possible because it is giving me more of a chance to really capture his likeness in my painting. By the time I have done that, I'm looking forward to breaking out the more colourful paints in my arsenal to tackle the garden. Greens, yellows and oranges will all be used to capture the grass and flower beds, although it won't be as creatively taxing to paint them as it was to paint the car and its owner just now.

It's amazing how quickly I can work once I have a good picture of what I want to create in my mind, and after almost a week of producing very little, I have now almost finished my latest masterpiece. I move my brush away from the canvas and lean back on my stool to get a better idea of how my work is looking. And when I do, I have to say I'm surprised. This might be one of the best paintings I have ever done. I might be biased, but it definitely looks like I have captured a small slice of suburban solitude in this image of one man and his car on his driveway in the middle of the day.

It's not long after I have finished that I see Chris put the bonnet back down on his vehicle and wipe his hands on a greasy rag before picking up his toolbox and heading back inside his house. It looks like his work is finished for the day, and I think I can say the same about myself. It feels good to be ending the week with a finished product that I can hopefully sell to somebody one day and generate some income to contribute to my daily living expenses. I've never expected to get rich from my artwork, but it would be nice to be able to pay a few bills every now and again from the profits of any sales I have made. And I'm sure Sean would appreciate that too, even if he would never come and say it directly to me.

I leave the painting behind and take my brushes and palette downstairs to the kitchen sink where I wash them all carefully so that they are ready to be used when I come to sit back down on that stool on Monday morning. My very first art teacher taught me how important it is to keep your equipment clean and in good condition, and I have always made sure to follow that advice. Besides, that's the easy part of being an artist. Anybody can wash some brushes. It's the process of getting them dirty for a worthwhile reason that's the hardest part.

With my equipment restored back to cleanliness, I deposit it all back upstairs in the spare bedroom before taking another moment to admire the work I have just created. I really am happy with this one, and I take a photo on my mobile phone with the intention of uploading it to my website as soon as possible so that a customer might see it and potentially make me an offer on it.

I'm just about to return my phone to my pocket and leave the painting to finish drying when I hear the knock at the front door. I ordered some new plates and cutlery online yesterday, and I paid for next day delivery, so I'm assuming it's a delivery driver dropping those items off for me now as I make my way to the staircase and head down it. But when I open the door and get a look at the man on my doorstep, I see that it isn't a delivery driver holding a box full of kitchenware. It's Chris, the man I have just spent the last hour painting.

'Oh, hi,' I say, my surprise apparent in both my voice and I expect the look on my face as well.

'Hey, me again. Not a bad time, is it?'

'No, it's fine. Is everything okay?'

For some reason, I entertain the paranoid thought that he has seen me spying on him out of the upstairs window, and now he's coming to ask me what I have been doing. If that is the case then I will have to tell the truth and say that I was using him for inspiration in my artwork, and then he will most likely ask to see that artwork. That would be very awkward for both of us, I imagine, so I really hope that's not what is about to happen.

'Everything's fine. It's Friday, and I've had the afternoon off, so I can't complain,' Chris replies breezily. 'I've just been working on my car. I like to tinker with it when I have the time.'

'Oh, right, I see,' I reply, hoping that I'm doing a good enough job of pretending like I had no idea that he has spent all afternoon underneath his vehicle's bonnet.

'But I was just calling round to see if you and Sean would be interested in coming around to ours for a meal tomorrow night. Abi is a great cook, and she suggested we have you guys over for some food and maybe a bottle of wine or two. But only if you guys are free, of course. No worries if not.'

I was caught off guard by Chris' appearance at my house just now, and I'm just as surprised by his invitation for Sean and me to visit their house as dinner guests. It's a lovely gesture, and we don't have anything planned for tomorrow evening, so in normal circumstances, I'd just thank him, say yes and go and pick out a bottle of red for us to take over tomorrow. But these aren't normal circumstances, and I'm still aware of the warning Albert and Eileen gave to us when we first moved in here.

"Don't let them get too close to you."

It doesn't get much closer than going around to theirs for dinner and drinks on a Saturday night, does it? So I guess I should say no and leave it at that.

'No pressure. I'm sure you have lots of exciting plans. It was just an idea,' Chris says, and he seems genuinely nice, as well as genuinely expecting me to turn down his offer and make it clear that I do have something more exciting to be doing than sitting with him and his partner on my Saturday evening. But I don't, and I feel bad for saying no to him after he has come over here to extend the invitation.

So I don't say no. I say yes instead, and by doing so, I choose to completely ignore Albert and Eileen's warning.

But I'm sure it will be fine.

Won't it?

That's why I'm already looking forward to this bottle in my hand being uncorked, and I'm certainly looking forward to learning more about our hosts this evening. Albert and Eileen said we should be worried, but I'm not.

Instead, I'm intrigued.

The door is answered by Chris, who is looking much smarter than I am in a sharp black shirt, which makes me instantly regret putting on the casual t-shirt I have on now. Katie did tell me that I might want to wear a shirt tonight, but I told her I didn't want to look too formal in case Chris had opted for the casual look himself. But he hasn't and now I'm the one who looks scruffy out of the pair of us.

'Come in guys and make yourselves at home,' Chris tells us as we step inside, and I hand him the bottle of wine. 'Thank you, but you really didn't have to bring this. We have plenty of bottles here. I'll have to show you our wine rack. It's quite something.'

I smile as I kick off my shoes, and Katie does the same before we follow Chris into the kitchen where we find Abi standing in front of the oven looking less like a chef and more like she is just about to go out for dinner in one of the finest restaurants in Monte Carlo. She is wearing a figure-hugging red dress, and the look is complemented by the expensive-looking necklace and earrings that she has also chosen to put on this evening. Part of me is impressed by the effort she has gone to for us tonight, and the other part is feeling a little smug at Katie's situation because just like me, she is now not looking as formal as she could do. My wife did opt for a dress tonight, but it was a very casual one, and even though she looks beautiful as always, it's still a far cry from the amount of effort that Abi has obviously gone to tonight. I guess this meal really is a big deal for our hosts, and I wonder how often they have people over on a Saturday night. I presume they have plenty of friends but maybe not. For us, this is the highlight of our week, but looking at these two, it could be the highlight of their month.

'Can I get you guys a drink?' Chris asks after we have been warmly welcomed by Abi, and we politely tell him that he can, allowing him to grab a couple of fresh wine glasses from the cupboard and pour us a couple of measures to go along with the ones I can see he and his wife have already started.

'Wow, this is lovely,' I say after I have taken my first sample of the wine that he has given us, and Katie thinks the same.

'If you think this is nice, wait until you try the food,' Chris replies with a warm smile. 'Abi is making a casserole, and it's her speciality. It's to die for, trust me.'

It certainly looks like Abi has got everything under control on the food front, and so much so that she asks me if I would like to take a closer look at the home gym she has constructed in her garage. I feel like I can't say no, so I follow her out of the kitchen, leaving Chris and Katie chatting about something to do with the use of space in the kitchen and how the colour of the countertops compliments the colour of the cupboards.

I'm quite glad I don't have to partake in that conversation, if I'm honest.

Reaching the garage, Abi turns on the light and the fluorescent bulb kicks in, revealing most of what I saw the other day, which was an exercise bench, some dumbbells and a medicine ball. But being in here now, I notice there is even more equipment than I had initially realised and I'm very intrigued by the machine in the back corner of the room.

'Oh, wow. You have a mountain climber,' I say, referring to the tall black contraption against the wall that allows a user to walk up and down its moving steps as if they are walking up a mountain.

'Yeah, I use it every day,' Abi tells me as she turns it on and allows me to get a look at it in full motion. 'It's hard work, but it's great for the glutes, and what woman doesn't want good glutes?'

I smile as I watch the steps moving round and round on the machine, but it's pretty familiar to me as I've seen plenty of people using machines just like this one in the gyms that I have been a member of over the years. I've never actually seen a man use it before though because, like Abi said, it's for the glutes, and I'm not sure there are too many men who care about having a pert behind. I know it's definitely way down the list on my priorities when I go to do a workout anyway.

'I'd give you a demonstration, but I'm not really wearing the right attire for it,' Abi says as she leans over and turns the machine off, and I laugh and tell her that it's fine. She definitely isn't wearing the right clothes to use a machine like this, although I can tell that she does use it a lot, but I quickly avert my eyes away from the back of her dress as I probably shouldn't be noticing things like that.

'Like I said, you're welcome to use some of this equipment anytime you want to,' Abi tells me as we look around at the impressive array of kit.

'Thanks again, but I've just joined the gym on Westgate Road, so I'll probably do most of my workouts there now,' I tell her, relieved that I have a decent excuse to avoid having to come around here and use the spare key to access her garage. It is true that I joined the gym this week, and while I haven't actually been and used any of the facilities there yet, I am planning on doing so when things quieten down in our new house over the coming days and weeks.

'Oh, I know the one you mean. That's a great gym. Lovely big swimming pool.'

'Yeah, that's what I've heard.'

'Are you a swimmer?'

'Sometimes, although I'm more a fan of the jacuzzi, if I'm honest.'

Abi laughs and brushes a hand against my arm as she does.

'I know what you mean. That's why I try not to go swimming too much these days. I just end up sitting there in the bubbles watching all the other people swimming lengths.'

'Well, it looks like you've got everything you need here anyway,' I say, looking to wrap things up because I feel like I probably should be getting back into the house to see how Katie is getting on before either of our conversations start to dry up. But before I can go, Abi turns to me and asks me for my opinion on something.

'Do you think I look nice tonight?'

I'm surprised by the question, which is why I don't do a very good job of answering it.

'I'm sorry. What?'

'I said do you think I look nice tonight?'

I notice that Abi looks genuinely interested in hearing my opinion on her appearance, and I'm not sure why, although I have a feeling that maybe Albert and Eileen might have an idea now that it's happened.

'Erm, yeah, of course. You look lovely,' I tell her, hoping I'm treading the right line between being polite but not seeming like I'm too enamoured by her looks.

'Thank you. This is a new dress, and I wasn't sure if it would be the right occasion for it, but I'm glad you like it. I think Chris likes it too.'

'I'm sure he does.'

'And you look nice too,' Abi tells me as her eyes move from my face down to the t-shirt on my torso.

'Oh, this old thing. I probably should have put a shirt on,' I say, waving a hand dismissively and feeling bad that she is wearing a new dress while I am wearing something that I have owned for years, and even then, it has spent most of that time screwed up in a ball at the back of my wardrobe.

'No, I like the casual look. Not everyone can carry it off, but you definitely can.'

She returns her eyes to my face again as I start to wonder if she is flirting with me or just being nice. It's hard to tell what is real and what is my imagination running away with itself after what Albert and Eileen said about the people who live in this house. But I don't allow the moment to linger any longer than it should do, so I smile awkwardly before turning towards the door, looking to get back into the house and back in the company of my wife as quickly as I can.

Abi follows behind me and turns off the light as we leave, and by the time we make it back into the kitchen, I feel like I'm ready for a second glass of wine. Then I see Chris and Katie sitting at the kitchen counter laughing away, and it looks like they have already started on theirs.

13

KATIE

Chris was right. Abi's casserole is to die for. That explains why I haven't said a whole lot since we sat down at the table and started eating. I'm simply enjoying the food too much. Add on top of that the delicious wine and my taste buds are getting a real treat this evening. I can tell that Sean is enjoying the dinner too because he has been uncharacteristically quiet since it began. Instead, he's just chomping away on his casserole and glugging his wine and looking like he hasn't had a meal this good in a long time. But Chris and Abi are more than making up for our lack of speech over these last fifteen minutes as they have regaled us with all sorts of tales ranging from how they met to where they went on their honeymoon and even where they are hoping to go next year.

It was interesting to hear that they met at university, and it was certainly interesting to hear about their time in South America after their wedding because it sounded very adventurous and certainly a lot more adventurous than where Sean and I went to ours. We ended up staying in a small chateau in the North of France because it was the best thing that we could afford, but it turned out to be in the middle of nowhere, and it rained almost every day. We made the best of the situation, like most newly married couples would, but compared to Chris and Abi's story, it was certainly different. There were no steaks in Santiago and beaches in Brazil for us, that's for sure, and I'm not sure there ever will be because it seems like an awfully long way to fly for a holiday. I prefer to take trips closer to home, and if I'm really honest, I'd be happy just going to the artsy places like Vienna, Berlin and Florence every year. But that's not really fair on Sean, who prefers the beaches and bars of Spain and Portugal over the Rembrandt's and Van Gogh's on display in Central Europe, so I make sure to compromise and have our holidays cater to his tastes too.

I'm just enjoying yet another scrumptious piece of casserole when Chris asks us where we like to go on holiday, and even though I'm not snobby in any way, I feel strangely compelled to answer before my husband because I worry he might make us seem a lot less worldly than they are.

'We like to go different places,' I say as I swallow down my food. 'We try to go somewhere different every year. Our last holiday was Italy, wasn't it?'

'Yeah,' Sean replies, picking up his glass of wine and preparing to take a sip. 'But it was less of a holiday and more a tour of several art galleries, so don't get too jealous of us.'

Abi laughs at my husband's joke, but Chris doesn't.

'Which galleries did you go to?' he asks me, seemingly intrigued, which I'm not sure was what Sean was expecting.

'The Galleria Borghese and the Musei Capitolini.'

'Wow, I've always wanted to visit those. They're both in Rome, right?'

'Yeah, that's right,' I reply, impressed at Chris' knowledge of some of the most famous art galleries and museums in the Italian capital.

'How wonderful. We'll have to take a trip there someday,' he says before looking to his wife for her opinion on the matter.

'Maybe,' she replies, and I can tell she isn't as keen on the idea as I am.

'Let me guess. You prefer chilling by the pool or on the beach with a good book?' Sean pipes up, and Abi nods her head enthusiastically.

'That's more like it,' she says with a smile, and even with all the red wine and food she has consumed so far this evening, her teeth still look dazzlingly white, just like her husband's do. I really must ask them where they had them done, but only once I've got to know them a little better.

'I think the perfect holiday has just the right balance of relaxation and culture,' Chris says, twirling the base of his wine glass over the tablecloth. 'That's why Rome is perfect. You'd get the weather and the art scene.'

'Exactly,' I say, warming up now that I have somebody on my side at the table. 'There's so much to see in old cities like that. It beats lying on a beach in a tourist trap any day of the week.'

'Well I'm sold, but I think these two might need a little more convincing,' Chris chuckles, and he is referring to Sean and Abi, who don't look enamoured with the idea of using any future holidays to wander the cavernous rooms of a prestigious art gallery.

'It's lucky my husband doesn't get a say in anything then,' I joke, putting my hand on Sean's lap and giving him a cheeky smile, which gets a laugh out of Chris more than it does out of my partner.

'I can see why people would want some culture,' Sean says as he shifts a little awkwardly in his seat. 'But surely you can see why some other people just want to lie on the sand and soak up the sun when they go away. It's usually the only chance we get at good weather all year, especially if we live in England.'

'Exactly!' Abi cries a little loudly, and it maybe gives away how much she has already had to drink this evening. 'Why leave the grey skies of England behind and go somewhere warmer only to spend most of it stuck indoors looking at old pictures?'

I'm tempted to say that there is a lot more to art than just looking at some old pictures indoors, but I'm a guest here, so that means that I'm on my best behaviour, and I choose to just take a sip of wine instead. But Chris seems more than ready to fight the corner for the art lovers of the world.

'It's an acquired taste, and I understand that it's not for everyone but to me, spending an afternoon walking around a good art gallery is just as enjoyable as any other leisure pursuit,' he says, and I nod my head because I'm very much in agreement with him. But I stop nodding when Abi comes back with her retort.

'Well, I guess there's no other option for it then. You two can go to Rome and look at some paintings while Sean and I will go and lie on a beach somewhere and get a good suntan together.'

Sean laughs, obviously because it is a joke, and I try my best to do so too, but I'm also a little conscious of how things have been developing here. Chris seems to be agreeing with everything I like while Abi is sticking firmly on Sean's side. That could just be a coincidence and a reflection of their true personalities and interests. Or it could be for the reason Albert and Eileen warned us about. They might be trying to impress us as a way of getting closer, and they might be looking for a lot more than just good food, good wine and good conversation in the long run.

But I'm feeling emboldened by the alcohol in my system, so I decide to make a comeback to Abi's suggestion.

'You might think that sounds fun, but try spending more than ten minutes with Sean abroad. He'll start moaning about sun cream and midges and probably the price of a beer too.'

I'm only teasing my husband, but it is also a subtle attempt at making Abi think that Sean isn't as appealing as she might think he is. But I'm not sure it works because Abi just laughs and tells us that she hates sun cream and midges too and that she is willing to pay any price for a cold beer when abroad, which certainly makes her sound like she would be good fun on holiday.

'It's fine, Katie,' Chris says as he sits back in his chair and fixes me with a warm stare. 'We'll leave these two to the sunburn and the overpriced drinks while we open our minds and feed our creative souls in the presence of some of the best artists who have ever lived.'

I notice that Chris holds my gaze for a moment or two longer than might be considered normal when he has finished telling me his 'plan', and I'm the first one to break away from it and lower my eyes back down to the table. There's no doubt that this evening is going well in terms of the rapport that Sean and I have fostered with our hosts. But maybe it's going too well. Sean and Abi obviously have plenty in common, and it's clear Chris and I do too. If everything was normal then this could be the beginning of a beautiful friendship between us all. But not everything is normal. Albert and Eileen told us that, and no amount of casserole, red wine and holiday chat can make me forget what they did tell us.

I wonder if they saw Sean and I come over here tonight for this meal.

And I wonder if they are shaking their heads and preparing to say "I told you so" if things go wrong because of it.

14

SEAN

I drop the house keys on my first attempt at getting them in the lock, and I have to carefully bend down and scoop them up off the doorstep before trying again. Katie laughs at my poor try, and I have to admit I find it a little funny too. That's because we're both drunk, and when that's the case, everything seems funnier than usual.

I'm able to get my coordination skills working a lot better the second time around, and with the key in the door, I'm able to open it up and get us inside. As I close it behind us, Katie is already making her way down the hallway in the direction of the kitchen where she is going to get us a couple of glasses of water for our bedside tables.

I hold onto the wall beside the staircase for support as I take off my shoes, all the while thinking about the last few hours my wife and I have just experienced and what it might mean going forward. To say the dinner party with Chris and Abi went well would be an understatement. We got on like a house on fire, sharing stories, jokes and plenty of food and wine, and there was barely an awkward moment of silence to be had once we had got past the initial few minutes. I had a great time, and I'm sure Katie did too, and normally that would be a good thing. But all of the excitement and anticipation of future dinner dates to come is tempered somewhat by the knowledge of the people in the house we had to walk past on our way back home from Chris and Abi's this evening. That was Albert and Eileen's house, and while I didn't say anything to my wife at the time, I'm pretty sure I noticed Albert in an upstairs window looking out at us as we staggered back across the street in the direction of our house. I only noticed the man's shape in the window for a moment before he disappeared back behind the curtain, but I definitely saw him, and he definitely saw me, and it definitely had me thinking again about what he said to us when we first met him.

Sorry old chap, but we've gone against your advice and made friends with Chris and Abi, and I have to say, I'm not sure what all the fuss is about. As far as I can tell, they are a lovely couple who are keen to make new friends, and I'd say exactly the same about us. We're all of a similar age, and we have more than our fair share of things in common. Abi and I share a passion for fitness as well as cocktails on a sandy beach on holiday, while Katie and Chris are more into culture and visiting galleries and museums over pools and bars. But as a collective foursome, we all found common ground over the course of the evening and all enjoyed each other's company, and that is why we have already decided that we should do it again. Of course, next time it will be our turn to host, and while we haven't set a date for the evening yet, I'm sure we will get around to it in due course.

With my shoes off, I put my feet onto the steps of the staircase and make my way up to the bedroom, bumping into the wall slightly as I go, and it's another reminder of how inebriated I am right now. It's been a while since I had this much to drink, but I can also say it's been a while since I had such a good time, and the two things so often tend to go hand in hand, or at least they do for me anyway.

Reaching the bedroom, I pull my t-shirt over my head before making a bigger job out of removing my jeans than I need to. But finally, I am stripped off and lying on the bed, and all I have to do then is close my eyes and the room should stop spinning.

It works until I have to open them again when Katie tells me to drink some water before I fall asleep, and I sit up on the bed and take a thirsty gulp from the glass she has just provided me. It won't be enough to stave off the dehydration and the hangover that will be waiting for me when I wake up in the morning, but it's better than nothing, and Katie does the same thing before we place our glasses on our bedside tables and turn off the lights.

As we both lie there in the darkness, I know it won't be long until we are both fast asleep. I'll most likely end up snoring because that's what I do when I've overindulged on the alcohol front, but it's okay if Katie has been drinking too because she'll fall into such a deep sleep that my heavy breathing won't wake her. That's good because if not, she would wake me up, and I'd end up getting a terrible night's rest. But just before we drop off, Katie rolls over to face me and puts a hand on my chest.

'We don't have anything to worry about, do we?' she asks me with a hint of concern in her voice.

'What do you mean?'

'With Chris and Abi. They're just nice people, right? Just friends.'

'Of course they are.'

Katie goes quiet for a moment, and I wonder if that is it before we slip into sleep. But it's not.

'I know I don't look as good as Abi, but you love me, don't you?'

Even though I've had too much to drink, I recognise when my partner is being needy and requires some extra affection, so I make sure to roll over and face her myself before taking her hand and holding onto it as I look at her face in

110

the small amount of moonlight that is seeping through our curtains.

'I love you. Stop being silly.'

I move my head forward from my pillow onto my wife's, and we kiss for a moment. It starts off as a tender, loving kiss but soon turns into something more passionate and animalistic and before we know it, we are making out like two hormonal teenagers who have found themselves alone while both sets of their parents are away.

Sleep is suddenly off the menu as we become intimate, and our inebriated states do wonders for loosening up our inhibitions and giving us both the excuse to put a little more gusto into our performances than usual. Blame it on the wine, the fact it's Saturday night or maybe just the fact that we are finally unwinding after a hectic house move, but Katie and I are making love like we were when we first met, and I have to say, I'm enjoying it.

By the time we're done, we're both sweaty and out of breath and lying on our backs, looking up at the dark ceiling again. I'm not sure that enthusiastic performance will do as much good for our impending hangovers as the glasses of water beside us will, but it was definitely worth trying, and we both roll over on our pillows feeling even more satisfied with the evening than we were before.

111

I let out a relaxed sigh as I close my eyes and feel my heavy head sinking deeper into my pillow, and I'm almost asleep without a care in the world. Almost. That's because right before I drop off, I get a wave of guilt washing over me, and I know exactly where it's coming from.

It's coming from the fact that I wasn't entirely present when I was with my wife just then. I wasn't fully thinking about her in every moment that we were physical together.

There were a couple of moments when I was thinking about Abi instead.

15

KATIE

I tend to have lots of weird dreams when I go to sleep after drinking too much. They're not nightmares, but they're not exactly pleasant either. All sorts of weird things race through my mind behind my closed eyelids, no doubt a consequence of my brain's attempt to purge itself of the liquid drug that I ingested and indulged in a little excessively. One of the things I see in my slumber tonight is my neighbour, Chris, and just like he was in my painting, he is in front of his car with the bonnet raised, and he's working away on the engine.

It seems so vivid, presumably because it's a reflection of something I have already seen in the real world before, and I definitely feel as if I'm really awake right now and watching Chris from my window. But I also get the sense that he knows I am watching him, and every movement he makes is done for my benefit rather than his own. Like when he drops his wrench on the floor and bends down slowly to pick it up. Like when he takes off his t-shirt and reveals his toned body before taking a long swig of water. And like when he turns around and looks towards my house, spotting me watching him from my vantage point and making intense eye contact with me which he holds for an unbearably long time.

Then he starts walking towards my house, and I already know what to do. I head for the staircase, descending to the front door, which I unlock and pull open as the topless man gets closer and closer. When he reaches the open doorway, I step aside to allow him to enter, and he accepts the invitation without so much as a word.

Then I close the door and turn to face him.

And then I lean in for a kiss…

I wake up with a jolt and roll over quickly as if I need to confirm that I am lying in bed beside my husband and not my neighbour. Thankfully, it is Sean who I see beside me, snoring away loudly and looking a lot more settled than I am right now.

Letting out a deep breath, I reach over to my bedside table and pick up my glass of water before chugging the remainder of it down my parched throat and feeling the guilt that comes when you dream a dream that you shouldn't have done.

I replace the empty glass on the table quietly so as not to wake Sean, although maybe it's an unnecessary gesture because judging by the sounds he is making now, he is in such a deep sleep that not even a train passing by our bedroom window could wake him at the moment. Then I lay my head back down on my pillow again because it's still dark outside, so it's obviously far too early to think about getting up. And there's also the fact that my head is banging too, which is likely to put me off getting out of bed anytime soon.

But that all changes when I hear the loud crash at the back of the house.

Sitting bolt upright because the noise was both loud and close, I listen out for any further sounds. There are no more at first, but then I hear something again. It sounds like broken pieces of something on concrete. Maybe a broken plant pot on the patio. But why would I be hearing that in the middle of the night?

Unless somebody is in our back garden right now.

'Sean,' I say with urgency as I shake my husband awake so that he can join me in figuring out what the hell is going on outside.

'What!' he cries, and he sits up in the bed looking very confused about things.

Bless him, he's never much use when he first wakes up at the best of times, but after all the wine he has had this evening, he's going to be even groggier than normal now. But I don't have time to wait for him to come around more peacefully. I need to tell him what the problem is right away.

'I think there's someone in the back garden,' I tell him as he rubs a hand over his weary face. 'I heard a crash. It sounded like a broken plant pot.'

'What?'

'I said I think there's someone in our back garden!'

'It's probably just a fox.'

'Will you go and check?'

'What time is it?'

'It doesn't matter what time it is!'

'I was asleep!'

'Fine, I'll go and check it myself. But if I get murdered then it's your fault.'

I pull back the duvet in a huff and put my bare feet onto the carpet, annoyed at my husband and his inability to wake up immediately in the middle of the night and go and do as I say without questioning it. In hindsight, I might look back and say I was perhaps a little unfair to demand such a thing of him, but right now, all I am concerned about is making sure we don't have a burglar trying to get into our home.

I fumble around for the switch on the bedside lamp before finding it and lighting up the room, causing Sean to moan and cover his bloodshot eyes with his hand. But I don't have time for letting my own eyesight adjust, and I get out of bed and stomp towards the bedroom door to prove it.

116

'Where are you going?' Sean asks me as I open the door.

'Where do you think? I'm checking who's in the garden.'

'I told you. It'll just be a fox.'

'And what if it's not? What if somebody is trying to get in?'

I'm just about to step outside the bedroom and onto the dark landing when I pause, aware that it might not be the most sensible thing for me to go out there alone when I'm not sure who else might be out there too. It's easy to be brave and bold in the light of the bedroom, but it's not so easy in the darkness of the rest of the house.

Thankfully, Sean gets his act together and gets out of bed, and I feel much better about stepping out of the bedroom now that he is in front of me and leading the way. He turns the landing light on and heads to the bathroom window that looks out over the back garden, and I follow him in until we reach the closed curtains at the back of the room. I'm hoping that when we look out, there will be nothing of note to see in our garden. But we won't know that until we take the plunge and look.

Sean reaches for the curtains and opens them enough for him to peep outside, but I find myself hanging back a little, a little anxious about what I might see if I look too. In my mind, I'm imagining there to be two or three men in balaclavas standing on our lawn with rucksacks on their backs, and crowbars in their hands, so it's probably best that I don't look out and confirm that is the case. But Sean doesn't seem so worried, and then I find out why.

'There's nobody there,' he tells me after a tense few seconds.

'What?'

'I can't see anybody.'

'But I heard something.'

'Well, I don't know what it was, but there's nothing there.'

I move beside my husband and join him in looking out of the window down into our dark garden. But there's enough moonlight for us to be able to see the lawn, and it looks clear. So too does the patio, although I can only see a portion of it from this angle.

'See, there's nobody there,' Sean tells me again with a definite hint of "I told you so" to his voice. 'It was probably just a fox. Like I said.'

With that he turns away from the window and heads back towards the door.

'Are you coming back to bed?' he asks me when he notices that I'm still at the window looking out at the garden.

My eyes scan the hedges and the flowerbeds for any sign of movement or just a shadow that shouldn't be there, but just like Sean, I can't see anything untoward. I guess that's it then. There's nothing else to do but go back to bed.

'Fine,' I say as I close the curtains and follow my husband back out of the room.

Sean wastes no time in getting back under the duvet and closing his eyes, and he tells me to hurry up and turn the lamp off so that we can go back to sleep before we make the morning's hangovers any worse. I do as I'm told, but there's no way I'm going to be able to sleep now. I'm too wired after the noise I heard in the back garden. But there's something else causing me to keep my eyes open too.

It's because the last time I closed them, I saw myself being intimate with Chris.

16

I could do without any work today after the copious amounts of red wine I consumed last night, but before I can crawl onto the sofa and spend my entire Sunday watching sports on television, Katie wants me to go out into the garden and check everything is alright. She still seems a little worried after what she apparently heard in the middle of the night, and that's funny because I'm still feeling exhausted after she disturbed my sleep so dramatically in the middle of the night too. But I'll do anything for an easy life, and especially when my head is pounding like it is now, so I tell her I will go out and check the garden now that the sun has come up and I'll be better able to see what I'm doing.

Unlocking the back door, I step out onto the patio, and I'm instantly met with the sight of several broken plant pots sitting in piles of scattered soil.

I guess Katie was right.

Something did happen in our back garden in the early hours of the morning.

I let out a deep sigh as I inspect the mess and wonder why I bother trying to get my

120

garden looking nice. I should just get a gardener and let them deal with it. I'd be happy to pay them because no matter how hard I try out here, it doesn't seem to be improving. Not only has the local neighbourhood fox obviously had his way with the flowers I planted earlier in the week, but the lawn doesn't seem to have responded to the seeds I sprinkled on it earlier. I've been watering it regularly to try and breathe some life into it, but the blades of grass still look like they have been burnt and butchered beyond repair. With all that in mind, I add calling a gardener on my to-do list for the upcoming week as I grab a dustpan and brush from the garage and start sweeping up the mess on the patio.

It's not a big job but it's an annoying one, and I'm expecting Katie to come outside any minute now and tell me how she knew something had happened in the night and I should have been less grumpy with her. But to my surprise, it's not her voice that I hear a few seconds later. It's an unfamiliar one instead.

'What happened to your garden?'

Turning around, I initially fail to see where the question came from until I notice the face peering at me over the garden fence. It's Jackson, and he looks happy about something, though I'm not sure what.

'Erm, I guess a fox must have got in here last night,' I say with a shrug of my shoulders. 'It's annoying, but it's part of the fun of having a garden, I suppose.'

'It looks like it made a right mess,' Jackson comments, and he still seems to be smiling about something.

'Yeah, I guess it did.'

'Did it do that to your lawn too?'

Jackson nods his head towards my yellowish patch of grass, but unfortunately, I can't blame the state of that on any animals.

'No, I think that was the old owners,' I tell him with a resigned shake of the head.

'Unlucky. It looks terrible.'

'Thanks.'

I'm not sure Jackson's presence is making either my hangover or my current task any easier, so I'm just about to turn back around and carry on tidying up when he speaks again.

'You should look after your garden more. People can make all sorts of mess. Oh, and foxes can too, I guess.'

He flashes me another smile, and he's just about to disappear back on the other side of the fence when I wonder if he is trying to hint at something.

'Do you know what happened here?' I ask, suddenly remembering what Albert and Eileen had to say about the teenager at Number One.

'How would I know?' Jackson replies with all the confidence and cockiness of youth.

'I don't know. You just seem like you're enjoying seeing all the mess. It's almost as if you're feeling smug about something.'

I study Jackson's youthful face to see if I can get any clues as to what he might really be thinking behind that grin of his, but I can't know for sure.

'I'm just saying hello to my dad's neighbour,' he replies.

'So this wasn't you?' I ask, gesturing to the soil and broken pottery around my feet.

'No, it was a fox, like you said.'

With that, Jackson drops back down on the other side of the fence, and I'm left staring at the space where he once stood and wondering if he was winding me up. Maybe on another day I would have just left it and gone back to cleaning the patio before retiring inside to where my water, snacks and sports shows awaited. But with the grumpy mood I am in, no doubt enhanced somewhat by my lack of sleep and hydrating liquids, I decide that I'm not going to leave it there. Not after the way Jackson was with me just then. It was like he was enjoying seeing me cleaning up the mess.

The mess he might very well have created himself.

Putting down the dustpan and brush, I walk around the side of the house and out to the front, where I make my way next door to where the teenager resides. But it's not him that I want to speak to now. It's his father. I want to ask Ian if he heard anything next door during the night, and while I'm not expecting him to say that he did, it will be a good way of letting his son inside the house know that I'm not just going to let these disturbances go without investigation. Maybe it was just a fox, and maybe Jackson was just being curious when he poked his head over the fence and commented on the mess. Or maybe he was revelling in seeing me be annoyed about something he might have had a hand in. I won't find out by asking him directly, and I definitely don't want to go starting any fights with his father by making any accusations yet, but I'm annoyed, and most of all, I'm thinking about what the couple at Number Three told me.

"He has no regard for other peoples' privacy or property. I've seen him in our garden before, and I've even caught him trying to steal something from my garage before, after I left it open by mistake."

Albert and Eileen were talking about Jackson, so what if it's no coincidence that barely a week into being in our new home and we've already had an issue on our property?

Reaching my neighbour's front door, I knock three times before stepping back and taking a deep breath. I must stay composed and polite. I'll ask Ian if he heard anything and if he has ever had any problem with foxes before. He might wonder what the hell I'm on about, but he also might have a word with his son if he suspects him of being involved, which I do now. But there's no answer to my knocking, so I try again, almost certain that Ian is home because his car is parked on the driveway behind me.

However, that fails to get a response from inside the house either, and that irritates me because I know at least one person is home. Jackson could answer the door even if his dad wasn't able to. But what can I do? I guess I'll just have to leave it.

I walk away up the driveway, but I glance in one of the front windows as I go, and when I do, I see Ian sitting in an armchair watching television. He's home, after all. So why didn't he answer me? That's when I remember another thing that Albert and Eileen told us about the people at Number One.

"Ian doesn't tend to get too involved in what his son gets up to when he's staying with him. He mainly just sits in his armchair and drinks lager, leaving Jackson free to roam around and cause trouble where he sees fit."

Maybe Ian knew why I was coming around and couldn't be bothered to deal with it. Or maybe he is just lazy and isn't planning on making any more effort with his new neighbours after that brief 'chat' we had on his driveway the other day.

I grit my teeth because if there's one thing I can't stand then it's laziness, and Ian sitting in his chair while I knock on his door and get no response from him smacks of laziness, as well as perhaps arrogance too. That could be where Jackson gets that smugness from, I suppose.

But what can I do? I can't force a man to answer his front door and talk to me, can I? I'll just have to see him around. I guess I'll be seeing Jackson too. But one thing is for sure. If I see him in my back garden when he shouldn't be there then I'll be doing a lot more than just knocking on his father's door next time.

I'll be knocking him out, full stop.

17

KATIE

The house is quiet on this sunny Monday morning, and the weather is just one of the reasons why I'm feeling a lot better today than I was yesterday. Sunday was a long day, thanks to my hangover from Saturday night, my lack of sleep after being woken up in the early hours by the noise in the garden and most of all, because of Sean's grumpy mood.

He had gone out into the garden yesterday to clean up the broken plant pots that he initially believed to be down to a pesky fox, but he had come back inside with a different opinion altogether. It seemed he then blamed our neighbour's son, Jackson, for the damage and to make matters worse, he had apparently gone next door to potentially voice that opinion. But that hadn't gone how Sean had hoped it would, and he had spent the rest of the day in a grouchy mood on the sofa, not really talking much about anything after that. I know how irritable my husband can be when he's overindulged the night before so I left him to it, but that didn't mean I had an easy day myself. That's because I know what caused Sean's mood to really turn yesterday, just like I know what caused my own insecurities about Chris and Abi, and how we should be around them in our early days. It's because of what Albert and Eileen said. They warned us about Jackson, and they warned us about the couple at Number Three. They have given us a reason to doubt other people and their intentions, and with that, they have left us with a lot of insecurity going forward.

Sean left for work this morning, feeling marginally better than he did yesterday but still not his usual charming self, and that is why I feel compelled to leave the paintbrushes in their packaging this morning and make the short walk next door to Number Two.

I'm going to try and have a word with Albert and Eileen and see if I can get them to expand any more on what they told us last week.

I'm going to try and put my mind at ease.

And I'm hoping to put my husband's mind at ease too.

Reaching their front door, I knock lightly on it, not wanting to startle the elderly couple inside. I'm not sure how many visitors they get, particularly on a Monday morning, so I don't want to make them jump too much. But then I note that their car isn't on the driveway, so I wonder if the house is empty, and this has been a wasted trip. That is until I see movement on the other side of the frosted glass and hear a key turning in a lock.

'Oh, hello dear,' Eileen says when she sees me on her doorstep. 'Is everything okay?'

'Yes, it's fine. I just wanted to pop round and say hi,' I reply, wishing at that moment that I had come up with a better excuse for being here, like bringing some food round as a gift or asking for advice like when the window cleaners are due in the area.

'What a pleasant surprise. I was just about to do some washing up while Albert is out, but this seems like a good excuse for a cup of tea. Come in, dear.'

Eileen beckons for me to enter her home and I do, warmed by her welcome while also feeling a little anxious about being here simply to broach the subject of our other neighbours.

'Albert's just popped to the shops, but he'll be gone a while, so we have the place to ourselves,' Eileen tells me as I walk in. 'Truth be told, I like it when he gets out from under my feet every now and again.'

'I'm the same with Sean,' I say with a laugh as I wipe my shoes on her doormat.

As I close her front door behind me while she scurries into the kitchen to put the kettle on, I take a look around at the furniture and décor in the hallway. The first thing I notice is how dated it is, although that's not exactly a surprise considering that this home belongs to those in the older generation. The flowery wallpaper and the antique-looking cabinet at the foot of the stairs reminds me of my grandparents' home when I would visit there as a child, and it feels homely, but still very different to what I'm used to.

I'm about to follow Eileen into her kitchen when I notice the photos on the cabinet, and I lean in for a closer look. There are two frames on here, and the first one shows the homeowners on what was presumably their wedding day. I smile as I see Albert with a full head of hair looking resplendent in a smart suit as he beams beside his beautiful bride. Eileen really was quite the looker back in her heyday, and her wedding dress was beautiful. Then I look at the second photograph, but this one is of somebody who I don't recognise. It's a young man, and he definitely has the same smile as the two people in the photo beside him, but I don't know who it could be.

'That's my son, George,' Eileen says, and I turn around to see her standing in the kitchen doorway, having just caught me snooping at her photos.

'Oh,' I say, a little caught off guard that she saw me before quickly recovering. 'He is very handsome. How old is he?'

'That photo was taken when he was twenty-one. He's forty-two now, and as you can imagine, that makes me feel very old.'

I laugh before she asks me if I would like a piece of shortbread to go with our tea, and I say, 'That would be lovely, thank you,' before walking away from the photos on the cabinet and following her into the kitchen.

As she opens a cupboard and takes out a packet of shortbread biscuits, I look around at the small kitchen table, the garish green tiles on the wall and the lino covering the floor that looks like it was laid sometime in the sixties. This kitchen looks a lot different to mine, but everybody has different tastes and ideas about how they want their house to look, and I'm sure Eileen is very happy with how hers is. It certainly is homely, if a little tired.

Eileen asks me how I take my tea, and I tell her just a dash of milk and two sugars before she puts four pieces of shortbread onto a plate and asks me if I would like to sit out in the garden as it's such a lovely day out there. I like the sound of that, and we head outside into the sunlight that is bathing her beautiful back garden in its warm rays.

'Help yourself, dear,' she tells me as she pushes the plate of biscuits closer towards me after we have taken a seat on her patio furniture, which is a plastic table and chairs set positioned with a lovely view of her immaculate lawn and her well-tended-to flower beds.

'It's been a while since I had a visitor over,' Eileen admits to me after I have taken a

131

bite from my piece of shortbread and washed it down with a perfectly made cup of tea.

'Do you have family in the area?' I ask, hoping that she does because I can't think of anything worse than someone her age feeling lonely, even if she does have her husband around most of the time.

'Not as much as I used to. A couple of nieces and nephews. But most of my family moved further out. They like to be closer to the city. It's too quiet for them around here.'

'I like the quiet,' I admit, and Eileen tells me that she does too before I ask her where George lives now.

'Oh, he's all the way over in Australia,' the proud mother tells me, beaming from ear to ear as she talks about him. 'He's an engineer, and he's working on a very big tunnelling project in Queensland.'

'Wow, that sounds fun.'

'Yes, he works very hard, but he loves it out there.'

'Have you and Albert been out to visit him?'

'We went in 2015 for a month. It was a wonderful trip. But it's such a long way to go, and I dare say we'll never make it again. Twenty-four hours is too long to be sitting on an aeroplane with my back these days. And Albert suffered terribly with the jet lag last time too.'

'Oh, I see. Does George come home often?'

'He's not been back for almost a decade,' Eileen admits. 'But he's very busy, and we understand he has his own life over there. He doesn't need to be coming back to check on his mum and dad all the time.'

I smile before taking another sip of my tea, and as lovely as this conversation is, I know I came here today to talk about something else entirely.

'Is it okay if I ask you a little more about what you said to me and Sean last week?' I ask, approaching the subject cautiously.

'What was that, dear?'

'About what you told us regarding the other neighbours on the street.'

'Oh, I see. Yes, of course. What would you like to know?'

I fiddle a little awkwardly with my teacup as I watch a beautiful blue butterfly fluttering around at the bottom of the garden before just going for it.

'Were you serious about what you said?' I ask, hoping this will be the part where Eileen confesses to it all just being one big joke that her and the rest of the neighbours are in on.

'Deadly,' she replies, and she keeps her expression stern as she picks up her cup and takes a sip.

That really wasn't the response I was hoping for.

'Oh, I see.'

'Has something happened, dear?'

'No, not at all. Well, possibly. There was a bit of a mess in our back garden when we woke up on Sunday morning, and I'm not sure if somebody was out there.'

'Jackson,' Eileen says with a shake of the head.

'Well, it could have been a fox, I suppose.'

'We don't have many foxes around here. Just a troublesome teenager with a penchant for sneaking onto other people's property and leaving a mess behind.'

'So you think it was him?' I ask, although it's fairly obvious at this point that she does.

'Albert and I wouldn't have said those things if they weren't true,' Eileen replies before reaching out for her first piece of shortbread.

I think about what she has just said as she nibbles on her biscuit, and just like the butterfly that is still flying around in this garden, I feel jittery and unable to keep still. The last thing any person wants when they buy a new house is to find out afterwards that they might have nuisance neighbours. It's not as if it's exactly easy to just sell up and move, nor should anybody have to because it's not fair for someone else's behaviour to force a person out of a home they love. But I do worry now that there will be more incidents on our property, and if so, I worry that Sean won't be able to control his temper as well as I can about it all. He was certainly frustrated yesterday, and this was just over a few broken plant pots. What if Jackson does something worse? But before I can worry anymore about that, Eileen moves on to the other problem we might have.

'How have you been getting along with Chris and Abi?' she asks me after finishing her biscuit and the butterfly has flown away over the garden fence.

I can tell by the tone in which she asked the question that she is insinuating something, but I decide to be honest and say things as they are.

'Really well,' I admit. 'They had us over for dinner on Saturday night.'

'I see.'

'It was nice.'

'I'm sure it was.'

'You think we shouldn't have gone?'

'I didn't say that.'

'But you're thinking it?'

Eileen turns away from looking at her picturesque garden and looks at me instead, and I see that her stern expression is back again.

'You and Sean are a lovely couple, and you remind me a lot of the couple who lived in your house before you,' she says. 'It's such a shame what happened between them but make no mistake, it wouldn't have happened if Chris and Abi hadn't made it happen.'

The gentle breeze that was blowing in the garden seems to stop for a moment as the two of us sit there quietly at the table, and not even the reappearance of the beautiful butterfly can make me feel any better after what I just heard.

'You seem like lovely people, and you have a good home,' Eileen goes on after I have failed to come up with a response. 'But people are only as good as their actions, and a home is only as good as the people who live in it. I'd hate for either of you to do anything you'd regret but make no mistake about it, you will be pushed to your limits here. The other neighbours will see to that.'

18

SEAN

It's Friday night, and I'm home alone. I've just dropped Katie at the train station where she is travelling to Nottingham for a weekend catching up with her uni friends. That means that I've got a couple of nights to myself, and while I have plans to catch up with a few mates tomorrow, tonight is going to be a quiet one. Just me, a movie and a 14" pepperoni pizza from the local takeaway.

As I tuck into my first delicious slice with no regard for what it might be doing to my arteries, I savour the peace and quiet that one can only get when they have the house to themselves. Katie doesn't go away often, but I like to make the most of these times when she does. I miss my wife when she's gone, but I also miss those carefree times from my single days when I would just lounge around on my own eating junk food and watching whatever I wanted to watch on the TV, so I will make sure to savour this time now. It won't be long until Katie is back, and we'll be eating healthier meals and watching something we have both compromised on, but that's Sunday.

Right now, thank God it's Friday.

I use the remote control to browse the channels on the hunt for a great movie to go with my great pizza. As I do, I receive a text message from Katie telling me that her train is arriving in Nottingham and she is looking forward to going for a drink with her friends as soon as she gets there. I write back a quick message telling her that I hope she has a good time as well as sending her a photo of my pizza to show her that I am already having a good time myself.

I'm pleased that Katie is going to have a fun weekend, and I'm also quite pleased she is having a short break away from here. I feel like it will do her good to get off this cul-de-sac because, with her work from home job as an artist, she has pretty much been here all day every day since we moved in. That wouldn't necessarily be a problem in itself, but it hasn't made things any easier when it has come to the situation with our neighbours.

My wife told me that she went round to Eileen's earlier in the week and probed the older woman on the small matter of the warning she gave us about our other neighbours, and from what I've seen since, it's only made things worse. Katie seemed very paranoid after that, and I really wish she hadn't gone around there and given herself more to worry about. Speaking for myself, I am not at all bothered about anything that might happen here. If Jackson does anything in my garden then I will sort it out with his father or the police, and if either Chris or Abi try to make a move on Katie or me then we will politely but firmly decline the offer and carry on with our lives. None of it has to mean it's the end of the world, and a lot of it is still ifs and buts at this stage anyway. But Katie seems very troubled by the thought of it all, and that's why I'm glad she has gone away for a change of scene this weekend. I'm hoping she will come back with a fresh perspective on things when she returns from Nottingham and realise that no matter what anyone else on this cul-de-sac might say or do to us in the future, it's only the two of us who can ultimately control our fate. As long as we stick together and don't do anything stupid then everything will be fine, if anything else does happen at all, and that's a big if.

I include myself in that because I know I have the tendency to get a little angry and overreact at times like I did when I stormed around to Ian's house after getting the feeling that his son was revelling in the 'misfortune' of the broken plant pots in my garden. In hindsight, I should have just left it, and I'm quite relieved now that Ian didn't answer the door because it might not have ended up going well if he had, considering the mood I was in. But there will be no repeat of that, even if Jackson gives me any more reason to believe that he might have trespassed on my property and caused damage. If that happens then I will just call the police and let them deal with it. Things might be difficult after that between us and the residents at Number One, but sometimes that's just how it is with neighbours.

I don't know many people who are best friends with the people who live beside them. People just tolerate their neighbours most of the time rather than become best friends with them, and if that's what we have to do then so be it. As for Chris and Abi, Katie and I have decided to hold off on inviting them round for a meal to return the favour of when they had us around for dinner. We're not saying we won't do it at some point in the future, but we're not going to be in a rush to do it either. The decision is more for my wife's benefit than my own because I'm sure we have nothing to worry about when it comes to the couple at Number Three, but I'm happy to do whatever will set her mind at ease at this time. But I'm definitely glad Katie is off this street for a few days, and I'm hoping that when she returns, we'll spend a lot less time talking about our neighbours and more time talking about ourselves and all the fun things we are going to do in the future, like redecorating projects around the house and holidays in the upcoming summer.

I'm halfway through my pizza and ten minutes into a classic Nineties action movie when I hear the doorbell. It makes me jump, one because it was unexpected, and two because I'm still getting used to the sound of it after only installing it a couple of days ago. It's definitely loud, and I need to figure out how to turn the volume down on it a little bit or I'm going to be jumping out of my seat every time somebody comes along and presses it.

Getting up off the sofa and reluctantly leaving my pizza and movie temporarily behind, I walk through the hallway and reach the front door before unlocking it and pulling it open. But when I do, I fear that it might be a while before I get back to my quiet evening alone. That's because Abi is standing on my doorstep, and she is holding a bottle of wine.

'Oh, hi,' I say, unable to hide my surprise.

'Hey, I saw you take Katie out earlier and figured you were home alone. Me too. Fancy some company?'

She flashes me the bottle of red, as well as a dazzling smile, but all I'm thinking about is why she was keeping tabs on mine and my wife's movements.

'Erm…' I say, stalling even though I know that there's no way that I can say yes to her. I can't allow Abi in here while Katie is away, regardless of how innocent it would be, because to do so would only feed my wife's paranoia even more. I'll just have to come up

141

with an excuse as to why I can't be a sociable neighbour tonight.

'This is a great wine,' Abi says, showing me the label. 'One of my favourites. I'm going to drink it tonight regardless, but it's always better to drink with company, isn't it?'

It is, but that's not helping me get rid of her.

'I'm sure it's great, but I can't,' I say, scratching my head and sounding about as convincing as a guilty man on the stand when all the evidence is against him. 'I've got an early start tomorrow, so I'm not drinking.'

It's a poor attempt at a lie, and anyone with half a brain cell would be able to see straight through it, which of course, Abi does.

'Come on, you mean to tell me that you aren't having a little tipple or two on your Friday night alone?' she says, testing me and I fold easily under questioning.

'Well, maybe one or two,' I admit with a nervous laugh, and she has all the encouragement she needs to shake the bottle of wine at me even more.

'Then you won't want to be drinking alone either. So come on, go and get a couple of glasses, and we'll put the world to rights while our partners are out having their fun.'

I sometimes wish it was socially acceptable to be rude to people who are just being nice. If it was then I would just slam the door in Abi's face and disappear back into my house, where I would spend the evening alone at no risk of stressing out my darling wife. But it's not socially acceptable to do such a thing, and having already failed at coming up with a convincing story about not wanting to drink tonight, I'm not sure what else I can do other than be polite and allow Abi in.

I'll just have one glass with her and then tell her that I need to get an early night.

Just one glass.

And a quick one at that.

19

KATIE

It's good to be back in Nottingham, where I spent three fun-filled years as a student at the city's university. I'm here to catch up with my old uni friends, and so far, I have seen three of them. We are sitting around a table in a plush wine bar that we definitely wouldn't have been able to afford to drink in back when we were cash-poor undergrads, and it's been a fun evening so far. Tomorrow will be the highlight of the weekend when two more of our old friends will join us, and we will spend the day floating down the River Trent on a boat, sipping champagne and scoffing snacks before a night out in one of the city's many trendy hotspots. But that doesn't mean that this evening has to be a quiet affair, and we have certainly ensured that it's not. The clock is approaching eleven, but my friends are showing no signs of wanting to retire to their beds at the hotel, and neither am I. We're having too much fun, and that's why we have just made sure to get another round of drinks in when the last orders was called by the barman a moment ago.

I decide to make a quick trip to the ladies' room before the waiter brings our new drinks over, so I pick up my handbag and put the strap over my shoulder before making my way through the busy bar in the direction of the door at the back. Entering the bathroom, I find myself a vacant cubicle and take a seat but not before removing my mobile phone from my bag so I can make a quick check on my messages at the same time. I'm expecting Sean will have replied to my last text to him, which was around two hours ago, and it will be good to read it and fire back a response of my own before I return to my friends at the table. But to my surprise, there is no message from my husband, and not only that but he hasn't even read my last one to him. I wonder if he has had an early night, and it is possible although I would have imagined he would have stayed up a little later than this and made the most of having the house to himself by watching several movies that he wouldn't get a chance to watch if I was there with him.

I consider calling him but decide against it in case he is asleep, so I make do with sending him another text telling him that I'm feeling a little tipsy but will be going back to my hotel soon and that I'm missing him like I usually do whenever we are apart. After pressing send, my thumb finds its way to the app for my favourite social media site, and I spend a few seconds scrolling through some of the updates from my family and friends who use this site too. I see the photo I have been tagged in by one of the women whom I am with this evening, and I make sure to Like it before scrolling on. But then I see something that I definitely do not like, and it's the thing that my husband has been tagged in this evening.

"Movie night at my new neighbour's house. Good wine and great conversation!"

There is no photo accompanying the status update, but the name at the top tells me who has written it. Abi Cromwell, as in Chris and Abi Cromwell. She's tagged Sean in her update, which is why it has appeared on my feed, and going off what she has posted fifteen minutes ago, she is at my house with him right now.

So I guess Sean isn't sleeping after all. This must be why he hasn't messaged me back. He's been busy entertaining our neighbour.

But why is she there?

And why was it happening while I am away?

I waste no time in finding Sean's number on my contacts list and call him, holding the phone to my ear as I wait for him to pick up. While I do, my mind is running away with itself and thinking all sorts of paranoid things based on what Eileen said to me when I visited her home earlier in the week. This isn't just any woman who is at my house with my husband while I'm away. It's a woman who I have been specifically warned about, and now I want to know what is going on in my absence. I'm also curious as to why Abi posted the status update because she must have known that I would see it if she tagged my husband in it.

Is she deliberately trying to make me jealous or worried?

I grind my teeth together when it seems like Sean isn't going to answer my call, but he eventually picks up the phone, and I hear his voice at the other end of the line.

'Hey, are you okay?' he asks me, not sounding sleepy like I might expect at this time on a Friday night, nor sounding nervous or sheepish about having another woman around when I'm not there. If anything, he just sounds a little drunk.

'What's going on?'

'What do you mean?'

'I mean why is Abi at our house with you tonight?'

The line goes quiet for a second.

'Sean? What's going on?' I repeat.

'Hang on a second,' he says, and I wonder if he is leaving whichever room he is in to continue this call somewhere more private, out of Abi's earshot.

'Sean, tell me what's happening,' I plead with him, and I'm sure I'm sounding a little drunk myself, and that is no doubt

147

contributing to my anxiety levels right now. Maybe if I was clearer minded then I wouldn't be jumping to conclusions right away, but as it is, I'm sitting in this toilet cubicle in a wine bar in the middle of Nottingham city centre, and I am demanding to know what my husband is doing with our attractive neighbour while I am away.

'Sean!'

'Calm down,' my husband tells me, and I hear the sound of a door closing at the other end of the line. I guess I was right about him taking this call somewhere more private. But whereabouts in the house is he now, and more importantly, which room has he just left?

The living room? The kitchen?

Or the bedroom?

'How do you know Abi is here?' he asks me as if that is the more important question that needs answering.

'She posted something online,' I tell him. 'Movie night at my new neighbour's house. She tagged you in it.'

'I had no idea,' Sean replies, but that's hardly a source of comfort.

'What is she doing there? Did you invite her round?'

'No, of course not!'

'Then why is she there?'

'She just turned up at the door with a bottle of wine.'

'And you let her in?'

'Yes, I mean, I said no at first, but she said she was on her own, and I felt rude turning her away when she knew I didn't have anything better to do either.'

'How did she know I was out?'

'She said she saw me taking you out in the car earlier.'

'She's been watching us?'

'No, I don't think it's like that. She probably just looked out of her window when we were driving off.'

'And when you got back without me, I presume?'

'I don't know, Katie. But there's nothing to worry about. We've literally just sat on the sofa and chatted while we watched a film.'

'And drank wine.'

'What?'

'Her status said good wine.'

'Yes, we've had a couple of glasses. I told you she brought a bottle round, remember?'

'I want you to get rid of her. I don't want her there when I'm not around.'

'Katie, calm down. You're overreacting. Everything is fine.'

'Is it? Not according to Albert and Eileen. According to them, Chris and Abi are going to try and break us up.'

'Not this again.'

149

'Yes, this again! I want you to get rid of her now!'

'Seriously, you're overreacting.'

'I don't care. I want her gone!'

'Fine, I'll tell her to go when she's finished her drink.'

'No, screw her drink! Get rid of her now, and I want you to call me when she's gone.'

'You're acting like a crazy person.'

'Just do it!'

'Fine!'

With that, Sean hangs up on me, and I'm left looking at my phone in my hand and waiting for him to call me back to let me know that Abi has left our house. But until he does, my mind will continue to think all sorts of things about Abi and her real intentions for going around to my home this evening to see my husband while I am away. Sean might think that I'm acting irrationally, but I'm sure plenty of other husbands have thought the same things about their wives until suddenly it's too late, and things have happened that cannot be undone.

I don't want Sean to do anything stupid, and while I feel like I trust him, I don't trust Abi, and that's why I want her out of my house.

The only question is, will she go?

20

SEAN

I've ended the phone call with my wife in no uncertain terms about what I need to do next. I need to walk back into the living room and ask Abi to leave. Or as my wife put it so eloquently, "get rid of her." That's why I head for the closed door, planning on doing exactly that when it opens and Abi enters the kitchen.

'Is everything okay?' she asks me, and she is concerned enough to put a hand on my arm as I stand in front of her at a close distance.

'It's fine,' I tell her, making sure to take a quick step back to make her remove her hand from my skin and increase that distance between us again.

'Was that Katie?'

'Yeah.'

'Is she having fun?'

'I think so.'

'That's good. I'm glad we're not the only ones. By the way, I paused the movie when you went out, so you didn't miss anything.'

'Oh, thanks,' I say, thinking of the thriller film we were about halfway through before we got interrupted by Katie's call. I was enjoying the film, and I have to say I was enjoying the bits and pieces of conversation that interspersed my viewing of it too because Abi is good company, and I find her insights on certain things to be fascinating. But unfortunately, this is going to have to be where the fun ends. I'm not going to have any more fun chats this evening with Abi, nor are we going to be able to watch the end of the movie together. That's because I have to ask her to leave now before my wife calls back and gets even more worked up than she already is.

'I'm really sorry, but we're going to have to call it a night,' I tell the woman in my kitchen. 'I'm feeling pretty tired. I think the busy work week has finally caught up with me.'

'Oh, that's a shame. Are you sure?'

'Yeah, I hope you don't mind.'

'No, not at all. We can finish the film another time.'

I smile at Abi because she just seems genuinely nice, and it is frustrating that Katie is believing the word of Eileen over me when I say that there is nothing to worry about. But I don't want to incur the wrath of my wife, so I follow Abi out of the kitchen, where she gathers up her belongings in the living room before heading for the front door.

'Do you want to take your wine with you? There's enough for one more glass in there,' I say, picking up the bottle and calling after her.

'No, it's okay. You have it as a nightcap if you want,' Abi tells me as she puts on her shoes. 'Besides, I feel a G & T coming on instead.'

She gives me a wink as I stand in the hallway and watch her get ready to go. As I do, I check my mobile phone for any sign of another call from my wife, but there is none yet.

'Well, I've had a great time,' Abi says when she is finally ready to go. 'We'll have to do this again soon.'

'Yeah, when Katie and Chris are back,' I say before wishing that I hadn't because I'm worried it might have come across that I didn't enjoy just spending time alone with her, which is definitely not the case.

'Of course,' Abi says as she opens the front door. 'Well, enjoy the rest of your weekend, and if you're feeling lonely at any point, you're welcome to come over. There's plenty more wine and movies over there.'

She flashes me that brilliant smile of hers before stepping outside, and I give her a wave as I reach the front door and stand in the space where the cold air is seeping in and mixing with the warm air that was already inside.

'Goodnight,' I call after her, and she gives me a wave as she heads up the driveway and onto the street, her heels clip-clopping across the concrete as she goes.

Closing my front door, I lean back against it and let out a sigh, feeling a mixture of both relief and disappointment. I'm relieved to have been able to execute my wife's wishes so quickly but disappointed because I was enjoying this evening with Abi, as I feel like I had a right to do. Katie is having fun on her Friday night, and I should be able to do the same. Abi is a friend, it's as simple as that, and why can't I have a glass of wine and a chat with a friend when my wife has gone to Nottingham tonight to do exactly the same thing?

But before I have time to think about it anymore, I hear the ringtone from my mobile phone again and see that Katie is calling me back.

'Has she gone?' she asks me as soon as I have answered.

'Yeah, she's just left.'

'Good.'

'Is it? She wasn't doing anything wrong.'

'We'll talk about it on Sunday. I need to get back to my friends.'

'Yeah, go on, you enjoy your Friday night, and I'll just sit here on my own.'

'Don't be like that. You said you were looking forward to having the place to yourself.'

'Yeah, I was. But then our neighbour called round and was nothing but friendly.'

'I wonder why.'

'Don't be sarcastic.'

'I'm not. You heard what Albert and Eileen said, and you know what happened to the last couple who got too close to Chris and Abi.'

'I don't care. We're not those people. We can make our own mind up about things!'

'I really need to get back. But I'll call you when I get back to the hotel later, okay?'

'Whatever,' I say, and I hang up after that, which might not have been the best thing to do in the circumstances, but I'm irritated as well as emboldened by the red wine in my system.

It's the red wine that I return to now, and I re-take my seat on the sofa and pour myself the last dregs from the bottle before picking up the TV remote and pressing play on the film that Abi had kindly paused for me. It's a shame I couldn't watch the rest of this film with her but never mind.

I'm about ten minutes further into the action on screen when I hear a noise that almost causes me to spill my glass of wine all over the carpet. It was the sound of shattering glass, and it sounded like it came from the kitchen.

Putting my glass down and rushing out of the room, I enter the kitchen and look towards the window, or rather, where the window used to be. But as I feared, the glass is now broken, and

I see why when I look down at the floor. There is a brick lying on the ground on top of the shards of glass. Somebody just threw that straight through from the back garden.

But who?

It might be safer to just stay in the house and call the police, but I'm far too angry to do that after seeing my property damaged, so I rush to the back door and unlock it quickly before pulling it open and peering out into the darkness.

'Who was that? Who's out here?' I call out in my gloomy garden, but I don't see or hear anything in the way of a response.

Stepping outside, I can feel my heart hammering in my chest as I stand on the patio and look around for any sign of the vandal. But it's too dark out here, so I turn on the torchlight on my phone and move it around, hoping that will shine some light on this shocking event. But the garden seems empty. There's nobody out here, at least not anymore. But there definitely was, and I know that because I have the broken window and the brick to prove it.

It's time to call the police.

What a Friday night this is turning out to be.

21

KATIE

It took two hours to get back to my hometown on the train from Nottingham, followed by a fifteen-minute car journey when my husband collected me from the station, but it's the latter that felt the longest. As Sean parks up on our driveway and I gather up my belongings, feeling tired after a busy weekend of socialising, I'm glad to be home. But mainly, I'm just glad to be getting out of this car.

Things are still obviously awkward between my husband and I since the events on Friday night when I had a go at him for allowing Abi into the house while I was away and demanded that he make her leave immediately. We actually hadn't spoken properly to each other since then until I arrived into the station today and found him waiting for me in the short-stay car park outside. Our communication over the weekend had been reduced to just a few text messages, and they weren't quite as long and chatty as they usually were.

"How's your weekend going?"
"Fine. You?"
"Yeah, it's okay."

"Cool. See you Sunday."

Like I said, not exactly as long and chatty as they usually were. Now we are back together again in person, it is a chance for us to be a little more expressive with each other and put to bed any lingering thoughts and feelings that are still residing in us after what happened on Friday. But it's only a chance, and it won't be seized if neither one of us is willing to actually open up and talk about it.

As I step into the house and put my weekend bag down onto the hallway floor, I realise that Sean isn't going to be the one to bite the bullet, so that leaves me with little choice but to do it myself.

'Come here,' I say as I approach my husband and open up my arms, inviting him in for a hug.

He accepts the gesture, and we embrace for a moment before sharing a quick kiss and a couple of apologies. Then I lead him into the living room, where we take a seat on the sofa, and I decide that honesty will be the best policy going forward.

'You might think that I overreacted on Friday night when I found out that Abi was here,' I begin, holding Sean's hands and looking him in the eye. 'And maybe I did. But it was only because I was afraid. I'm afraid of losing you.'

158

'Don't be silly. You're not going to lose me.'

'Just listen to me for a second. I know you are attracted to Abi.'

'What? I didn't say that!'

'It's okay. I understand. She's very attractive, and you guys obviously have plenty in common. I could see that on the night we went to theirs for dinner.'

'Katie, seriously. I don't know what you think-'

'Listen to me for one minute. It's okay. I'm not mad at you, and I don't blame you for liking her. Just like I don't blame myself for liking Chris.'

That last comment catches Sean off guard, and he suddenly stops being defensive.

'What?'

I take a deep breath and then repeat what I just said about how I find my male neighbour attractive, and I do that because it's the truth. I do like Chris, just like I know Sean likes Abi. Because they're ultra-friendly and ultra-attractive, and we're only human.

'I can't believe you're telling me this,' Sean says as he removes his hands from mine and gets up off the sofa. 'I can't believe you're telling me that you want to be with our neighbour.'

'That's not what I said at all,' I say as Sean paces across the carpet in front of me.

159

'What I said was that I like him. But that doesn't mean that I like him more than you or that I'm going to do anything about it. It just means that I'm being honest and acknowledging my feelings, and that's all I want you to do too.'

'What do you mean? I am being honest with you!'

'Are you? Do you mean to say that you don't find Abi even slightly attractive?'

'No!'

'Why are you lying to me?'

'Why are you forcing me to say it?'

'Because it's important that we're honest with each other. That's how couples stay together!'

Sean stops pacing and stares at me from his spot on the carpet over by the window, the window that looks out to the house where the two people live that have caused us to have this conversation right now. Chris and Abi. I wonder if their Sunday is going as wildly as ours is so far.

'I've no idea what's going on here,' Sean admits with a shake of the head. 'But I'm not sure I like where this is going.'

It wasn't my intention to make my husband feel worried, so I get up off the sofa and go over to him where I re-take his hands and force him to look at me so he can see how serious I am about what I am trying to tell him.

'The reason I told you I like Chris is because I want you to know that it's okay if you like Abi too. It doesn't mean anything, and it doesn't mean that I'm going to be unfaithful. It's just me acknowledging my honest feelings with you so you can do the same.'

'What do you want me to say? That I like her? That I was having fun on Friday night until you called and made her leave? Is that it?'

'If that's the truth then yes, I suppose I do.'

'Fine! I like her, and I was having fun with her!'

'Okay,' I say, looking into my husband's eyes and keeping hold of his hands. 'That's absolutely fine. Thanks for being honest. Now do you see why I have to be like this?'

'Not really, no.'

'It's because I know I can trust you, and you can trust me. But we can't trust them. Chris and Abi, I mean. We can't let them come between us and change this amazing thing that we have here together, you understand?'

'But they're not. They're just our neighbours.'

'But they're a temptation, and from how it seems to be going, they will become more of a temptation the longer we're here. Unless we acknowledge it honestly and make a plan to avoid it.'

'What kind of plan?'

'I think it's sensible if we agree not to see them anymore. We'll be polite but firm. Cordial but not chatty. Wave, say good morning and good evening, but that's it. No more dinner dates. No more borrowing things off them and certainly no more being around them when one of us is away.'

'I still think you're overreacting.'

'I don't care. All I care about is making sure that we don't end up like James and Sarah.'

'That's not going to happen.'

'I know it's not, and the reason for that is we are too smart to let it happen to us. Okay?'

I'm being forceful with my husband, but I mean every word I am saying. I don't care about Chris and Abi, or Albert and Eileen's warning or the previous couple who lived here and ended up getting divorced. All I care about is the man standing right in front of me and making sure that nothing or no one ever comes between us.

'Okay,' Sean says with a nod of the head. 'We'll keep our distance from our neighbours. All of them. But that doesn't guarantee that they will keep their distance from us.'

'What do you mean?'

With that, Sean leads me by the hand out of the living room and into the kitchen, and when he does, I see the cardboard covering the hole where the kitchen window used to be.

162

'What happened?' I cry, rushing over to it to get a closer look.

'Somebody threw a brick through the window on Friday night.'

'What? Why didn't you tell me?'

'I didn't want to ruin your weekend. And I was fine. I wasn't in the room when it happened.'

'Who did it?'

'That's what I was hoping the police would help me find out. But they said it's unlikely they can catch the perpetrator if I didn't see anything.'

'Who the hell would throw a brick through a person's window!' I cry as I shake my head and turn back to my husband. 'It could have killed you.'

'Like I said, I'm fine. I was in the other room when it happened. I'm just waiting for the glass company to come out and fix it tomorrow.'

'This is awful. I thought this was a safe neighbourhood.'

'So did I until Albert and Eileen told us about Jackson.'

'You think this was him?'

'Could have been,' Sean says with a shrug. 'But I don't have any evidence. Not yet anyway. Come here.'

With that, Sean leads me outside into the back garden, where he points up to something on the wall on the back of the house.

163

'I had that camera installed yesterday. If it is Jackson coming into our garden then we should be able to see him now.'

'This is so bad. We shouldn't have to get cameras to protect our home.'

'I'll do whatever it takes. Just like you will.'

Sean and I share a moment of mutual respect as we stand there and think about all the things we have spoken about since I got back home. I'm looking out for our marriage by having us avoid Chris and Abi going forward, and Sean is looking after our home by installing the camera in case the neighbour's son is the one causing the damage. I guess that means we are both doing as much as we can at the moment to keep our home and our relationship intact.

Hopefully, that will be enough.

Hopefully, things are going to be okay.

22

I never thought I'd say this, but I'm glad it's time to go back to work again. I'd usually be spending these last few minutes before leaving the house on a Monday morning rushing around in a sleepy state trying to get my act together. But I was actually up before my alarm today, and I'm preparing to leave without so much as a concern about being late to the office.

The reason for my uncharacteristic eagerness is a result of me feeling like I could use a little space from this street, this house and even the woman I share it with. But it's not the brick through the window that has me keen to get away, nor is it the awkwardness of Friday night after Abi's visit ended so abruptly and I incurred my wife's wrath. It's because of what my wife told me when she came home from her weekend away yesterday. She admitted that she liked Chris, as well as saw through my poor attempts at pretending that I didn't like Abi either, and that was unexpected, to say the least. Katie always has been brutally honest, and that's surely a good trait to have, but sometimes she can be too honest, and I feel like yesterday was an example of that. Did she really have to tell me that she was attracted to Chris, and did she really have to call me out about liking Abi too? What's wrong with keeping some things private, even between a husband and wife?

It wasn't great to hear that Katie admired our handsome neighbour, but it doesn't really mean anything. I know she admires several Hollywood actors too, because she always drools over them whenever they come on screen during our movie nights together, but it doesn't mean she is going to act on it and leave me for any of them. So why do things have to be any different when it comes to Chris? So what if she likes him, and so what if I like Abi? We're married, and that means we can't and won't do anything about it.

Doesn't it?

I pick up my briefcase and head for the door, calling out a goodbye to my wife upstairs as I go. She calls back to wish me a good day before I open the front door and step out into the early morning drizzle that I'm hoping will be doing wonders for my parched lawn today. Heading to my car, I can't help but glance in the direction of Chris and Abi's home, but I instantly wish I hadn't done when I see Abi leaving her own house at the same time as me.

Damn it. We've made eye contact now, and I really hope she doesn't want to chat. I'm supposed to be avoiding her, and for all I know,

Katie might be peeping out of the bedroom window right now watching me.

Abi offers me a wave, and I wave back, albeit barely before I unlock my car and pull open the door, tossing my briefcase onto the passenger seat and getting in behind the wheel. I'm hoping she will take my rushed behaviour as a sign that I'm running late for work rather than because I'm trying to avoid conversation, but I guess I won't know. All I can do is start the engine, reverse off the driveway and get going.

As I do, it seems silly that I'm going to have to be this way with a neighbour for presumably the rest of the time we live here. But that's what Katie has said we need to do, and the fact that she was so honest and raw yesterday tells me that she really thinks it is for the best. Of course, much of that has to do with what Albert and Eileen told us about the couple at Number Three being on the prowl for new couples to sink their teeth into, but it is what it is. This cul-de-sac is obviously full of characters, and it seems that Katie and I are best served not tempting fate and just keeping to ourselves.

But it's not easy to keep to yourself when someone on a bicycle rides out right in front of your car, and that's exactly what happens to me before I can drive off this street.

Slamming on my brakes, I narrowly avoid hitting the bike and its rider, but then I see who it is, and maybe it wouldn't have been a bad thing if I had hit them. It's Jackson, and he looks annoyed that I almost ran him off the road.

'Hey, watch where you're going!' he shouts at me when I wind down my window beside where he has come to a stop.

'You came out right in front of me!'

'Whatever,' Jackson replies in a grumpy tone, and he looks like he's ready to pedal away. But just before he does, he pauses and looks back at me.

'Why were the police at your house the other night?' he asks.

I study his face as the drizzle continues to fall around him and my car to see if he is asking from a place of genuine curiosity or because he knows full well why and just wants to revel in my misfortune. But I can't read him or his mood. Damn teenagers.

'Someone threw a brick through my kitchen window,' I tell him while making sure to keep eye contact with him to see if he looks away nervously. But he doesn't. He just looks towards my house and then shrugs.

'Know who did it?'

'I have my suspicions,' I reply, testing the teen on the bike to see if he crumbles. But he doesn't. He's as annoying as this light rain.

'Well, good luck catching them, whoever it was,' he tells me before putting his feet back on his pedals and racing away down the road.

I watch him round the bend and disappear and wonder where he is off to. School, perhaps, but he wasn't dressed for it. But he must be going there if he's only fifteen. Who knows? Not me, that's for sure.

Before I drive off, I glance at Jackson's home, or rather, his father's home, and wonder when Ian will be going away on the rigs again. According to Albert and Eileen, he is away quite a lot, and he's been back a while now, so he should be due to leave any day. That will mean Jackson will be gone too, back to his mother's house wherever that is, and it will certainly be interesting to see if there are any further disruptions in my garden while he is gone. If so then I guess it wasn't him causing the trouble. But if not then maybe he is the person I should have told the police to look into.

As I drive away, I slightly regret not mentioning to the police my suspicions of the teenager next door when it came to the brick through the window. I was close to doing so, but without any actual evidence, I thought it was pointless, and all it would do would either make me look stupid or cause Ian to get angry with me for accusing his son. But with the camera on the wall now, I'm hoping there will be some hard evidence in place should anything else happen in the future.

Considering I was supposed to be avoiding my neighbours, I've managed to spend the first two minutes outside of my house waving at Abi and having a 'chat' with Jackson. That's not the best start to mine and Katie's plan, so I better get moving.

Leaving the street, I drive through the rain in the direction of my office, strangely feeling more relieved the further I go from home. Surely it's supposed to be the opposite way around but whatever. Right now, I'll take any good feeling I can get, however it comes, and at least I have the chance to get off the cul-de-sac whenever I need it. Katie will be working from home all day again, so she's stuck there in our house with that view and those neighbours.

There have been plenty of times during our relationship where I have envied my wife's more peaceful working situation when compared to my own. Getting to work from home is surely better than fighting through rush hour traffic in the rain to go and sit at a desk in a stuffy office all day.

But not today.

Today, I feel like I'm the lucky one.

23

KATIE

Despite the distractions of the weekend, my mind is surprisingly clear as I sit in front of my easel and paint. There are always good days and bad days when it comes to creativity, but today is definitely a good day, and my paintbrush is moving across the canvas without much resistance, which is a relief because this is supposed to be my job after all. I wish I could bottle days like this up and use them on the days when things aren't so well, but that's just the mystery of art. You never know when inspiration will strike and everything will flow, but you better make sure you're ready for it when it comes.

I was certainly ready today, and so much so that I have almost finished this painting and will still have time to move on to a second one. It's only two o'clock, and Sean told me he is going to the gym after work, so I estimate that I've got at least five more hours until he is home. That means I could technically sit here and keep painting until then, and while I'm in a mood like this, there's no reason why I shouldn't. I could sit back here again tomorrow and hit the creative wall again, so I should capitalise on this while I can.

Feeling good and painting even better, there is not much that can stop me when I'm like this. But then the doorbell rings, and that is something that can cause me to lower my paintbrush and sit back in my seat. I don't know who it is, but I'm reluctant to get up and leave my workstation when things are going so well, so I decide to wait and see if the visitor tries again. The sound of the doorbell a second time tells me that they are trying again, and I let out a sigh before standing up and leaving my brushes by the side of the palette.

Reaching the top of the stairs, I peer down to see who it might be and when I do, I catch a brief glimpse of the man outside. It's Chris, but this time, he hasn't seen me.

Stepping away from the staircase again so that I'll be out of view if he looks back inside, I wonder what it could be that he wants. But whatever it is, it's not important. What's important is that I don't answer this door. That's because I've told my husband that we should do our best to keep our distance from the couple at Number Three going forward, and I can hardly expect him to do that if I don't do the same. That's why I won't go downstairs and answer the door now. I'll just stay up here on the upstairs landing until I'm sure Chris has gone.

I feel slightly pathetic for being afraid to answer the door to my own house, but I'd feel even worse if I did anything that could encourage Chris to get closer to me and keep coming round here when my husband is not home. It's plausible that Chris will just think that nobody is in, so he won't even know that I'm actively avoiding him, and that's fine by me. I don't want him to know, just like I don't want Abi to know that Sean is now avoiding her because that would make things awkward whenever we bump into each other out on the street. I just need them to think that we're busy and we don't have the time to see them as much anymore. Surely they'll appreciate that because everybody's busy these days, right?

Everybody except Chris it seems, because he has just rung my doorbell for the third time.

He really is keen to see me open the front door, but that's why I have to be even keener to not do that. Surely a normal person would have given up after two rings and left. Three pushes of anybody's doorbell seems a bit excessive, doesn't it? But the fact he is still out there makes me even firmer in my belief that he isn't just some friendly neighbour and is, in fact, just a man with one thing on his mind, like so many other men out there in the world. He is here because he wants to get closer to a woman.

He wants to get closer to me.

173

Well I'm not going to let him do that. He and his wife might have had their way with the last couple to live here, but they aren't going to get so lucky with us. Sean and I are too smart to let our guard down and make a mistake that could blow up our marriage and see the pair of us have to sell this house and split the proceeds during our divorce. We're one step ahead of the couple at Number Three, and we will stay one step ahead of them for as long as we live here. They might think we can be put under their spell with friendliness mixed in with flirting and kind gestures that are really just ways to bridge the gap between them and us so that they get what they want. But they are wrong. I wasn't born yesterday. Neither was my husband, and the elderly couple who live next door to us certainly weren't either, so between us, we are on to Chris and Abi's game, and we are going to beat it.

I'm really hoping that I won't hear a fourth ring of the doorbell any second now because that would move this from the territory of slightly strange to suspiciously stalkerish, but the house is silent, and I suspect Chris has gone. I'm just about to peep around the top of the stairs again to make sure when I hear what sounds like something being pushed through my letterbox.

I guess he is still out there, so I avoid poking my head around the top of the staircase for a little while longer, but after another minute has passed, I feel like it should be okay to look. When I do, I see that there was something that came through my letterbox. It's a card, and it's lying on the doormat.

What is it? I guess there's only one way I'm going to find out.

Creeping down the stairs as if I'm scared of what I might find waiting for me at the bottom, I reach the doormat and bend down to pick up the card. When I do, I see that it is a ticket to an art exhibition at a local gallery tomorrow lunchtime. Is this why Chris came around? Was he hoping to give me this ticket in person?

I have to assume so because it came through my letterbox while he was outside.

Then I turn it over and see that there is something written on the back.

I thought you might be interested in this. Chris.

Yep, it's definitely from him then. Damn, I really wish that he hadn't pushed this through. That's because I feel like I can't just ignore this ticket as easily as I could ignore the ringing doorbell. A doorbell doesn't have to be answered, but a ticket invitation to an event does. I presume Chris will have spent money on this, so even if I don't go, and I am planning on saying no, the right thing to do would be to return the ticket so he could either gift it to somebody else or sell it and get his money back.

But how can I return it without going over there and giving it back?

Damn it. I guess it's not as easy to avoid people as I thought.

Of course, I could just ignore the ticket, not go to the event and then when I do see Chris at some point on the street, just thank him but say that I wasn't able to make it. That's not exactly the best way to deal with it, but it is surely better than me going to his house and handing it back.

Unless I don't hand it back. I could just post it back through his letterbox and walk away without knocking on the door so that I don't have to see or speak to him. That will mean he won't have the chance to change my mind, nor will he have the chance to flash me that smile, engage in some gentle flirting and seize the opportunity to get to know me any more than he already does.

That's what I will do. I will just go round to his and push this through his letterbox with a small note on the back saying thank you, but I'm unable to attend. But I can't do it now because one, I know he is in now, and two, I am supposed to be out considering I failed to answer my doorbell. I'll do it later, preferably when it's gone dark, so he has less chance to see me coming and be waiting by the door. Yes, I'll leave it until tonight. That will be best.

Putting the ticket on the kitchen counter and heading back to my artwork upstairs, I shake my head at how ridiculous this whole situation is. I can't believe that I'm having to figure out the best time to go around to a neighbour's so that I might not be seen. What's next? Putting out the bins in the middle of the night to avoid doing it at the same time as them?

This is stupid, and the more I think about it, the more I'm not entirely convinced that my plan to avoid Chris and Abi is a viable one. We live on the same street, and it's a very small one at that. We're going to see them, and even if we stay away from them, they obviously aren't shy in coming to us. Abi with her bottle of red wine when I was away and now Chris with his invite to an art exhibition while my husband is at work. They seem to want to spend more time with us than they do with each other. But Sean and I just have to make sure that no matter what we do, we spend more time with each other than we do with them.

That will be easy enough to do, right?

24

SEAN

It's good to try and decompress after a long day in the office. Some people use television, some use alcohol and some use exercise. I've been known to use all three over the years, but tonight, I am going for the healthy option.

Walking into the changing room at my local gym, I'm instantly met with the sight of at least half a dozen naked men standing around in front of their lockers, drying themselves off with a towel, putting on their gym gear or just standing around and seemingly basking in the attention that their toned torsos are getting from the other gym users. I love coming here and working out three to four times a week, but it does have its downsides, and no doubt the worst one of all is the fact I have to see so many male appendages flapping about before me.

Reaching my locker after doing my best to keep my head down and avoiding eye contact with any of the nude men around me, I enter the combination on my padlock and open the door to take out my rucksack inside. Rummaging through it, I remove the towel, swim gear and pair of goggles from within and proceed to remove my clothing, joining the rest of the other men in this room in a state of undress.

I've just completed a thirty-minute exercise circuit in the main gym area, but my workout isn't over yet. I'm going to go for a quick swim now, and I'm very much looking forward to getting in the water for some front-crawl action. It's been a while since I went swimming, but this gym is supposedly well known in the area for its impressive pool facilities, so it's high time that I sampled them for myself.

Having changed out of my sweaty t-shirt and shorts into my soon to be soaking Speedos, I re-lock my locker and throw my towel over my left shoulder before walking barefoot through the changing rooms and out to the pool area. I'm relieved to see that the four swimming lanes here are not too busy, but there are just enough people using the pool this evening to warrant me having to share one of the lanes with another swimmer. But that's okay. Like most pools, this one operates with a clockwise system, meaning that even if two people are swimming in the same lane together, they will be able to easily avoid getting in each other's way during their respective exercise.

I hang my towel on a spare peg and stretch my arms above my head to get loose before slipping into the water and beginning the next part of my workout. The water is warm, and

179

it feels good to be gliding through it as I pick up the pace and head for the other side. I presume this pool is the same size as the one in my old gym, so I know that I should be able to get around twenty-five lengths in without too much bother over the course of the next half an hour or so, not that I'm in a rush or anything. The big clock on the wall tells me that it is approaching seven, but I should be home by half-past, and I'm sure Katie won't mind me being a little later than I predicted I was going to be. It's not as if we have any big plans for this Monday evening other than having dinner and getting ready for another day of doing the same thing tomorrow.

I was on length five when I saw the other person in my lane climb out of the pool, and I enjoyed having it all to myself right up until I was on length twelve. That was when I saw somebody else climbing in, and I knew I would have to go back to sticking to the clockwise system so we wouldn't bump into each other at some point. With my goggles on and my head under the water half the time, I didn't really get a good look at the woman who I was now sharing this lane with when we first passed each other. But gradually, over the course of the workout, I was aware that she was swimming faster than me and was starting to catch me up. I wasn't going slow, it was more that she seemed to be going really fast. I guess I wasn't as fit as I thought I was, but I wasn't going to let pride get in my way. Rather than try and speed up myself and risk giving myself a stitch, or worse, a heart attack, I decided to slow down a little more so it would be easy for the rapid swimmer to overtake me on the next length.

It was a minute or so later when I could hear her moving through the water behind me, and I fully expected to see her passing me on my left-hand side any second then. Sure enough, I saw a flash of an arm in my peripheral vision before a white swimming cap and a pair of goggles came next, covering most of the hair and face of the person wearing them.

I was impressed at the way the athletic body cut through the water so effortlessly, and it was a far cry from how I imagined I looked as I swam up and down this pool, trying to execute my front-crawl technique efficiently but really just slapping each arm in and out of the water as my weary legs kicked through the churning water in my wake. But as the swimmer passed me, she turned to look at me and gave me a smile, and it instantly threw me off my stroke.

That's because it was a smile that I recognised.

It was the one that belonged to Abi.

She slowed down her own stroke as she came alongside me, to the point where I stopped entirely and put out my hand to hold onto the lane divider that was floating on the water beside me. It was too deep in this part of the pool to touch the bottom with my feet, so I would need to use the divider for support. But Abi didn't seem to need it. She just bobbed beside me, treading water easily and demonstrating just how fit she really was.

'Hey! Fancy seeing you here!' she cries as she lifts her goggles up to get a better look at me.

'Oh, hey,' I reply, lifting my own goggles up but managing to get some chlorine-filled water in my eyes as I do, forcing me to squint as my vision stings briefly.

'Are you enjoying your swim?'

'Yeah, it's my first time using the pool.'

'Oh, I'm sure it won't be your last. It's a great pool. Definitely the best in the area.'

'Yeah, that's what I've heard.'

I'm doing my best to hang on to the lane divider and keep my head above water as my tired legs kick beneath me, all the while wondering what the odds were on me ending up swimming in the same lane as the neighbour I was trying to avoid.

'I thought you did your workouts at home?' I ask as Abi continues to bob gracefully in the deep water beside me without so much as a sinew of effort on her face.

'Yeah, but I sometimes come here and buy a pass for the pool,' she replies. 'I thought I told you that.'

Now she mentions it, I do recall her saying something like that, and I realise how foolish I was in thinking that it would be so easy to avoid Abi by coming to the gym. Just because she exercises in her garage, it doesn't mean that she doesn't use the local facilities from time to time, and for a woman as fit as her, I should have known there might be a chance I would end up seeing her down here at some point. But that's not much help to me now that we're beside each other in the pool. So much for my promise to my wife that I would avoid Abi. Now here we are, our half-naked bodies only inches apart from each other.

'How many lengths are you doing?' Abi asks me, and before I answer, my brain seems to tell me to make up a bigger number than the one that would be the truth. But I don't do that. Instead, I just try to extricate myself from this situation as quickly as possible.

'I don't actually keep count,' I lie. 'But I've finished now. I was just about to get out.'

That was a lie too because I still had at least another dozen laps to do, but now I'd rather just get out and get home to Katie, who I will probably have to tell about this in case she finds out from Abi at a later date and gets all worked up again. But before I can swim away, Abi wipes her wet face with a hand and looks a little serious all of a sudden.

'Is everything okay between us?' she asks me.

'What? Of course it is,' I say, probably trying too hard to convince her.

'I hope I didn't cause any trouble when I came around on Friday night. You seemed a little stressed when you asked me to leave. Is everything okay with Katie?'

'Yeah, it's fine. And I wasn't stressed. I was just tired.'

'Oh, I see. Well as long as everything is okay.'

'Yeah, it is.'

I hate lying, and I'm sure Abi can see right through my awkward demeanour but whatever. At least she looks like she is about to swim away herself.

'That's okay then. I'll see you around,' she tells me, and I nod my head like some stupid sealion as I prepare to watch her turn and swim off. But just before she does, she turns back to look at me one more time.

'Look, I know not everyone is as open and friendly as Chris and I are,' she says. 'But if we're not yours or your wife's cup of tea, you can just let us know. We won't be offended, and we'll keep to ourselves.'

I feel instantly awful after what I have just heard. Abi has obviously picked up on the tension between us and has mistaken it for me not liking her, which isn't the case. She couldn't be nicer. Neither could Chris. It's just…how the hell am I supposed to say the truth?

'No, are you joking? We love you guys,' I tell her, saying what I can to make her feel better about herself. 'Sorry if we've come across as impolite. We've just had a lot on with the house move, and we're tired, stressed, all the usual stuff, you know.'

Abi looks relieved and smiles at me again.

'Well, that's good because Chris and I think you and your wife are great, and we'd love to see more of you. Maybe we can do something at the weekend?'

Damn it. How have I got myself into this situation? Katie is going to kill me.

'Erm, I'd have to check with my wife but possibly,' I mumble, and Abi flashes me another smile before telling me not to forget to stretch after my exercise. Then she swims away, as quickly and as easily as she arrived. But swimming is over for me tonight. I now need to go home and tell Katie that I've not done a very good job of sticking to the plan that she came up with earlier.

25

KATIE

I peer out of the living room window in the direction of Number Three while thinking about how I am not doing a very good job of sticking to the plan that I came up with earlier. I'm looking at this house because I'm trying to see if Chris is inside or not. That's because I need to go over there and return the ticket for the art exhibition tomorrow, and I'm hoping I will be able to do it without him seeing me and opening his front door to chat. But there's no car on the drive, and I can't see any lights in the house. That suggests to me that nobody is home, and that means the coast might be clear for me to scurry over there and drop this ticket back through his letterbox along with the short note I have written in which I thank him for the offer but politely decline due to a prior commitment.

Heading to the front door, I put on my shoes and coat before stepping outside onto my dark driveway. Sean will be back from the gym any minute now, and I'd hate for him to return and see me either going or coming back, but I wanted to wait until the sun had gone down before I made this attempt. The cover of darkness can be my friend, but I'm aware it's not just anybody at Number Three who I am hiding from. It's the couple at Number Two as well because I'd hate for Albert or Eileen to see me going over there because that would suggest that I was ignoring their warning to stay away from Chris and Abi, and I am definitely not doing that.

I creep across the cul-de-sac feeling like I'm some kind of spy on a secret mission, and in a way, I suppose I am. I'm trying to stay in the shadows as if some enemy sniper is out there looking to pick me off, and I'm doing my best to stay quiet as if Chris, Abi or indeed Sean have supersonic hearing and know where I am going. But in reality, it's less Mission Impossible to get across the street unseen and more Mission Accomplished because I reach the front door, take out the ticket and note from my pocket and push them both through the letterbox before turning to leave.

There, that was easy, wasn't it? I don't know what I was so bothered about. It was a piece of cake. Speaking of cake, I might treat myself when I get home and…

The sound of the door opening behind me almost causes me to jump out of my skin, and I turn around to see Chris standing with the ticket and note in his hand.

'Hey, Katie,' he says as he looks down at what I have just pushed through his letterbox, but it won't take him long to figure out what it is and what it means. The note was only a short one, and nobody returns a ticket they are planning to use, so I'm sure it will only take him a few seconds to get the idea.

'Oh, hey. I wasn't sure if you were in. I didn't see the car.'

'Abi's taken it to the gym.'

'Oh right.'

I stand there awkwardly as Chris reads my note, wishing I just left posting it until the dead of night because then Chris would have been in bed, and he would never have been able to open the door so quickly. Come to think of it, how was he able to open the door so fast? I'd barely let go of the ticket and note before he popped up. Had he seen me walking over? Possibly, and it could have just been bad luck on my part that he happened to glance out of his window as I was making my way over here. Or he could have been watching me, knowing exactly what I was doing and lying in wait for when I got closer. Oh, hello, paranoid thoughts again.

'You can't make it tomorrow?' Chris asks me as he looks up from the note.

'No, unfortunately not. I'm really sorry. But it was a lovely offer though, so thank you for that.'

'No worries. Another time maybe.'

'Yeah, another time,' I say, halfway up his driveway and just itching to get home.

The part of my brain that always fears the worst is currently telling me that there are going to be car headlights arriving on this street any second now, and they will belong to my husband's vehicle. He will see me standing here talking to Chris, the man I admitted to fancying and also the man I promised I would stay away from, and then what will he think? And how will I be able to tell him to stay away from Abi if I can't keep my end of the bargain?

Glancing over my shoulder to nervously check the entrance to the cul-de-sac, I fail to see any car arriving, and that is a relief, but I really do need to get going and stop tempting fate. But before I can, Chris speaks again.

'While you're here, you couldn't do me a favour, could you?' Chris asks me.

'What kind of favour?'

'I've just been making something for Abi and would like your creative opinion on it, if you don't mind?'

'Oh, erm. I really should be getting back,' I say, without expanding at all on what it is that I should be getting back for because, of course, there is nothing.

'It'll only take a second. Please. You'd be doing me a huge favour.'

'I'd love to, but like I said. I have to get back.'

I feel bad, but I expect that to be it, so I turn around to walk back home.

'Katie?'

I can't walk away after he has just said my name because that would be plain rude as well as plain obvious that I am trying to avoid him now, so I turn around again and face him.

'Yeah?'

'I'm not sure what you think Abi and I are like, but I can assure you that we're good people.'

Damn, can he tell that I'm feeling awkward around him and his wife?

'Sorry, I don't know what you mean.'

'Have Albert and Eileen been talking about us to you?'

'What?'

I doubt I'm doing a very good job of playing dumb, but I'm going to keep trying anyway.

'Is this about what happened with James and Sarah?'

I can't play dumb there because I know exactly who he is talking about. They are the couple whom Sean and I bought Two A from. They are also the couple who split up after apparently breaking their marital vows with the couple at Number Three.

'I'm not sure what you mean,' I try, but it's a poor attempt because I know my face is giving away my true thoughts.

190

'Look, I'm not proud of the part Abi and I played in the breakdown of their marriage, but we're not bad people, and we didn't make either of them do anything that they didn't want to do. And Abi and I have suffered too. I'm not sure if you could tell, but we're not as close as we could be after what happened.'

I'm tempted to say that's probably to be expected when married couples stray, but I don't, deciding instead that I'll stick with my fairly useless tactic of still trying to play dumb. But I am surprised by Chris' honest admission. And I am even more surprised by what he says next.

'I bet Albert and Eileen warned you about us, didn't they?' Chris asks me, and I'm not sure how I'm going to be able to get away with not answering that one.

'Erm…' I begin, but Chris obviously knows, and he nods his head.

'I'm not surprised. They got on well with James and Sarah, and they blamed us for them splitting up and moving out. They even came around here and had a go at us both.'

'Albert and Eileen did?'

'Yeah, they're such busybodies. Always sticking their noses in other people's business. I tend to stay away from them as much as I can these days, but it's not easy to avoid people on a street as small as this one.'

I know exactly what he means.

191

'Look, I just want you to know that you have nothing to worry about. Abi and I are no threat to you and Sean. I can see how much you guys love each other, and I'm sure nothing would ever get in the way of that.'

I didn't need Chris to give an endorsement of my relationship, but I appreciate it, nonetheless. I also feel bad about the way I have been lying and being closed off with him in trying to avoid him and declining the exhibition invite now that he has just been so open and honest with me. Maybe he is right. Maybe Albert and Eileen should stick to their own business and not worry about other people's.

'You said you had something you wanted to show me?' I say, figuring this might be a good way to show that I'm not just taking the word of my elderly neighbours over the words he has just said to me right here on his driveway.

Chris' face lights up when he realises that I am offering to do him that favour he just asked of me, and he beckons me inside quickly because apparently he needs to show me this thing and put it away again before his wife gets back from the gym.

Having followed him into his house and into the kitchen, I see what it is that he wanted to show me. It's a drawing, and I presume it's supposed to be of Abi. The problem is, it's not very good.

'What do you think?' he asks me as I look down at the picture on the table. 'I've been doing a drawing class online, and I'm trying to have a picture ready for her birthday next week. Is it any good?'

It's a decent attempt, I almost say, but I'm not sure I'd call it good.

'Erm, I think it's got potential,' I offer, but I guess that doesn't cover up my real thoughts.

'I knew it was rubbish. I should never have bothered.'

'No, I didn't say that.'

'But you're thinking it, I can tell. You're a terrible liar. I knew that the second you told me nothing was wrong earlier.'

I see the wry smile on Chris' face, and I can't help but laugh because he has rumbled me. But it's enough to ease the awkward tension between us after what we have discussed tonight and so much so that I tell him that I will help him out and have a go at painting Abi, and if it goes well, he could give that to her as her birthday present instead.

Chris is thrilled at my suggestion and accepts the offer before I tell him that I really must get going. Then I leave his house and feel relieved not to see Sean's car on our driveway yet as I do.

I make it home and close my front door before kicking off my shoes and hanging my coat on the hook. Then I think about what just happened. Chris was vulnerable with me and admitted to his past mistake. He also suggested I shouldn't listen to Albert and Eileen because they liked the last couple who lived here and therefore blame Chris and Abi for them leaving.

So what does all this mean? Are Chris and Abi really as dangerous as we were told? Or could they just be our friends after all? And should I tell Sean about what has just happened?

I guess I should. No secrets, remember. But maybe I'll edit the story a little. Maybe I'll tell him everything except the part where Chris admitted his and Abi's mistake with James and Sarah as if it was a regret and something that would never happen again. That's because I'm not sure I want Sean to know that. If he does, he might think it's okay to be friendly with Abi again, and despite how I have just been with Chris, I still feel jealous when it comes to his wife. I guess I don't see Chris as a threat anymore, but for some reason, I still see Abi as one. Call it female intuition or perhaps just plain paranoid envy, but I'll still ask him to stay away from her to be on the safe side. But as for Chris and I? Would it do any harm if we were friends? I have just offered to paint a picture for him, so I guess that's a friendly thing to do.

I'll have to think about that one.

I can think about it while I'm painting his wife.

26

SEAN

I'm really not happy about having to come home from a busy Wednesday in the office to get the ladders out of the garage and climb up to check on the guttering again. But that's what I'm going to have to do because Katie has told me that there seems to be another blockage up there again after she noticed problems during the heavy rainfall today. I thought I'd got all the dead leaves and rubbish out of there last week, but I guess not, so here I am again, looking to do yet another repair job on this house that is slowly but surely testing my will. If it's not the blocked gutters then it's the burnt lawn, and if it's not the burnt lawn then it's the broken window and the smashed pot plants.

Propping up the ladders against the side of my house, I decide to climb up and make a quick check on the guttering before I get any tools out of the shed because hopefully, I might not need any, and it will be a few minutes work with just my hands.

I'm about halfway up the ladder when I look to my left at where my newly installed camera is supposed to be positioned and pointing at the garden. But to my shock, the camera is not there. All that remains of it is the wire coming out from the brickwork. It's as if the camera has been ripped off the wall completely.

'What the hell?' I say as I lean over and inspect the situation, but there really isn't that much to see. Just a wire hanging uselessly where there was once a fairly expensive piece of equipment instead.

'I don't believe this,' I say as I shake my head and grit my teeth.

This has to be Jackson. He must have seen me put the camera up and thought he would take the opportunity to come around and take it back down again. It was obviously him who broke the plant pots and him who threw the brick through the kitchen window, and he knew he needed to get rid of the camera so that he was free to carry out more damage on my property without consequence. I'm being directly targeted here, and it's time it stopped.

The problem is that Jackson is no longer next door. I saw Ian packing up the car this morning and presumably heading out for another stint on the oil rigs, and that means Jackson will have gone back to his mother's house. I presume he will have taken my camera as his parting gift.

Number One is presently empty, which means I can't go around there and confront Ian or his vandal of a son. All I can do is wait until they return, whenever that may be. That's annoying, but it is what it is. At least things should calm down around here. I seriously doubt anything else will happen now until Jackson is back, and at least that's something.

Realising that there isn't much I can do about the camera now, I carry on with the task at hand by climbing up the final few rungs of the ladder and looking into the guttering. But it seems I'm due a little good news because there is nothing up here that suggests a blockage. I'm not sure what Katie saw earlier, but it must just have been excess water running off the end of the house during the storm rather than an issue with the gutters again. It's about time I had something go my way when it came to this house, so I'm not going to be disappointed about not having to do any DIY work this evening after all. All that remains for me to do now then is climb back down off these ladders, put them away in the garage and go inside for my dinner.

But before I do, I take the opportunity of being at my high vantage point to look over into my neighbours' gardens. Turning in the direction of Number Two first, I look down over Albert and Eileen's immaculate garden and marvel at the colourful array of flowers on display, as well as how Albert has been able to get such perfect lines in the grass from the last time he cut it. I'm not sure how either of them came to be so good in the garden, but it obviously helps being retired and having more time on their hands than the average person, and I guess my time will eventually come when I get to leave my job behind and give more hours to my little slice of nature.

As well as the pristine flowers and grass, I see the table and chair set on the patio, and that must be where Katie sat when she was next door for a cup of tea and some shortbread last week. She told me that Eileen had taken her out into the back garden where they had chatted, and it looks like it would have been lovely. But I've probably snooped on their garden enough for one night, and I'd hate for Albert or Eileen to catch me looking from up here, so I turn around and look the other way, this time in the direction of Number One.

I don't have to worry about being caught looking here because I know that the house is empty, so I take my time and take in the view. This garden is definitely not as nice as the old couple's, but it's not bad considering that Ian is away half the time. That fact galls me because I'm here every day, and I still can't get my lawn looking as good as his, as well as my flowerbeds which are still looking feeble in comparison to my neighbour's. I'm surprised to see a couple of gnomes on the edge of his grass, and I didn't take Ian for the kind of guy who would have things like that in his garden, but then again, I barely know him. I'm more surprised that

Jackson hasn't broken them already, but then again, I suppose he prefers damaging other people's property over his father's. But then I see something else just behind the gnomes, and it's even more surprising to see. That's because it's something that belongs to me. It's one of my plant pots, one of the last remaining ones that didn't get broken the other night. I recognise the distinctive green tiling on the pot and know that it is definitely one of mine.

What the hell is it doing in next door's garden?

Jackson. A vandal and a thief. Just wait until I get my hands on that kid. He'll wish the police had got to him first, that's for sure.

27

KATIE

There's been a lot of unexpected things I've had to do recently. Like convincing my husband not to go into next door's back garden and take back the plant pot that he says they have stolen. Or telling myself and my partner that we should probably avoid the couple at Number Three as if they are a pair of Sirens from Greek mythology seducing us with their songs, only to cause us to crash and burn on their rocks. But perhaps the most random thing to have happened is the thing that is happening right now. I'm sitting here in front of a canvas painting an image of Abi, the woman I told Sean to stay away from, as a kind gesture for Chris, the man I am supposed to be staying away from.

Dabbing my brush into the black paint, I glance again at the photo of the beautiful woman that Chris has provided me with before returning to the canvas and completing another section of the painting. I'm surprised how well it seems to be going so far, and I'm almost done. I'm also surprised at how excited I feel about showing Chris my work as if I can't wait for him to view my talents and compliment me on them. But I remind myself that I am doing this only as a kind, neighbourly gesture and nothing else. It's also a way of me alleviating some of the guilt I felt when Chris was so honest with me the other night after I had treated him as if he was some leper to be avoided at all costs. But I'm also aware that this is just another example of me trying and failing to reduce my interactions with the man at Number Three, just like Sean seems to be failing when it comes to Abi too.

My husband told me how he had bumped into Abi at the swimming pool, just like I told him how I ended up talking with Chris after I had gone back to return the exhibition ticket, and it was clear to us both then that it's not as easy to avoid these people as we thought. But I had also told Sean about how Chris had been remorseful about what happened with the previous owners of our house and how it seemed like he had learnt his lesson and would not make a repeat of past mistakes. Sean was a little sceptical, but to be honest, he was less bothered about the people at Number Three when we spoke than he was about the people at Number One. He is still very much on the warpath after discovering that not only has his camera been taken away, but one of our plant pots has ended up next door. He blames Jackson, and then he blames Ian by association, and I know he can't wait until they both come back home so he can have it out with them. I'm urging him to be calm and cautious, and reminded him what happened to a previous occupant of this house in Greg, who got angry with Ian and ended up with a restraining order, but it remains to be seen what will happen when Ian and Jackson return. There's not much stopping my husband when he gets a bee in his bonnet, just like there isn't much stopping me when I get the creative urge to paint. And I definitely have that urge now.

My paintbrush is positively flying over the canvas as I continue on this piece for Chris, and Abi's image is starting to form more and more as I go. Of course, it helps to have such a beautiful subject to work with, and I certainly have that thanks to the image that Chris provided me with of his wife. The photo I am using for inspiration shows Abi sitting on a wall in front of a clear blue sky, smiling in a white flowing dress. Chris told me the image was captured on a holiday to Greece last summer, and he says it's his favourite picture of his wife, and that is why it is the one he has asked me to use as the basis for my painting. I'm no stranger to painting seascapes, so I've had no problem capturing the beautiful blue sea, but it has been more of a challenge to capture the beauty of the woman standing in front of that sea because she really does look like a Goddess, and those aren't so easy to paint.

This will be the fourth attempt I have made on painting this image, and my first three tries ended with me shaking my head and removing the canvas from the easel before putting a clean canvas in its place and starting again. I'm aware that I have gone through rather a lot of my materials since beginning this project, as well as an awful lot of time of which I'm not going to be paid for, but I made a promise to Chris that I would do this for him, so I have to honour my word.

But I'm confident that this fourth attempt will be my last one because I feel good about how this painting is turning out. I'm so close to finishing it now, and I can feel the familiar feeling of butterflies in my stomach as I approach the home straight, as I worry about making a silly mistake so close to the end that will render all my previous good work useless and force me to start all over again. It's a typical concern for an artist to have, but there is only one way to defeat it, and that is to keep concentration and have the courage to keep painting because no good piece of art ever came from playing it safe and taking the easy way out just to get it finished.

I glance at the photo of Abi a couple more times as I work, but truth be told, I feel as if I have already committed the image to my memory, having spent so long looking at it recently. I could even see it when I closed my eyes in bed last night because I'd been studying it so much beforehand, so I don't have to worry too much about checking it in between strokes of my paintbrush. But I do so anyway out of some kind of respect for my subject and what I am trying to achieve here.

I'm not sure how much longer it takes me to finish the painting, but eventually, the time comes when I sit back on my stool and inspect my work, and when I do, a wide smile spreads across my face. I've done it, and not only that, but I've done a good job too. I think Chris is going to love this, and hopefully, Abi will too. But before all of that, I need to show it to somebody else. I need to show it to Sean. That's because I haven't actually told him yet that I am doing this painting for Chris. I kept it from him because I was still feeling a little foolish about agreeing to do it when we spoke earlier, so I withheld the information at the time. Sean was so worked up about Jackson and what he may or may not have done that I didn't want to drop it on him then. But I will have to tell him. I can't keep this a secret, nor is there any reason why I should. I've done nothing wrong. This is just a favour for a neighbour.

A neighbour I'm supposed to be avoiding.

But if Sean is refusing to listen to me when I tell him to stay away from Ian and Jackson when they get back then why should I stay away from Chris, who seemed so honest and genuine with me when we spoke outside his home the other night? And why should I listen to Albert and Eileen too? I'm an adult, and I can make my own mind up about things, and besides, it's been fun to paint this picture and why should I deny myself that pleasure as an artist?

Studying the painting for any small errors that I might have made, I relax when I am sure there are none. It's definitely finished, which means it's definitely time to show it off to other people. But as I sit there and think about it, I'm not sure who I'm most nervous about showing it to. Sean or Chris? Sean might ask me why I've done it, and he might even get a little jealous, and that would be bad. But Chris might tell me that it's rubbish and that I've let him down, and for some strange reason, that almost seems just as bad too.

It shouldn't do, should it?

Surely I should be more worried about my husband's opinion than my neighbour's?

So why aren't I?

28

SEAN

I've always been proud of my wife for following her passion of being an artist. That's why I've always been happy enough to leave her to pursue her craft while I've been going out into the world to do a slightly less inspiring job. There have been ups and downs with her chosen career, from lack of sales to issues with getting the right equipment, but that can happen in any business, and we have both learnt to take the rough with the smooth. But in all the time that she has been painting professionally, one thing has always stayed the same. She has always been shy in showing me her work. No matter how much I show an interest and ask to see what she has been up to, she very rarely lets me into her workspace to show me what she has been doing. So much so that it's been a long time since I even asked to see any of her paintings. I just assumed she'd say no anyway. That's why it was a surprise to come home from work this evening and hear Katie tell me that she had a painting she would like to show me.

'I'm in shock,' I say as I follow her up the staircase. 'I can't remember the last time you showed me one of your paintings.'

Katie laughs, a little nervously I note, but says nothing as we reach the upstairs landing and head for the spare bedroom, a room in which I have barely set foot in since we moved in here and my wife claimed it as her studio. I presume the nervous laughter is because she is anxious about showing me the fruits of her labour, and I can understand that because I assume most creatives are very precious about their work and are constantly living in fear of what other people might think of it. But she has nothing to worry about because I'm sure that I'm going to love whatever it is she has painted. And even if I don't, I'll just be a good husband and say I love it anyway.

Katie opens the door to the spare bedroom slowly, as if having doubts about letting me in here to see her work after all, and I wish she'd hurry up because I'm starving, and the sooner we are done here then the sooner we can get started on making dinner. But then I see what it is that she is showing me this evening, and when I do, all thoughts of food go out of my mind and are replaced instead by a mixture of awe and surprise.

'What do you think?' she asks me as she stands beside her painting of a beautiful brunette woman sitting on a wall in front of a clear blue sea.

'Wow, it's stunning,' I say, and I mean every word. I knew my wife was talented, but this is something else.

'Really? You think so?'

'Are you kidding? It's amazing!'

Katie seems relieved by my seal of approval, but I'm being serious. This really is amazing work, and I'm not only proud but also a little curious as to how much she might be able to sell this piece for. I never thought my wife's earnings from her art might one day allow me to take early retirement, but if she can produce content like this then who knows?

I step a little closer to the painting to get an even better look at it, and I'm still in awe of how such a beautiful thing could have been produced by my wife. But the more I look at it, the more the woman in the painting seems familiar somehow. It's like I know her, but I'm not sure where from. But maybe that's what a good artist can do. They can make you feel things about a painting, and I guess this one makes me feel like I know the subject captured within it.

That is until Katie speaks again and explains why exactly it is that the woman seems so familiar.

'It's Abi,' she tells me unexpectedly.

'What?'

209

'This woman in the painting. It's Abi.'

I look away from the perfect portrait and back at my wife beside me.

'Why have you painted her?'

'Because Chris asked me to.'

'What? When?'

'The other day. When I went round to return the ticket.'

'You didn't mention anything about a painting.'

'I know, and I should have done. But I wasn't sure if I was definitely going to do it then or how it would turn out. I didn't expect it to end up being my best ever painting.'

'It's your best ever?'

'By a mile.'

I look back at the painting, and now that I know it's Abi, I can definitely see her in it. Her posture. Her confidence. *Her smile.*

'I don't understand. I thought we were meant to be keeping our distance from them. Now you're painting them?'

'I know, it's stupid, and I shouldn't have done it. But I told you how Chris seemed sorry about what had happened with James and Sarah, and I felt bad for him. Then he showed me a picture of Abi he had drawn for her birthday but bless him, it wasn't very good. So I offered to help.'

I'm not really sure if I'm supposed to be annoyed at my wife or not. She has broken the

210

rule about us staying away from Chris and Abi, yet it was her rule to begin with. I never put much stock in Albert and Eileen's warning, or at least not their one about the couple at Number Three anyway. I've been more bothered about Ian and Jackson and the damage being caused on my property. But maybe this is the bigger problem.

'So what are we saying now? That we can see Chris and Abi again?'

'I don't know. I'll just give him the painting and see how it goes. But maybe they're not as bad as we think.'

'Fine, whatever,' I say with a shrug before turning and heading out of the bedroom.

'What's wrong?' Katie calls after me.

'Nothing. I'm just hungry,' I reply, and at least that's my excuse for leaving the bedroom anyway. Really it's because I'd rather not look at that painting of Abi anymore. That's because I feel strangely drawn to it as if it's somehow making her seem even more beautiful than she does in real life. I'll be glad when it's out of this house and in theirs.

'Is everything okay?' Katie asks me before I can make it all the way downstairs.

'Yeah, it's fine. Why wouldn't it be?'

'I don't know. I thought you might be mad at me for what I've done.'

'I'm not.'

'Promise?'

'Yeah.'

I smile at my wife, and I guess I mean it. It's just a painting, and it's just a favour for Chris. It's not that big a deal. My wife is a great artist, and she should be proud of her work, as should I. And I am. I just wish I could get that image of Abi on that seawall out of my head. It feels like it's stuck in my head now.

Just like the image of her at the pool the other day is too.

29

KATIE

I knock on Chris's front door with a mixture of excitement and dread. I'm excited because I get to show him the painting I have done for his wife. But I'm also dreading what will happen if he tells me that he doesn't like it and that I've wasted my time. He probably has this idea of me in his head of being some super talented artist who lives across the street, but after this, he might just think that I'm some hack who needs to get a proper job. I guess I'll find out soon enough.

I came around here when I saw Abi leaving in the car a moment ago, seizing my chance to drop the painting off while she was out so that it can be kept a surprise for her ahead of her birthday in a few days. That's assuming Chris still wants to give it to her for her present, and I guess I'll find out if that is the case when he opens the door and lays his eyes on the painting.

The front door is suddenly unlocked, and Chris appears before me, his top half looking smart in a black shirt while his bottom half looks decidedly more casual considering he is wearing a pair of green shorts and no socks or shoes.

'Wow, that's quite the outfit,' I tell him with a laugh, and he looks a little embarrassed to have been caught looking like this.

'Oh yeah. I had a video call with the office, so I put a shirt on. But I guess I didn't make quite as much effort with the part of me that wasn't on camera,' he admits with a sheepish grin.

'Well, I like it. I had no idea you were so fashionable.'

Chris laughs at my teasing before looking down at the large canvas I am holding under my left arm. But he won't be able to see the whole painting yet because I've covered it in a protective coat which will be unzipped when the picture is somewhere safer than out here on the street.

'So I've finished the painting!' I tell him, trying to stay positive even though I'm feeling more and more nervous about his reaction to it by the second.

'Oh wow, that was quick!'

It didn't feel quick to me considering how many attempts I made at it, but I don't disagree with him.

'So, erm. Do you want me to show you? Or I can just leave it with you?'

'No, come in, please,' Chris offers, and I take the invite, stepping into his home and following him into the kitchen.

'Sorry about the mess,' he tells me as I see the laptop and paperwork on the kitchen table. 'Busy day today.'

'Don't apologise. You should see the state of my spare bedroom where I work,' I tell him with a laugh. 'How about I set it down over here?'

I nod towards the large kitchen counter as a good place to put the painting when I reveal it, and Chris agrees that's as good a spot as any.

With the painting on the counter, I put a hand on each zipper of the protective coat and prepare to reveal my picture to its potential new owner. In a couple of seconds I will be able to tell whether he likes it or not, and really, it is he and his wife who will be the most important critics. I know Sean told me that he thought I had done a great job of this portrait, but he's not the one who will have to live with it. Presumably, it will hang on a wall somewhere in this house, so it's more important that Chris and Abi like it more than my husband does.

I guess it's time to find out.

Pulling on the zippers, I peel back the coat and pull the painting out until all of it is on show for Chris to inspect. He takes a step closer towards it as he gets his first look at it, and I find myself holding my breath as I try and gauge his first reaction. It's only when I see the smile spreading across his face that I find myself exhaling again.

'This is wonderful!' he cries as he runs a hand over the image on the canvas. 'It's perfect!'

It's an extremely positive reaction, just like I got from Sean, and I guess I don't need to worry anymore. I really have done a good job.

'Thank you so much for this, Abi is going to love it,' Chris tells me. 'I can't wait to give it to her.'

'You're welcome,' I say, feeling all the tension leaving my body and being replaced by relief.

'I have to pay you for this,' Chris suddenly says, walking away from the counter and going over to his wallet on the kitchen table.

'No, don't be silly. I told you it was a present.'

'But you've gone to a lot of trouble. And it is your job, so you should get paid.'

'No, seriously. It was my pleasure. I had fun, and I didn't expect anything for it.'

Chris looks at me with his hand in his wallet, presumably trying to figure out if I am being sincere or if I am just being polite and really would like some money for my troubles. But he must see that I mean it because he closes his wallet again and puts it back on the table.

'Okay, if you won't accept money then you will have to accept something else instead,' he tells me as he steps closer. 'There's another exhibition coming up at the gallery. I'll get us both tickets, and this time I'm not going to take no for an answer.'

I could refuse, just like I did last time, but unlike then, I don't feel like I want to. Besides, I've earned this. I did work hard on the painting, and while I don't want paying for it, it would be nice to get something, and a ticket to an art exhibition will more than suffice. Of course, I'll have to run it by Sean first to make sure he doesn't have any problems with it, but I'm sure it will be fine. I think we've moved on from the part where we were treating Chris and Abi like a danger to be avoided. I can see now that Chris is just a nice guy who made a mistake in the past, but that doesn't have to define him. I'm sure Abi is the same. And who hasn't made a mistake in the past? I know that Sean has made a few, and so have I.

That's why I accept the ticket to the exhibition right there and then.

And that's why this moment can also be looked back on with hindsight as being the latest mistake I made in my life.

And the biggest so far.

30

SEAN

There's not a much more mundane job to do around the house than taking out the bins for the weekly collection. But that's what I'm doing right now as I drag my wheely bin down to the end of the drive in anticipation of the collection tomorrow morning. It's only when I'm turning back to my house that I see Albert doing the same thing next door, and he gives me a wave as he spots me too.

'Evening,' he says as he drags his bin near to where I have left mine, and I feel like I should offer to help him with his manual task because it seems like the right thing to do considering I'm the much younger man. But I don't, mainly because I don't want to feel patronising to him but also because I have the feeling that he would just turn down my offer anyway and carry on doing it himself. He must do it himself every week anyway, so he can obviously manage.

'Good evening. How's it going?' I ask, preferring to be inside by now but doing my neighbourly duty of making small talk whenever I bump into one of the people I live beside. It's actually been a while since I saw Albert, and come to think of it, I might not have actually spoken to him since the night he came around just after we had first moved in. That was the same night he gave us the tip-off about the other residents on this cul-de-sac, and maybe that explains why I haven't exactly been in a rush to catch up with him since. He seemed a little crazy that night, and even though I've since had reason to believe that some of the things he said that evening could be true, namely Jackson and his penchant for property destruction, I haven't made the effort to talk with him since. But I guess I have my chance now.

'I can't complain,' Albert tells me once he has deposited the bin at the end of his driveway and taken a deep breath from the exertion. 'How are things with you guys? Eileen told me about the brick that went through your window. I hope everything's okay. We saw the police visit your house, but we didn't want to pry.'

I assume Katie has told Eileen what happened that night because I definitely didn't, but that's okay because it doesn't have to be a big secret.

'Yeah, that was a bit of a shock,' I admit.

'Do the police know what happened?'

'No,' I say with a shake of the head. 'Has anything like that ever happened to you?'

219

I'm probing because I want to see if Albert is going to suspect Jackson of throwing the brick just like I do.

'I can't say it has. But like I told you before, we have had trouble in our back garden. Broken furniture. Things going missing. And you know who caused all that trouble?'

'Jackson.'

Albert nods.

'I mentioned my suspicion to the police that night,' I tell him. 'But they said I couldn't make accusations without any evidence, so they didn't look into it.'

'Yeah, evidence is the thing that has always stopped us from getting anywhere too.'

'I did try and get some,' I confess, and Albert looks intrigued, so I go on. 'I put a camera up a while ago in the hope of catching him, but that got broken. I have to assume he spotted it and threw something at it to bring it down.'

Albert raises his eyebrows before shaking his head.

'He's a nuisance, but he's not dumb.'

'Yeah, I'm just waiting for his dad to get back from the rigs again, so he is around again. But surprise surprise, there has been no trouble in our garden since Jackson went away.'

Albert nods his head as if this is something he already knew, and I guess it is. I might be fairly new to this situation with

Jackson, but he's been putting up with it for years.

'How are things with our other neighbours?' Albert asks me, changing the subject from the people at Number One to the people at Number Three.

I know what he will be trying to get at here, which is to find out if we are following his advice of staying away from Chris and Abi as much as possible, but I'm not sure what I can say there. How do I tell him that instead of following his advice I've instead been swimming with Abi while my wife has painted a portrait of her as a gift for Chris? Not to mention the dinner date we had with them or the time Abi came around and shared a bottle of wine with me while Katie was out of town.

'Erm, things are going okay,' I say, hoping to just leave it at that. But Albert is old enough and smart enough to know when somebody is holding back on him, and he furrows his brow before speaking again.

'Look, feel free to tell me and Eileen to mind our own business if you want to. But before you do, I'll tell you this. You're playing with fire if you get close to that couple. And what happens when you play with fire?'

I know the answer is that you get burned, but I don't say it because it doesn't need to be said. I just stare at Albert until he says goodnight and shuffles away back up his driveway.

I keep watching him until he goes inside and closes his front door before making a move myself, but before I re-enter my home, I glance over at Number Three across the street. The lights are on inside and the car is on the driveway, presumably meaning that both Chris and Abi are home. Then I look at Number One and see the empty driveway and the dark windows with the curtains closed and know that Ian and Jackson are gone.

Four different neighbours posing two very different problems.

I really didn't expect this cul-de-sac to be as interesting as this.

Closing the front door and finding my wife in the kitchen putting the finishing touches on our evening meal, I give her a kiss before telling her about my little chat with Albert a moment ago. I'm expecting Katie to have an opinion on it, but she doesn't. Instead, she tells me that Chris has offered her a ticket to an exhibition tomorrow and that she has accepted it.

'Wait a minute, let me get this straight. You had a go at me for being alone with Abi, but it's okay now for you to be alone with Chris?'

'We'll be in a busy gallery in the middle of the day. That's a little different to being alone together in a house on a Friday night with a bottle of wine.'

'That's not the point! One minute you're telling me we need to stay away from Chris and Abi, the next you're painting them a picture and going to events. So what does this mean? I can hang out with Abi again now?'

'I didn't say that.'

'So it's one rule for you and another for me?'

'No, that's not what I mean.'

'Well, what do you mean?'

Katie looks like she has something she wants to say, but she holds back on delivering it.

'What is it?' I ask, pressing her on it. 'Come on, what do you want to say?'

Katie tries stalling again by pretending to be busy with the boiling saucepan of pasta, but I tell her to leave it and ask her again about what is really going on here.

'Why is it okay for you to be around Chris, but it's not okay for me to be around Abi?'

'I didn't say that.'

'But you're making it clear that that's the case, so why is it?'

'I don't know.'

'Yes, you do. Come on, spit it out.'

'Because I'm worried about her.'

'What do you mean?'

'I'm worried that I can't trust her around you.'

'But I'm supposed to trust Chris around you, aren't I?'

'He feels bad for what he did to James and Sarah.'

'But he still did it.'

'At least he has shown some remorse. I don't know if Abi has.'

'What does it matter what they do anyway? As long as we don't do anything then it's okay, isn't it?'

That's when the penny drops, and I realise what my wife is really trying to say here. It's not just Abi whom she doesn't trust.

It's me as well.

'You think I might be tempted,' I say, shaking my head. 'You think that you can control yourself around Chris, but I might not be able to around her. That's it, isn't it?'

'No, I didn't say that.'

'But it's what you're thinking, and it's the only thing that makes sense. You feel like you and Chris can be friends, but that Abi and I can't because something might happen. I don't believe this.'

I storm out of the room, ignoring my wife's calls to come back into the kitchen. But I'm too angry about this to stay and hear what she has to say. Not once have I done anything to give my wife reason to worry about my loyalty to her, yet she thinks I'm the risky one out of the two of us? How dare she. I'm not the one painting pictures for presents and accepting tickets to events, but you know what? If Abi invites me somewhere then I'm going to go, and I don't care what Katie says. She can trust me or not, but it won't change who I am and what I can do in my own free time.

Katie keeps calling after me as I climb the stairs, telling me that dinner is ready and that I should come back, but I've lost my appetite, and I'm not turning around. Instead, I enter the bathroom and lock the door before turning on the shower and tearing off the tie that has been hanging limply around my neck all day. Then I strip off and get in the shower, feeling the hot water on my skin, and it's almost as hot as the anger that is bubbling within me.

I'm mad at my wife for thinking that I can't be trusted.

And I'm also mad because deep down, I know that she might have a point.

31

KATIE

The gallery is filled with the sound of quiet chatter and the clinking of champagne flutes as I enter with Chris alongside me. We've just handed our tickets to the well-dressed man on the door, and now we are inside this exhibition and eager to see the various works of art that are on display here.

'I knew I should have worn a tie,' Chris confesses to me as he notices most of the other men in attendance here this afternoon are wearing one themselves.

'Don't be silly, you look fine,' I tell him, and he does. Then I make a quick check on the other women in the room to make sure that I look just as acceptable. Thankfully, I feel like I do because while I haven't made quite as much effort as some of the ladies here today, I am more than passable in this red dress that I pulled out from the back of my wardrobe, especially for this fairly exclusive occasion. I haven't worn this dress in years, more from a lack of having a suitable event to wear it to rather than anything else, so it feels a little strange to be sporting it now. But it still fits me well, and I know that because I spent half an hour looking in the mirror earlier making sure it did, and it certainly feels good to be dressed up again. Being a work from home artist means I very rarely have the need to get changed into anything more flattering than an old t-shirt and a pair of jogging bottoms, but this is a nice change of pace. It definitely felt a little weird glancing in the mirror and seeing myself looking so good, and I think it even took Chris by surprise too because I noticed his raised eyebrows when he first saw me earlier, not that I have spent too much time thinking about his reaction to my outfit today.

'Champagne?'

I turn to see the pretty waitress standing beside me with a tray full of champagne flutes, and I am tempted to take a glass of fizzy bubbles, but then I remember that it is still early in the day. But Chris seems to have no qualms about starting on the strong stuff now, and he picks up a glass before thanking the waitress. I decide to join him and take my own glass before she moves on to the next ticketholders loitering nearby and the pair of us both take a sip before turning our attentions to the first painting on display.

'Hmm, what do you think?' Chris asks me as I study the image of the small boy sitting on a box in an otherwise empty room.

'I like the colours they've used,' I say, casting my allegedly expert eye over the artwork. 'But I'm not exactly sure what it's supposed to represent.'

'Yeah, me neither. I just hope the artist used her imagination and doesn't actually know some boy who lives on a box in an empty room.'

I laugh as we move on to the next painting, and this one is of a meadow, which looks rather lovely and has me inspired to take my brushes and canvas out to the countryside one day to try and create a landscape like this one in my own work.

'This is beautiful,' Chris says as he steps closer to the painting and reads the name of the artist that is written on the card underneath it.

'I agree,' I say in between sips of my champagne. 'Whoever painted this is very talented.'

I expect Chris to perhaps nod before we move on to the next painting, but he doesn't. Instead, he turns to me and asks me why I haven't entered any of my work in exhibitions like this.

'You're just as talented as these artists are, if not more,' he tells me, seemingly being sincere. 'That painting you did of Abi could easily be hanging in here today for people's enjoyment.'

'Oh, please. I'm not that good,' I say, but Chris doesn't seem to agree.

'You shouldn't put yourself down. You have a gift, and I think you should be doing much more with that gift than what you are currently doing.'

'What do you mean?'

'I mean that an artist like you shouldn't be sitting at home all day painting out of your spare bedroom. You should have a proper studio and your work should be displayed for the public to see more often instead of on some website that nobody is ever going to find.'

He's being quite blunt with me, but I don't tell him to stop.

'You have so much potential, and you need to capitalise on it. You know what your problem is?'

I shake my head.

'You see yourself as a struggling artist who depends on the support of her partner. But you need to see things as they really are. You have an ability that very few people have, and it's one that can far surpass anything Sean can hope to achieve in his workplace. You need to stop thinking of yourself as a poor painter toiling away at home and start dreaming of how far you could really go with this.'

It's quite the pep talk, and if I'm honest, it was the last thing I was expecting when I came here today. I just thought we'd wander around the gallery for a bit, check out some paintings and make small talk. I definitely didn't expect Chris to give me this kind of intervention where he effectively says that I am squandering my talents and wants me to push myself more. Come to think of it, I've never really had anybody speak to me about my career in this way before. Sean has never said these kinds of things to me, and I guess he assumes I'm happy enough just doing what I'm already doing. But am I? In a way, yes, but I do have ambitions of having my own studio one day, and it would certainly be a thrill to see some of my work on show in a gallery at some point for some of my peers to comment on. It seems like Chris can see that in my future, and I'm flattered that he does. It doesn't mean it's guaranteed to happen, of course, but it's nice that he thinks it could, and it's clear that I need to believe in myself more if I'm ever going to get there.

I thank him for his kind words and nod my head as if in agreement before taking another sip of my champagne, because putting that in my mouth means I don't have to say anything else as we move on to the next painting. I do that because I'm not sure what it is that I would say. I'm still thinking about what Chris has said to me, and the more I do, the more I see that he is right. I am limiting myself by just sitting in my spare bedroom and keeping most of my paintings to myself. Maybe it is time to expand. But that will take money, and that means it will involve risk. I wonder what Sean will think about that.

The rest of our time at the exhibition is mainly spent with me giving Chris information about some of the artists on display here because as much as he is making an effort, it's clear that he doesn't know that much about art. Certainly not as much as I do anyway. But he is obviously doing this today more for me than for him, and it's a thank you to me for the painting of Abi that I did for free. I'm grateful for that because I have a wonderful time and so much so that I am surprised when I hear the event organiser inform us all that the exhibition will be ending in five minutes' time. I had been rather hoping to see the last couple of paintings that I hadn't got to yet, as well as perhaps have one more cheeky glass of champagne, but I guess we better start making a move for the door.

They say time flies when you're having fun, and this has certainly been fun. But just as I think it's coming to an end, Chris grabs us both another glass of champagne each and tells me to down it. I think he's joking until he drinks his own, and then I see that he's actually up for some mischief, and then he proves it when he suggests finding a bar to go for another drink in.

32

It's not often my boss tells me and my fellow employees that we can take the rest of the day off and go home early, but that's what's happened today, and it's why I have a spring in my step as I walk towards my front door at the early time of three-thirty in the afternoon. I was surprised to get the offer from my employer, and I'm sure Katie will be surprised too when I walk through the door and let her know that I'm home. I know she was attending the art exhibition with Chris at lunchtime today, but she should have been back hours ago, so I expect she is upstairs in the spare bedroom painting again. I've done my best to not show how annoyed I am about the whole situation with Chris and Abi since the little argument I had with my wife about it because nothing good can come from it. Instead, I've decided to let Katie do whatever she wants, and that way, I'll be free to do whatever I want to. It's her jealously of Abi that caused her to want me to stay away from her, but I'm not going to act jealous about Chris and make her stay away from him. That way, she can't make me stay away from Abi in

232

future either, should I wish to spend time with her at any point.

Of course, the logical solution to all of this is that the four of us organise things when we are all present so that way there will be no opportunity for anybody to start getting jealous. And that's why I have had the idea of suggesting to Katie that we finally get around to inviting Chris and Abi over for dinner soon. I'll bring it up with her right now, just as soon as I get inside.

As I put my key in the lock, I make sure to glance over at Number One to double-check that the house is still empty, and sure enough, it is. Ian and Jackson aren't back yet, so I will have to wait a little longer to resolve my problem there. But that's okay. I'm enjoying them being away because it means there has been no dramas in the back garden, and long may that continue.

Entering my home, I call out to Katie to let her know that it is me so that she doesn't get a big fright when she hears the door opening. But she doesn't call back to me, so I presume she didn't hear me. Taking off my suit jacket and shoes, I climb the stairs and call out to her again, wondering as I go if she has her headphones in her ears because she sometimes likes to work with music playing. That must be the case today because she hasn't responded to my second call either, and she would definitely have heard that one normally because I'm at the top of the stairs now, so I head towards the spare bedroom and knock before I enter.

There's still no noise from within as I walk into the room, and that's when I see that Katie isn't here. Her stool is unoccupied, the paintbrushes are lying idle, and the canvas on the easel in front of all the equipment is blank.

Taking my phone out of my pocket, I call her number, but she doesn't pick up, so I send her a quick text letting her know that I'm home and asking where she is. Then I go to leave the room, but just before I do, I notice the painting that is propped up behind the door. It caught my eye because I recognise the landscape depicted within it, and I crouch down to get a closer look.

The painting shows a car on a driveway in front of a house, and I recognise the house as being Number Three on this cul-de-sac. I also recognise the person who is standing beside the car. It's Chris, and Katie has certainly done a good job of capturing his image. But why has she painted him?

Walking away from the painting and towards the window, I look outside, and sure enough, I see the exact view of Number Three from here as the one in the picture, which suggests to me that Katie was looking out of here as she was painting it. Presumably, Chris was out there working on his car at the time, and that was why she used that in the image. Does it bother me that my wife is painting another man? I guess it does or I wouldn't be feeling like I am right now.

Walking out of the bedroom, I decide that I'm going to grab my gym gear and go for a workout to let off some steam. But before I do, I try Katie on her phone again, eager to know where she is. That's because I'm wondering if she is still with Chris now even though the exhibition was supposed to end in the early afternoon and she had told me that she was coming home straight afterwards.

But Katie fails to answer again, and I'm still no nearer to knowing where she is. But right now, I'm imagining she is still with our neighbour, and that's why I have the idea of doing something that would only be fair in the circumstances.

Having finished packing my gym clothes, I head downstairs and leave the house, but I'm not going straight to my car. I'm going to Number Three, and I'm hoping that Abi is in because I'm going to ask her if she wants to come to the gym with me. She might not be home, or she might not fancy a workout and that will be fine, but if she does then I'll be happy to drive her there myself. Screw trying to avoid her and feeling awkward whenever I bump into her. Not when Katie is out there having fun with Chris.

I reach Abi's door and knock on it loudly, but there is no answer, and I feel a little disappointed that she must be out too. But then I see movement behind the door, and it turns out that she is home, and that makes me feel surprisingly happy as I see her face emerge from inside.

'Hey, stranger! How's things?' she asks me, seemingly pleased to see me whilst referencing the fact that she hasn't seen much of me lately. But I won't say that's because my wife has been telling me to actively avoid her.

'Not bad. Is Chris in?' I ask, deciding to check on that in case he might actually be home and not with my wife, just in case I've got the wrong end of the stick.

'No, he's still out. He went to that art exhibition with Katie, I think.'

'Oh yeah, of course. I forgot,' I lie before moving on to what else I came here to ask. 'So, I'm just heading to the gym, and I was wondering if you fancied tagging along? I could get you a free pass on my membership if you'd like?'

'You want a workout partner?'

'Yeah, if you're up for it?'

'Sure! Just let me grab my gear, and I'll be right out!'

Abi seems enthusiastic about my plan and rushes back into her house to get her gym clothes, leaving me waiting for her on the doorstep. While she's gone I take the chance to check my phone in case Katie has tried to return any of my calls, but there is still no word from her. Whatever. She's having fun with a friend, and now I'm going to be having fun with a friend too.

'Let's go!' Abi says as she reappears with her bag over her shoulder. 'And I brought my swimming gear too if you fancy hitting the pool after?'

'Sounds like a plan,' I tell her, and she locks her front door before walking with me across the street back to my car.

I'm almost too busy chatting with her to look up and notice the person watching me from the upstairs window at Number Two, but I just about manage to spot them, and when I do, I wish I hadn't. Albert is watching me, and now he will know that I'm definitely not following his advice of staying away from the woman at Number Three.

I give him a quick wave to be friendly, and Abi does the same when she sees him too. But Albert doesn't return the gesture. He just stands there and watches us as we get in the car and drive away.

33

KATIE

I can't remember the last time I sat with a cocktail on the table in front of me at four in the afternoon. I didn't even start drinking this early when I went to Nottingham with my uni friends recently. Of course, this cocktail isn't the first drink I've had today. There were two or three glasses of champagne at the exhibition to start me off earlier. But things have definitely gone up a notch now.

'Cheers,' Chris says to me as he lifts up his own cocktail and bumps it against my glass.

'I still can't believe you ordered that,' I tell him, referring to the bright pink Cosmopolitan that he is now holding in his hand.

'Why not?'

'It's quite girly, and I don't just mean the colour. I mean the umbrella too.'

'What can I say? I'm a man in touch with my feminine side.'

I laugh before taking a sip from my straw, careful not to poke my eye out with the umbrella that is sticking out of my drink too.

Looking around this bar, I see that it is surprisingly busy for a weekday afternoon, but the multitude of shopping bags under the tables of the other patrons in here suggests these are either tourists on holiday or locals who have booked the day off work to shop, eat and drink. Technically, I'm neither because I didn't book a day off, although being my own boss, I didn't really have to. But just because I can work when I want to, it doesn't mean I get lazy, and I have certainly never made a habit out of sitting in a busy bar in the middle of a weekday. But that doesn't mean that I'm not enjoying myself now.

'So, are you back at work tomorrow?' I ask Chris before the conversation is in danger of drying up, not that it would be awkward if it did because there has already been a couple of quiet moments between us today, and it didn't feel awkward then.

'Yeah, unfortunately,' he tells me while twirling the umbrella around in his drink. 'But that doesn't mean I can't enjoy today. These happy hour prices really are something, aren't they?'

I laugh as he picks up the menu again to presumably look for the next drink to order. But as much as I would love to sit here all day and work my way through the cocktail menu with him, I am aware that I should probably start thinking about making a move so that I'm home before Sean returns from work. He didn't take his gym bag with him to the office today, so I assume that means he will be coming straight home, so by my estimates, I have around an hour and a half to get back to the house before he does. That sounds like plenty of time, but I still have a cocktail to finish before then, as well as get back across town in a taxi and on top of that, it seems like Chris is happy to stay longer.

'I think I'll have to get going after this one,' I tell him before he can go ordering us any more beverages.

'Really? But there's still another hour to run on happy hour yet.'

He does seem disappointed, and I'm not sure if it's because he's having a good time or just because he's got the taste of alcohol now and wants to keep going while he can, not that it really matters.

'Yeah, sorry. But Sean will be home soon.'

'So?'

'Well, he'll be expecting me to be at home.'

'Why? Can't you go out and have a social life?'

'Don't be silly. Of course I can. It's just he knows the exhibition finished a few hours ago, so he'll wonder where I am.'

'Then give him a quick call and let him know.'

I'm not really keen on doing that, and I think Chris can tell.

'There's not still a problem is there?' he asks me.

'What do you mean?'

'I mean with you guys and spending time with me and Abi. I told you that there was nothing to worry about.'

'No, of course not. That's not it,' I try, but it's a bad lie, and he knows it.

'Forgive me if I come across as a little blunt, but Sean shouldn't be worrying about you having a drink with a male friend, just like you shouldn't be worrying about him spending time with a female friend either. You're grown ups, and you're married. Not a couple of teenagers who could break up at the drop of a hat.'

'No, it's not that, honestly.'

'Then what is it then? Why are you so anxious about getting home before Sean?'

'I don't know.'

'Look, if you're not having a good time with me then I won't be offended if you leave. Honestly, it won't be the first time I've ended up drinking alone, and I'm sure it won't be the last.'

'No, I am having a good time.'

'Then why leave? Let's get another drink. The night is still young, or rather the day is still young because I can still see sunlight out there.'

He gestures towards the large windows behind me, and I laugh as I turn and look at the daylight out there. It is weird to be feeling tipsy when the sun's not even gone down yet.

'Okay, fine. One more drink,' I concede with a smile. 'I'm off to the ladies. Don't order anything too crazy for me.'

'I can't make any promises,' Chris replies, and I laugh as I leave my seat and take my handbag into the toilets.

I take out my mobile phone as soon as I am inside one of the cubicles because I'm aware that I haven't checked it all afternoon and there might be a missed message or two on there. But I'm not expecting what I see when I look at the screen. That's because there are a couple of missed calls from Sean as well as a text message asking me where I am.

I don't understand. How can he know that I'm not home if he's still at work? Unless he came home early. But that's unlikely. He's always in the office until at least five.

I'm unsure as to how my husband could possibly know that I'm not at our house, but I decide to find out, pressing the button to call him in the hopes that he will pick up and enlighten me. But he doesn't, and even though I try again, there is still no answer. Damn it.

I decide to send him a message to let him know that I'm okay, but I don't mention where I am and who I am with. It makes me feel as if I am up to no good and have a secret to hide, which I don't really because I've done

242

nothing wrong, but I'm still aware that Sean isn't keen on the idea of me hanging out with Chris if he isn't allowed to hang out with Abi. That's why I don't mention anything about that and keep my message short and sweet.

I press send before flushing the toilet and leaving the cubicle, and by the time I have washed my hands and returned to the table, there is a fresh cocktail waiting for me.

'Don't worry, it's not one of the strong ones,' Chris tells me, and I smile as I retake my seat while making sure to leave my phone out so I can keep an eye on it for any incoming calls or messages from Sean. But before I can take a sip of my new drink and spend any more time wondering how Sean could know that I'm not home, Chris picks up his own phone from the table and holds it towards me so that I can see what is on the screen.

'You don't have to worry about Sean,' he tells me as my eyes read the text message in front of me. 'Abi just sent me this. She's on the way to the gym with him.'

I finish reading the message, and it backs up what Chris has just told me. Abi has texted him to say that she is with my husband, and while I'm not sure how that is possible considering that he should be at work, that's the least of my worries.

Why is Sean with Abi again? Is it because he knows I'm with Chris and he's feeling annoyed?

I don't know, but I've suddenly lost my appetite for my cocktail. That's because I feel as though I've made a complete mess of things here. I've gone from saying we should avoid Chris and Abi to a situation where we are almost spending more time alone with them than we are together. What would Albert and Eileen say? And is this how James and Sarah were before they were unfaithful and blew up their marriage?

I should leave and go home, and I should get Sean to come home too. Maybe everything is okay, or maybe Chris and Abi are up to their old tricks again, and everything is going right to plan.

'Cheers,' Chris says to me as he lifts up his new cocktail and waits for me to join him again. 'Here's to new friends.'

I smile weakly as I touch my glass against his.

"New friends." It sounds so innocent, doesn't it? But according to Albert and Eileen, there's nothing innocent about this at all, and maybe now it's too late for me to stop what is already in motion. I can control myself around Chris, no matter how many drinks I have had with him today. But what about Sean? Will he be able to stay strong if Abi makes a move,

particularly if he thinks I'm out here having fun with her husband?

I suddenly feel sick, and it has nothing to do with this drink.

I feel sick because I'm worried that I've spent so long trying to keep Sean from Abi that I've now ended up pushing him right towards her.

34

SEAN

I was pretty confident that I would win when this race started, but I'm not anymore. That's because I can see Abi ahead of me, and she's definitely going to reach the other end of the pool before me. I thought I was a decent swimmer, but she swims like a fish. But I won't concede defeat yet. I'll keep going because the only thing worse than losing is giving up.

Needless to say, Abi puts me out of my misery a few seconds later by touching the edge of the pool and confirming that our race is over. I follow behind her a few seconds later, much more out of breath than she is as I put my arms on the side of the pool and suck in some oxygen.

'Good race,' she says to me kindly, but I know that it wasn't. She was way too quick for me, and I feel silly for even suggesting the idea of the two of us competing.

'I'll get you next time,' I try, but it hardly sounds like the most confident statement in the world when I'm sucking in air at the same time.

Abi laughs and wishes me luck before turning around and suggesting we go again. But there's no way I can face swimming another length today, so I shake my head and instead gesture towards the changing rooms where a nice hot shower will be waiting for me. Abi sees what I mean, which is basically that I'm far too unfit to do any more exercise today, but before she can let me skulk away with my tail between my legs, she has another idea.

'How about a quick stint in the sauna?' she asks me, and I see her looking over at the wooden door on the other side of this pool area.

I've never actually used the sauna since I've been coming to this gym, and I'm not really a big fan of using them anywhere because of how uncomfortably hot they can be. I know that's the whole idea of them, but after some intense exercise, I've never seen the fun in forcing myself into a tiny room filled with hot, dry air. But obviously, Abi does.

'It's one of the best things to do after a workout,' she tries to convince me, but I'm not sold.

'I'm not sure. I always feel a little claustrophobic in a sauna,' I tell her, and it's true. There's just something about the tiny wooden benches condensed into a small square area in a dark, parched room that makes me want to get the hell out of there as soon as I have gone in.

'The thing with saunas is that it's all in the mind. It's supposed to be an uncomfortable place. That's the challenge of it. The rest of the gym is for the physical test. But the sauna is more about the mental one.'

I'm just about to ask her if she is some kind of motivational guru when she hauls herself up out of the water and onto the pool edge, leaving me still bobbing around below her.

'Come on, it'll be fun. I promise,' she tells me as she peels off her swimming cap to allow her long dark hair to fall down her bare back. Then she turns and walks towards the sauna, her bare feet padding lightly across the wet tiled floor.

I know I could just get out and go into the changing rooms, but Abi will be disappointed in me, and I don't want that, so I pull myself out of the water too before following her towards the wooden door. As I go, I notice a couple of the other guys in this pool area checking out Abi as she walks ahead of me, and I even see one of them give me a nod as if he approves of my companion and respects me for being with her. It's a silly, stupid thing, but then those words could describe most guys, I guess.

Abi holds the sauna door open for me as I catch her up, and seconds later I am leaving behind the cool, clear air of the pool area for the stifling, lowly-lit air of the sauna.

It feels as if all the air has been sucked out of my lungs as I enter the tiny room and look around at the wooden benches, all of which are unoccupied, meaning Abi and I will be the only ones in here. I presume she is going to take a seat, and I wait for her to do that so that I don't end up sitting too close to her in here, but she goes over to the small pile of sauna rocks instead and uses the scooper from the bucket to pour water over those sizzling rocks. I know this is done to increase the temperature in here because the steam from the hot rocks will mix with the dry air in the room, but in my opinion, it was already more than hot enough in here to begin with. But I guess Abi likes it hotter.

I take a seat on one of the wooden benches as far away from the hot rocks as I can get and tell myself that I need to last at least five minutes in here or I will look like a wimp. Fortunately, there is a clock on the wall in here, so I can keep an eye on that to gauge how well I am doing for time as this sauna session begins.

Abi finishes what she is doing with the hot rocks and comes to join me over on the same bench, her bare legs only inches from mine now as she sits beside me and lets out a long, deep breath.

'I love it in here,' she confesses. 'Sometimes it feels like the most peaceful place in the world.'

'I thought the most peaceful place in the world was on the sofa with a big bag of crisps,' I reply, and she laughs.

'I don't know. Sometimes I feel like home isn't the best place to truly relax.'

That sounds like quite a deep statement from Abi, and while I'm not exactly sure what she is getting at in her personal life, I feel as if I can relate to what she just said. That's because the way things have been in my home life lately means I've found it difficult to relax there too. I'd like to say all of that is down to the disruption of the issues in the back garden and my worries about Jackson, but much of it is also down to my wife and the way she has been with me lately.

'That's why I like coming here to exercise every now and again,' Abi goes on as I feel the water on my skin drying out. 'I can just get away from it all. People. The past. Everything.'

I wonder if she is referring to Chris as well as what happened with James and Sarah before that. But of course, I'm not going to say anything because it would be awkward enough at the best of times without being in a tiny wooden box set to 100 degrees.

'How are things with you and Katie?' Abi suddenly asks me.

'Erm, yeah. Fine,' I reply, not entirely convincingly. But Abi must buy it because she nods and seems a little envious.

'You guys seem pretty solid.'

'So do you and Chris.'

'Yeah, well, appearances can be deceiving.'

I'm not sure what she means by that, and I'm not sure that I want to find out either. I'm starting to sweat in here now, and I'm not entirely sure that it's all down to the hot rocks and the water vapour. Maybe I should think about getting out. It's only been two minutes, but I'm not sure anything good could come from the next three if I stick around and Abi keeps talking like this.

Then I notice Abi is looking at me, and I turn to see her face. It's gloomy in here, as most saunas are, but I can still make out her dark hair and her delicate features. And she seems to be studying mine too. I want to say something just to break the silence, but I'm not sure what. Abi doesn't seem to have anything to say either. She just keeps looking into my eyes. *Then down at my lips.*

The door to the sauna suddenly swings open, sending a cooling jet of air into this stifling room, and I turn to see an overweight man waddling in to join us. That's my cue to get out of here quickly and get up from the bench and tell Abi that it's too hot for me in here. She says she'll meet me in the reception area after we have showered and I nod my head as I leave the sauna and return to the cool pool area.

It feels good to have the cold air on my skin again after those intense few minutes, but

I'm aware it's not just the change in temperature that has made me relax again. It's because I have extricated myself from that slightly tricky situation just then.

What would have happened if that guy hadn't come into the sauna when he did? Would Abi have tried to kiss me? But as I reach the changing rooms and locate my locker, I know the most important question is the one I really don't want to know the answer to.

Would I have kissed her back?

35

KATIE

I pour myself a third glass of water from the kitchen tap before drinking it all and taking a deep breath. This is my attempt at sobering up before Sean gets home because I definitely overdid it on the drinks today, and while I'd like to say that was Chris' fault, I know there is no one to blame for overindulging but me. I could have said no to another drink at any point and come home but instead, I ended up staying out much longer than I anticipated and drinking far more than I thought I would do too. That resulted in me having to have the window down in the taxi on the way home because I was feeling a little nauseous, and it's also why I am now chugging water like there's a drought coming before my husband gets back and sees the state that I'm in.

I check the clock on the wall and notice that it's gone seven o'clock, and even though I know Sean is at the gym with Abi, I really would have expected him back by now. While his failure to return is giving me more time to get some water into my dehydrated system, it is also causing me to feel anxious about what could be keeping him out so long.

I'm just about to pour myself some more water when I hear the sound of a car door closing at the front of the house, so I put my empty glass down on the counter and head into the living room to check the driveway. I assume it is Sean getting back at last, but to my surprise, our driveway is still empty. Looking around, I notice that the sound must have come from the car at Number One because it looks like Ian has just arrived home again, and he has Jackson with him too.

I watch as the pair of them go into their house, and I know that Sean has been waiting for them to get back so that he can talk to them about our plant pot being in their garden, as well as all the other strange things that have been going on around here recently. But my husband isn't home yet, and the longer he is out, the more I will worry that something is happening between him and Abi.

Checking my phone for messages or calls, I see that there is still no word from Sean, and it's been a few hours now since he tried to get in touch with me. If only I had answered his calls earlier then he might not have gone out with Abi. Or rather, if only I hadn't gone for drinks with Chris after the exhibition then I would have been home when Sean got back and we'd probably be sitting down to a nice dinner together now. Instead, I'm standing here at this window looking out onto the dark street and wondering if my husband is having a better time with our neighbour than he would do if he came home.

There's suddenly a flash of light across the cul-de-sac, and I see car headlights approaching. This must be Sean, and sure enough, I see the car turning onto our driveway.

I quickly duck away from the window before the headlights can detect me standing there watching because I don't want him to see that I have been waiting for him to get back, nor do I want Abi to see me either because I presume she is in the car alongside him having come back from the gym together. That's why I just loiter in the kitchen until I hear the sound of the key in the front door, and a few seconds later I enter the hallway to see my husband with his gym bag slung over his shoulder.

'Hey!' I say as I approach him, doing my best to seem sober.

'Oh, hey,' he mutters as he drops his bag and locks the door, and that wasn't quite the greeting I was hoping to get from him.

'How was the gym?' I ask him before he can head upstairs.

'How do you know I went to the gym?'
'Chris told me. Abi sent him a message.'
'Oh, right.'
'Did you have fun?'

'It wasn't really fun. We were working out.'

'You know what I mean. Did you have nice chats?'

'Yeah, it was fine.'

I've known my husband long enough to know when he's not in the mood for talking to me, and he definitely isn't in the mood now. But that's too bad because I want to keep conversing, if only for my own benefit rather than his.

'I'm sorry I missed your calls earlier. I didn't know that you'd be finishing work so early.'

'Don't worry about it. As long as you were having fun with Chris.'

'Yeah, we went for a drink after the exhibition.'

'Just one drink?'

He studies my face, and I fear that despite my attempts with the water, I still look drunk.

'Well, a couple of drinks,' I confess, and Sean gives me a wry smile.

'So much for us avoiding those two then, hey?'

'Well, you just went to the gym with Abi.'

'Only because you were out with her husband. I came home to see you, not her, but you were out with him.'

'I'm sorry. But we're just friends.'

'Just like me and Abi.'

'Then what are we arguing about then?'

'I don't know!'

Sean and I stare at each other across the hallway, and even though we're only a few yards away from one another, it feels like there is a much bigger difference between us right now.

'Do you like her?' I ask because that's really the only thing on my mind right now.

I'm expecting Sean to say no because that's what I would say if he asked me about Chris, but to my surprise, he doesn't.

'Yeah,' he admits.

'As a friend?'

'I guess.'

'What do you mean by that?'

'I don't know. What do you think of Chris?'

'I think he's a nice guy, and he's a friend. But that's it.'

'Why are you painting him then?'

'What?'

'I asked you why do you have a painting of him upstairs? Isn't that a little weird?'

'Why are you snooping around my artwork?'

'I'm not snooping. It's my house, I can look at whatever I want. Now tell me why you painted him?'

'I don't know. I just looked out of the window one day, and he was working on his car, so I started painting. That's what I do. I see things, and then I paint them.'

'You've never painted me before.'

'That doesn't mean anything.'

'Doesn't it?'

'What's your problem?'

'My problem is that you seem to think it's fine to spend time with Chris and even paint him, but you don't like me seeing Abi.'

'Because I don't trust her!'

'Yet you trust Chris? That's weird because from what we know, they are both capable of adultery.'

'At least Chris apologised for it.'

'Oh, that makes it alright then.'

'Stop being like this.'

'Not until you tell me what your problem is with Abi.'

'Do you like her? In that way?'

'What way?'

'The same way in which you like me? Because I've seen you looking at her, and I know you do.'

'I don't know.'

'What does that mean?'

'It means I don't know! God, I'm sick of having these conversations with you about them. You've been out having fun with Chris, so I've been out with Abi. What's the big deal?'

'The big deal is that I feel like we're drifting apart, and I'm worried that what happened to James and Sarah is going to happen to us too.'

'Don't be silly.'

'I'm not! What if this is how they trapped them? They became friends, they got them alone individually, and then they made their move. Maybe James and Sarah never realised what was happening until it was too late.'

'Wow, you really have been drinking today.'

'I'm serious. Has Abi ever tried anything with you? Be honest with me?'

Sean pauses for a moment, and I'm not sure whether that's a good or bad sign, but surely it can't be good.

'No,' he eventually says with a shake of the head, but I'm not convinced.

'Really?'

'Jesus, what do you want me to say, Katie? I haven't been unfaithful to you. Is that it? What about you? Has Chris come on to you?'

'No, and if he ever did then I would tell him to get lost!'

'Well, good!'

'But would you do the same thing if Abi tried?'

I know that I'm pushing my husband, but it's almost as if I need to hear him say that he likes her, even though it would break my heart. At least if he did then we could figure something out before he went too far with her, and there would be no coming back for us then.

'I don't know,' Sean admits, and that's when I realise that my husband really is being honest with me. He has just told me that he doesn't know what he would do if Abi tried anything with him.

I appreciate the honesty, as much as it stings, and I step towards him to try to get him to be closer to me. But he heads up the stairs, clearly not interested in anything I can offer him right now.

'I'll sleep in the spare bedroom tonight,' he tells me as he goes.

'What? Why?'

'Because I need some space!'

I watch as he disappears upstairs, and then I hear a door slam, and that tells me that he doesn't want to see me for the rest of the evening. What a disaster that was. I feel like I have made a complete mess of today, and not only that but I have made a complete mess of the warning Albert and Eileen gave us. They told us to be careful of the couple at Number Three, and yet here we are, falling out over them because neither of us stayed away.

I head back into the kitchen, but it's not another glass of water that I'm after now. It's the wine in the fridge. Sean might be having an early night, but I'm not. I need another drink, and I also need to figure out what we do next. But as I pour myself a glass and take a seat at the table, the answer seems to be quite clear to me.

We need to get away from the couple at Number Three before it really is too late, and this time, I have to mean it.

36

SEAN

I'm tossing and turning, but I can't sleep, although it's got nothing to do with the fact that I'm in an unfamiliar bed. It's because I can't stop thinking about two women.

Katie.

And Abi.

Rolling over on the mattress for what must be the twelfth time this hour, I look up at the dark ceiling in this spare bedroom and let out a deep sigh. I don't want to check the time on my phone again because I got a shock the last time I did that. The clock said that it was 02:31, and that meant I had been lying here for at least three hours without having slept a wink. I estimate it must be closer to three o'clock now, but I'm not going to check the time again because it's just too depressing. Instead, I'm going to lie here and think about the messy situation I've managed to get myself in.

I haven't spoken to my wife since I stormed upstairs earlier and told her that I would sleep in this spare bedroom, and that was because I was mad at her for being out all day with Chris. But it's also because I was mad at myself, and the reason for that is I was stupid enough to put myself in a position where Abi and I almost did something we shouldn't have.

We definitely had 'a moment' in that sauna, and I dread to think what might have happened if we hadn't been disturbed by that man walking in. I have never thought of myself as being capable of cheating on my wife, and I still like to think that I'm not, but there is no doubt that the incident in the sauna was the closest I have ever come to making a mistake. That's why I'm mad at myself, and that's why I can't sleep tonight. I feel guilty even though I did nothing wrong, and it's because I put myself in a position to do something wrong, and that was foolish. Worst of all, I only ended up in that situation because I was jealous of Katie being out with Chris and felt like I needed to invite Abi to the gym to try and get back at my wife. That was immature, and I should be better than that. Yet here I am, sulking in the spare bedroom like some naughty kid who has been sent upstairs with no dinner as punishment for doing something he shouldn't have done.

I roll over onto my side, and in the darkness I can make out the silhouettes of all the paintings that are propped up in here, either against the wall or on the easel. There's not enough light for me to see them properly, but I don't need to. I already know that one of them in here is the depiction of Chris, and that is enough to make me grit my teeth and feel a pang of jealousy again about the fact that my wife has painted him while she has never felt compelled to paint me before.

I know I'm fighting a losing battle trying to get to sleep tonight, and the way I see it, I have two options now unless I want to spend the rest of the night tossing and turning on this mattress. I could go into the main bedroom and crawl in bed beside my wife before apologising and trying to make up. Or I could creep downstairs, get some snacks out of the fridge and watch some television until the sun comes up and it's time to go to work. The first option will require me to swallow my pride, while the second one will only require me to swallow some fatty foods.

The second option it is then.

Peeling back the duvet, I swing my feet out of bed and get up, treading slowly across the carpet while being careful not to step on any paintbrushes or bump into the easel and send it crashing to the floor. I don't want Katie to know that I am up because that will tell her that I'm not sleeping, and then she will think that she has won. It's petty, but when it comes to an argument between a husband and wife, petty is usually the order of the day.

Opening the bedroom door, I peer across the dark landing and listen out for any sounds from the main bedroom. But Katie has never been a snorer, so I'm not expecting to be able to hear anything that will let me know that she is asleep now. I'll just have to be as quiet as I can and hope she doesn't hear me go down. If she does then she might follow me downstairs, and then my snacks in peace will be substituted for a heart to heart chat, or worse, another argument.

Creeping across the landing, I pray that I'm not going to place one of my bare feet on any of the creaky floorboards in here. Being new to this house means that I still haven't figured out where all the noisiest parts are yet, so I'll be unable to avoid them and might end up disturbing Katie if I'm not careful.

But to my surprise, I make it to the staircase without treading on a noisy floorboard, and that is a relief. Now all I have to do is tackle the steps. Fortunately, I've already learnt that the third step from the top is the creaky one, so I can easily skip that one out and make it all the way down without too much trouble. The fridge has never been so close now, and I feel as though I can almost taste some of the delicious contents.

Entering the kitchen, I decide not to turn the light on and instead just rely on the moonlight seeping in from the new window that was installed to replace the old one that was broken. Opening the fridge, I reach inside and take out some leftover lasagne. It's been a while since I consumed food at such an early time in the morning, but needs must, and if I can't do it now when my wife and I are at war then when can I?

Closing the fridge, I plan to head into the living room and put the television on at a low volume to help me while away the next few hours until the black sky outside turns blue. But just before I do, I walk over to the kitchen window and look out into my back garden, and when I do, I notice a dark shape moving at the back by the shed.

The plate of food almost drops from my hands as I see the shape and realise that somebody is in my back garden. But they haven't seen me yet, and unlike all the other times when this intruder caused damage on my property, now it is me who has the element of surprise.

Rushing to put my trainers on over my bare feet, I no longer care about making too much noise because this is more important than waking my wife. I am finally about to catch Jackson in my garden, and when I do, that boy will get his comeuppance.

With my shoes on, I scurry towards the back door and turn the key, unlocking and pulling it open quickly so as not to waste a second that could allow the intruder to make his escape.

No sooner is the door open then I see the figure run away from my shed and head for the fence, but I give chase, determined not to let him get away this time. He is wearing a balaclava, and I'm half expecting him to climb over the fence and into his garden, but he doesn't, and instead, the dark figure disappears into the row of conifers by the back fence.

I'm not sure how he plans to make his escape by going that way because there is no way out there, so I'm feeling confident about catching him as I sprint towards the conifers and prepare to enter them. But when I do, I don't see the intruder anymore. All I do see is a broken fence panel lying on the ground which is obviously how they made their escape.

'Hey!' I call out, angry about the broken fence as well as frustrated at Jackson giving me the slip once again. But this time I'm not having it, and I turn around and run towards the front of my house, figuring that I'll catch the little beggar out before he can make it back to his bedroom in time.

Rushing towards Ian's house, I pound my fists on his door when I get there, no doubt startling the man because it's the middle of the night but determined not to waste any precious time in which Jackson might be able to worm out of this one. I have no idea what he was doing around my shed in the dead of night, but I presume he was preparing to steal something or break something, and either way, he had no right to do so.

I see a light go on in the house on the other side of this door, but I keep banging until Ian opens it. When he does I see that he looks as dazed and confused as anybody would be if they were woken up at 3 AM by loud knocking on their front door.

'What the hell is going on?' he asks me when he sees me standing before him in my pyjamas with running shoes on my feet.

'Your son was in my garden just then. I chased him out and he broke the fence panel. Where is he?'

'What the hell are you talking about?'

'Jackson? Where is he?'

I go to step into the house, but Ian prevents me from doing so with a firm hand across my chest.

'Your son was on my property. Again! I've had enough of it, and it's time to do something about it.'

'And what do you think you're going to do?'

The question from Ian is a loaded one because as angry and as desperate as I am to get to Jackson, he seems just as angry and desperate to protect him, and it's clear that I'm going to have to go through him before I get to his pesky offspring.

If only I hadn't argued with Katie last night, and if only I had been able to enjoy some restful sleep then I might have handled the next few seconds a little better. But that wasn't the case, so I made a right mess of it.

I pushed Ian back and tried to get into his house again in a bid to find Jackson, but Ian responded by pushing me back out and sent me tumbling back out of the door. I should have stayed there, but I didn't and I tried again, this time more forcefully. I took a swing at Ian and hit him on the left cheek but not as hard as he hit me a second after that.

The next thing I know, I'm sitting on the drive with my hand over my bloodied nose while Ian goes back inside to call the police.

37

KATIE

It was three-thirty in the morning when I was woken up by the doorbell. My eyes scarcely believed the time on the alarm clock on my bedside table, nor did my ears believe that somebody was trying to pay a visit at such an ungodly hour, but they definitely were, and the second ring on the door confirmed it.

I feel exhausted as I haul myself up and out of bed and throw on my dressing gown and slippers, but before I go downstairs to answer the door, I go into the spare bedroom to make sure that Sean is awake too. We might be fighting right now, but I could still use his help in dealing with whoever is outside the house in case it is somebody dangerous, although if it is, I doubt they would bother knocking first.

But when I check the spare bedroom, I find that Sean isn't in the bed. Has he already got up to get the door?

'Sean?' I call out into the house, but I get no response, and now I'm getting nervous. First the doorbell in the middle of the night and now I can't find my husband. What the hell is going on?

'Sean?' I cry again as I hear the doorbell go for the third time while peering down from the top of the stairs. I'm anxious about answering the door considering that it's the middle of the night, but whoever it is doesn't seem to be leaving, and I can't get my husband to do it for me if he isn't here.

In the end, my curiosity overpowers my fear, and I go downstairs to open the door. When I do, I see that there is a policewoman standing on the doorstep, and she looks like I feel. Tired, fed up and wishing she wasn't up before the sun was.

'Mrs Thompson?' she asks me, and I nod my head while wondering what terrible news I am about to be given.

Has somebody died? Am I in trouble? Is it something to do with Sean?

'What's happened?' I ask when I see the two police cars parked on the cul-de-sac behind her. Both vehicles have their blue lights flashing, and while there is no sound to accompany them, they are bathing the other houses on this street in blue and no doubt waking everybody up with their brightness.

'It's your husband, Sean,' the policewoman says, and my heart skips a beat.

'What's happened to him? Is he okay?'

'Yes, he's okay. Well, he's got a bloody nose, but he'll live. But we're going to be taking him down to the station for questioning.'

'What are you talking about?'

I look towards the cars again, but I can't see my husband out there, although now my eyes are adjusting to the light, I can see Ian talking to another officer on his driveway.

'Your husband has been involved in a physical altercation with your neighbour, Mr Mitchell,' the policewoman tells me. 'And at the moment, Mr Mitchell wants to press charges for trespassing and assault.'

'Trespassing and assault?' I cry. 'Where is my husband now?'

'He's in the back of the car over there.'

The policewoman points towards the second of the two vehicles, but I still can't make out my husband, so I step outside.

'I want to speak to him,' I say as I hurry down the driveway in my slippers. 'Sean!'

The policewoman scurries after me as I rush towards the car where my husband is apparently incarcerated, and I notice that Albert and Eileen are standing on their porch looking out at the surprising scene as I go.

'Is everything okay?' Albert calls to me, but I ignore him as I reach the police car and try to open the door.

'Wait, you can't do that,' a male police officer tells me, and I turn to see it is the one who was speaking with Ian a moment ago.

'I want to speak to my husband! Sean!'

I can see him in back of the car now, and I can also see the blood above his top lip which backs up what the policewoman told me about him being involved in a physical altercation tonight. He looks hurt, and I have no idea why.

'Okay, you can talk to him quickly, but we have to take him to the station,' the officer tells me, and he opens the back passenger door on the car, so there is now no barrier between Sean and I. That's when I see that my husband is in handcuffs, and this suddenly gets more real than it already was.

'Sean, what the hell is going on?'

'Jackson was in our back garden again. I chased him away and then came round here to tell his dad, but he hit me.'

'I hit you because you were trying to get in my home,' Ian suddenly shouts from behind me, having heard my husband's side of the story. 'And my son was not in your back garden. He was in bed!'

'Bullshit!' Sean cries again, but I don't think swearing is going to help get my husband out of handcuffs now.

'You need to let him go. He's done nothing wrong,' I plead with the policewoman, but she shakes her head and then gestures to the other officers on the cul-de-sac that it's time to get going.

'You can come down to the station if you like, but we won't have any further updates for you until we have spoken to your husband,' the officer tells me before closing the door on the back of the car and putting the barrier between Sean and I again.

'I can't believe this,' I say, and I turn to Ian to see if I can make him stop this from happening. 'I'm sorry for whatever my husband did, but he doesn't deserve to be arrested. Please, tell them to stop!'

But Ian remains stone-faced as he stands on his driveway with his arms folded across his chest and then I spot his son standing in the doorway behind him.

'This is your fault,' I scream at the teenager. 'You wouldn't leave us alone, and now look what's happened!'

Ian tells his son to go back inside, and he follows him in, but that only makes me angrier because they are getting to go back to their warm beds while my husband is being taken into police custody.

I hear the engines on the cars start and turn back to see both vehicles driving away. Sean's bloodied face peers at me from the back window of the second vehicle, and I feel like crying as I watch him taken from the street. I keep watching until the blue flashing lights fade from view, and then I turn back to my house with the intention of getting changed and getting down to the police station as quickly as possible to try and get Sean out of there. But when I do, I see Chris and Abi hurrying across the street towards me.

'Is everything okay?' Chris asks me, and I shake my head, feeling like I'm on the verge of tears.

'They've arrested Sean,' I say, and I hear Abi gasp. Even at this early hour of the morning and even in her own dressing gown and slippers, she still looks absolutely stunning, and I'm annoyed that it bothers me.

'Is there anything we can do?' Chris asks, but I feel like saying they have done enough considering what trouble has been caused by us spending yesterday with them. But I just shake my head and carry on up my driveway, eager to get out of view of the rest of my neighbours. But before I close my door I notice that Albert and Eileen are still watching me from their doorway, and they have sorrowful expressions on their faces.

If I had to give a phrase to how they are looking at me right now, it would be this one.

"I told you so."

38

SEAN

There's no good time to find yourself at a police station sitting opposite a uniformed officer asking why a serious allegation has been made against you. But somehow it feels even worse now because it's happening in the early hours of the morning and I've been awake all night. I'm tired, my nose hurts, and I just want to go home. But I can't because I have to answer the questions being put to me in this stuffy room by this stern-faced policeman.

'Please can you explain why you went around to Mr Mitchell's address and tried to gain entry at three o'clock in the morning?'

'I've told you this already! I chased Ian's son out of my back garden, and then I went round to his house to let his dad know before he could get back and worm his way out of it.'

'The son would be Jackson?'

'Yes!'

'And you saw Jackson in your garden? I mean, actually got a full visual I.D. on him?'

'Yes! I mean, no, I didn't see his face. But I knew it was him!'

'How could you know it was him if you didn't see his face?'

'Because he's been in my back garden before!'

'Do you have proof of this?'

'No, but I know it's him!'

'And how do you know that?'

'Because I was told about it!'

'By whom?'

I pause because I'm aware that what I am about to say might not come across as the most convincing story, but it is the truth, so I push on anyway.

'My neighbour told me,' I say before letting out a deep sigh. 'He told me that Jackson was trouble and that he liked to trespass and cause damage on other people's property.'

'Your neighbour told you that? And what might their name be?'

'Does it matter? The point is that ever since my wife and I moved into our house, we've had nothing but trouble. You should know about this because I filed a report recently after a brick was thrown through my kitchen window.'

The policeman checks one of the files on the table in front of him, and I wait for him to find what he is looking for.

'Okay, I see there was an incident on the evening of the fourteenth.'

'Yes, and that's not all! My plant pots were broken before that, and the camera I installed was destroyed too! And then I saw one of my plant pots in Ian's garden. That proves that Jackson has been doing all of this!'

The policeman lets out a sigh as he continues to look in the file, and I shake my head at the fact that I have ended up here in this situation when I have done nothing wrong. That's when I realise that maybe getting worked up isn't helping me and that I should perhaps try a slightly different approach to the rest of this interaction.

'Look, I'm sorry for going around to Ian's house and trying to force my way inside onto another man's property. But you have to understand that I'm just a homeowner trying to look after his home. How would you react if you got up in the middle of the night and saw somebody in your back garden?'

'I understand. But I'm sure you understand that we have to look into this and try and get both sides of the story.'

'Of course,' I reply with a sigh, and I sit back in my chair because I realise that this isn't going to be a quick and simple process.

As I sit there and watch the policeman making notes in his file, I think about how Albert and Eileen told me about the man who lived in my house before who ended up getting into a physical altercation with Ian and wound up with a restraining order against him. Despite that ominous tale, it appears that I am now headed down the same path as that poor chap, and I curse myself for not being smart enough and calm enough to avoid it. But then again, when I think back about how it felt to have my property damaged and to see somebody trespassing, I'm not sure I could have acted any differently. Something had to be done, and I only wish I had caught Jackson before he got away because now that he has, I'm not sure what I can do about it.

'It appears that there have been issues at your neighbour's address before,' the policeman suddenly says, and I realise that he must be referring to the time that Albert and Eileen told me about.

'Yes, that will be because of the same thing,' I say, sitting forward again and feeling a little more optimistic about things. 'That would have been about Jackson's trespassing too.'

'That resulted in the issuing of a restraining order,' the policeman says, and then he looks at me as if to say that it's the same situation repeating itself again.

'But don't you see that guy was just trying to stop the same thing that I'm trying to stop,' I plead. 'Jackson is trouble. I was warned about him, and now all of this has happened. So what are you going to do about it?'

'What do you want us to do about it?'

'Well, you could question him for a start!'

'And ask him what?'

'I don't know! You're the police officer!'

'So you want me to ask him if he has been trespassing on your property?'

'Yes! But he's hardly likely to admit to it, is he?'

'It's doubtful. So we would require some evidence.'

'I don't have any of that. Like I said, I did install a camera, but it was broken.'

'Then I'm not sure you can make these kinds of allegations against Jackson without any evidence.'

'This is ridiculous!'

'No, what's ridiculous is a man your age being questioned over an assault on a neighbour while your wife is at home on her own worrying about you.'

I'm struck by the statement from the policeman, but it is a bit of a reality check. Katie is home alone, and she will continue to be on her own until I get out of this mess. So I better start doing a better job of it. The problem is I'm not sure how?

'What's going to happen?' I ask the policeman rather meekly.

'We're going to have to speak to Ian and see if he wishes to continue pressing charges,' he says.

'Well, if he does then I want to press charges against him. He's the one who hit me!'

'Yes, but you were the one trying to get in his house, so I wouldn't go there if I was you.'

I stop talking after that and let the police officer finish.

'If you're lucky then he will drop this, and this won't go any further. Maybe this is all just a misunderstanding. But one thing's for sure, it's going to be awkward living next door to each other from now on.'

The policeman seems slightly amused at what he has just said, but it fails to raise a laugh or a smile out of me. That's because he is right. Things are going to be awkward when I go back to the street and not just with those who live at Number One. I'm sure my other neighbours saw the police car taking me away a few hours ago, and I can only imagine what they are thinking of me at this time. But I shouldn't care about Albert and Eileen, nor should I care about Chris and Abi. All that matters is what my wife thinks of me, and right now, I can't imagine that it's anything good.

39

KATIE

It's been a busy few days since I was rudely awoken in the middle of the night to find out that my husband was being taken to a police station for questioning. Thankfully, there have been no more rude awakenings since, just a lot of effort on my part to build back the relationship with Ian so that he would drop the charges and give Sean the chance to keep a clean record. That seems to have worked because Sean is home, and Ian has told me he will leave it at that, providing my husband stays away from both him and his son for the rest of the time we live here. I have assured him that he will, and hopefully, that is the end of it. But this doesn't mean that I have taken Ian and Jackson's side. Far from it. I believe my husband when he tells me that the teenager is trouble, and I have no doubt that Sean would never have acted in the way he did if he didn't have good reason to. But there comes a time when one has to bite down on their tongue and do what's best for them, and that's what I've done now. If Sean got a restraining order, or worse, a criminal record then he could lose his job, and he might not be able to find another one, so I'm glad I seem to have defused the situation. At least in that regard anyway. But there is still plenty of work to be done in mending my own relationship with my troubled husband.

Sean is in the back garden now hauling the lawnmower over our terrible grass, and I'm taking the opportunity while he is busy to pop next door and have a word with Eileen. I know she is in because I looked out of an upstairs window a moment ago and saw her sitting on her patio chair, so I know she will answer when I knock on her front door. Sure enough she does, and she invites me inside with a warm smile and the offer of a cold drink on this hot day.

By the time I accept the drink from her I'm already sitting on her patio looking out once again over her beautiful garden, and I wonder if it would be worth me asking Eileen if she could send Albert round to give Sean a hand with ours. But then she tells me that her husband is out fishing, so I guess I won't bother.

'How is everything, dear?' Eileen asks me as she eases herself into her seat beside me and takes a sip of her lemonade. 'I understand you've been having a rough time of things.'

'That would be the understatement of the year,' I reply as I put my delicious lemonade down and look to the woman beside me. 'I need your help.'

'You do?'

'Yeah. It's about me and Sean.'

'Oh, okay.'

Eileen takes the chance to put her drink down too as she obviously senses this is going to be a serious chat and not just a friendly catch up between two neighbours.

'How long have you and Albert been married for now?' I ask her as I listen to the sound of Sean's lawnmower still going over the garden fence.

'Fifty-one years,' she tells me, and I give a respectful nod.

'So that must mean you know the secret to a long and happy marriage then,' I say, and I look to Eileen with hope in my heart that she will tell me that she does and not only that, but she can furnish me with that secret too. But she just laughs and shakes her head.

'Oh dear, it's not as simple as that. There is no secret. Just a lot of hard work.'

'What do you mean by that?'

'Well, when you've been married to someone for as long as I have, you can't expect every day to be a bed of roses. There are always going to be ups and downs. Silly arguments, disagreements, awkward silences, the occasional cross word that you wish you could take back. But that is all part of it, and I like to think that the good times more than outweigh the bad.'

'But what if it's more than just an argument or a disagreement? And what if something is said that can't be forgotten?'

'What do you mean?'

I pause before replying because I know that when I do answer it then Eileen might have a very different view on me and my marriage for as long as we are neighbours. But I came here for her advice, and I can't expect to get the full benefit of that without giving her the full story, so I take a deep breath and then just go for it.

'Sean and I didn't really follow your advice when it came to Chris and Abi,' I say, but her sympathetic smile tells me she already knew that without me having to confess it.

'What's happened?'

'Nothing like that,' I reply quickly in case she is thinking that one of us has already strayed. 'It's just that I've been spending time with Chris and really enjoying it, and I know Sean has been doing the same with Abi. The problem is, we don't seem to be very happy when we spend time with each other.'

Eileen nods her head like some wise old sage, which I'm hoping that she is otherwise I wouldn't be here baring my soul like this.

'It's only natural that you would be attracted to them. They are both good looking people, and they know it. And it's only natural that you would get along so well because you're a similar age, and I assume you have some things in common.'

I nod my head, and Eileen keeps going.

'The problem comes when you feel like you are looking forward to seeing one of them more than your own partner, and by the sounds of it, you seem to be getting that way, right?'

I hesitate to nod my head again, but it is the honest answer, so I eventually do so.

'I know he likes Abi,' I say with grave acceptance. 'He almost admitted as much the other night. But I also know that he wouldn't do anything if things were great between us, and I always thought they were, right up until we moved here.'

'You haven't had the easiest of starts here,' Eileen muses. 'I see Jackson has been up to his old tricks again.'

'Yeah, and Sean was lucky not to get more than a warning after the other night. But I'm worried about what he might do if anything happens again. Sometimes, I think it might just be for the best if we were to move.'

I pick up my lemonade glass and take another sip, but the zesty flavour does little to boost my mood. I hear the lawnmower stop on the other side of the fence and presume that Sean has finished cutting the grass now. That means he'll be heading inside soon, and then he will wonder where I have got to.

'I should be getting back,' I say before finishing my drink and going to stand. 'Thanks for the lemonade and the chat.'

'You're welcome, dear,' Eileen tells me, and she follows me through her home as I walk back in the direction of the front door. But before I can open it to leave she puts a wrinkled hand on my arm and looks me right in the eye.

'You asked for the secret of a happy marriage, and I said there wasn't really one,' she says to me. 'But I might have been a little hasty there. I think there is something that is important, and it has helped guide me through my marriage with Albert. In fact, it can be applied to any area of life, not just relationships.'

'What's that?' I ask, feeling as if I might be about to be given the key to everlasting happiness, although I doubt I'll be lucky.

'You should always trust your instincts,' Eileen tells me with a serious expression. 'They are very rarely wrong.'

With that she opens the door and allows me to leave, and I do just that, walking up her driveway and then across onto my own while replaying her last words to me over and over again in my head.

She wants me to trust my instincts, and I don't think anybody could call that bad advice. So what are my instincts telling me now?

By the time I walk back into my own house I have a pretty good idea, and now I know what I have to do. I'm going to cook a meal for Sean this evening.

And then I am going to tell him exactly what my instincts are telling me.

40

SEAN

The smell of home-cooked food is wafting out from the kitchen, and I can hear music playing in the dining room, all of which leads me to think that Katie is preparing a special dinner for us. I'd have been happy enough with a piece of toast and a cup of tea tonight because I'm not really in the mood for sitting down at the table and making a big deal out of the evening meal, but my wife obviously has other ideas. I can't remember the last time we had a proper meal together, and maybe that's why she is cooking something up tonight. Recent meals have basically consisted of sitting on the sofa in front of the television and barely making conversation while we eat. But tonight looks like it's going to be a return to more traditional ways, and I suppose that can only be a good thing.

Entering the kitchen, I see Katie dishing up what appears to be a very appetising bowl of pasta before my eyes are drawn to the bottle of red wine she has already uncorked.

'What's the occasion?' I ask her as I take a couple of glasses out of the cupboard.

'I just thought it would be nice to talk over a proper meal,' she replies, and I smile because I have to agree.

Five minutes later and we are seated at the dining room table with our food in front of us, a flickering candle in between us and the dulcet tones of Barry White floating all around us. This feels more like a first date than a meal between a married couple. Or maybe it's a desperate attempt at a reconciliation. I guess time will tell.

'This is great,' I say after tucking in and getting a taste of the perfectly cooked pasta. 'Thank you.'

'You're welcome,' Katie replies, but I'm sure I'm not the only one who can't help thinking things are a little formal and forced between us right now. But not only has it been a long time since we had a meal like this together, but it's also been a while since our conversations were free-flowing. To highlight that, I'm just about to mention the weather when Katie thankfully takes the lead and steers our interaction in a more interesting direction.

'What do you think about moving?' she asks me, putting down her knife and fork and looking me right in the eye to show me how serious she is about what she has just said.

'What do you mean?'

'I mean selling up and moving house. Going somewhere new.'

'Why would we do that?'

'I don't know. I just think that things aren't great between us at the moment and all our problems started when we moved here. So maybe if we move away then things will go back to normal.'

'That's quite a drastic thing to do to get us back on track.'

'Do you think we're off track?'

'I didn't say that. You did.'

I put down my knife and fork too, and it looks like neither of us will be eating again until we have talked this over.

'I'm just worried about us,' Katie says, and while I am too, I'm not keen on the idea of moving house so soon after we have got here.

'I know, but moving is not the right thing to do. It's a lot of effort and we'll probably lose money on the sale.'

'Right now, money is the least of my worries.'

'What are you worrying about?'

'I'm just listening to my instincts, and they are telling me that we should leave before things get worse.'

'You mean with Ian and Jackson? I told you, I'm going to stay away from them and not let them bother me as long as they stay away from us.'

'No, it's not just that.'

291

I let out a sigh because I know what she is getting at here.

'Abi,' I say with a shake of the head. 'You still think something is going to happen between us.'

I expect her to reluctantly agree, and then that will be the end of this pleasant meal because I won't be able to sit here with my wife who doesn't trust me not to have an affair. But to my surprise, Katie doesn't do that. Instead, she looks down at the table and admits something else entirely.

'It's not Abi I'm worried about anymore,' she says as the candle continues to flicker in between us. 'It's Chris. I'm attracted to him and not just his looks. His personality. I know I've been harsh on you for spending time with Abi, but I've spent too much time with Chris, and I find myself thinking about him quite a lot now.'

I'm stunned, not only at what my wife has just said but at the honesty behind it. It takes serious guts to admit something like that, but before I go handing out any awards for nobility, I am too busy trying to figure out what this means for my marriage.

'I don't understand,' I say. 'Has something happened between you two?'

'No, I promise!' Katie replies defiantly, and I can guess I can take that as the truth as well.

'But you're worried it will?'

'I'm just trusting my instincts.'

'What does that even mean?'

'It means I have a feeling we should leave.'

'Because you're attracted to one of our neighbours?'

'And he's attracted to me.'

'Did he say that?'

'No, but I can tell.'

'So what you're saying is we have to sell our house and move to another part of town because your instincts are telling you to do so? What about your common sense? What's that telling you to do?'

'Don't be like this.'

'No, I think I'm right to ask because common sense is important. Let's just say we do move. What happens if you fancy our next neighbour? Do we move again? And what if I like somebody in my office? Do I have to change jobs?'

'That's not what I mean.'

'Well, it sounds like it is!'

I raised my voice just then, and I take a moment to calm down before speaking again.

'What happened to trusting each other?'

'I get that, but what about trusting our instincts?'

'Why are you so obsessed with your instincts all of a sudden?'

'Because Eileen told me that was the key to a lasting marriage!'

'What are you talking about now?'

'I asked Eileen for her advice because she has been married for so long.'

'You went to our neighbour about our marriage problems? Don't you think you should be keeping that between us?'

'I just wanted some outside perspective.'

'I think we've had enough outside perspective since we've been here! Albert and Eileen's warnings. Ian and his nightmare of a son. And Chris and Abi and their ultra-friendliness that has done nothing but driven a wedge between us!'

Katie looks frustrated at what I have just said, but now it's my turn to be honest with her.

'I don't know how many times I have to promise you that I won't cheat. But I can't make that promise for you. If you think you can't be around Chris then that's your problem, not mine, and while I appreciate your honesty, I don't appreciate the fact that you think moving house is the solution.'

'I just don't want us to end up like James and Sarah.'

'I know that.'

'And I don't want you to end up with a criminal record which almost happened.'

'Okay, I get that. But forget our neighbours for a second and just think about this house. Do you like it?'

'Of course I do.'

'Then we should stay.'

'I don't know.'

'Why did we move here?' I ask, deciding to go for a change of pace to seal the deal.

'You know why we moved here,' Katie replies.

'Yes, I do, but I want you to say it.'

'We moved here because we were planning to start a family.'

'Exactly. So don't you think we should get started on that?'

Katie seems surprised by what I've just said, but I show her I am serious by getting up out of my seat and holding out my hand for her to take. She does, and then I blow out the candle before leading her out of the dining room and up the stairs to the bedroom, where we spend the rest of the evening making up with each other in a much more enjoyable way than just eating pasta and drinking wine.

41

KATIE

So last night's dinner went well in so much as it allowed Sean and I to do some making up, although the food didn't really have much to do with it in the end. We ended up spending more time in the bedroom than the dining room, but the important thing is that I feel we're in a much better place in our relationship now. However, that doesn't mean that I got my own way, not entirely anyway.

I took Eileen's advice and listened to my instincts, and they told me that we should leave this house before things got worse. Then I relayed that information to Sean, but he wasn't quite so keen on the idea of us selling the house that we have barely finished moving into. I could see his argument because moving home at any time is a big stress involving lots of upheaval, never mind doing it so soon after the last move. But I had been wondering if he would see things from my point of view and agree to the idea. However, he did not, and we are staying. For now, anyway. But I still feel a little on edge about things with our neighbours and wonder if we might come to look back on last night's decision to stay as the beginning of the end for our marriage.

Let's hope not. I want many more nights like last night, and I hope Sean does too.

My husband is at work right now, and that means that I should be as well, but instead of being holed up in our spare bedroom painting, I am in the kitchen doing a spot of baking. For someone who loves to try their hand at being a chef, I haven't done half as much cooking or baking since I moved into this house. But I'm starting to change that now, both with last night's meal and with today's attempt at making some sultana buns that I know Sean will absolutely love to come home to later today. But I'm not just baking for my husband.

I'm baking for the neighbours.

Seeing as how Sean and I re-committed to staying in this house last night, I've figured it's as good a time as any to prove to our neighbours that we belong on this street and not only that, but we can fit in. That's why I have made extra buns, and I am planning to deliver them to the doorstep of the three other houses on this cul-de-sac so that I can spread a little neighbourly warmth and goodwill. Lord knows this place could do with some.

Putting four buns into three small containers, I leave a dozen buns for Sean and I, to cool down on the kitchen counter, before picking up the three containers and heading for the door. Feeling as if I am some kind of Samaritan of the baking world, I then head for Number One to deliver my first batch of goods.

Knocking on the door, I expect it to be Ian who answers, but to my surprise, it is Jackson.

'Oh, hello,' I say, wondering why the teenager isn't at school right now, considering that it's the middle of a weekday.

'Hey, I'll just get my dad,' the teen replies with a weary voice, and he looks like he's just woken up, which he may very well have done.

'No, it's fine. I'm just dropping off these,' I say, and I hand him the first container.

'What is it?'

'Sultana buns! I hope you like them!'

'Oh, right. Cool.'

'Enjoy!' I say breezily before walking away and leaving the sleepy teen to close his front door and go back inside, where he will presumably scoff the buns and get straight back into bed. But I don't care what he does as long as he appreciates the goodwill gesture. He might not have been very kind to us and our property since we moved in, but that could be because we haven't been very kind to him. He might just see us as nameless targets who he has no emotional connection to, but if I can change that with some friendly gestures then he might think twice about getting up to no good. Basically, I'm hoping that the way to a teenager's heart is through his stomach.

Crossing the street and reaching Number Three, I decide not to hang around too long here so as not to get into a conversation with Chris or Abi. Instead, I just place the second container on the doorstep, knock on the door and then hurry away, hoping that I'll be across the street again before they answer it. It works because I'm almost at Albert and Eileen's house before I hear a door open behind me, and then Abi shouts 'thank you' across the street to me.

'You're welcome!' I say before turning back around to show that I don't have time to chat, and then I make my final stop off of the day.

It's Eileen who answers the door here, and she looks thrilled at the prospect of being given some buns to go with her tea later today.

'Thank you dear, that's very kind,' she says as she accepts my last container. 'And Albert will be very happy too.'

'You're welcome,' I say before turning to leave. But just before I do, Eileen has something to ask.

'How is everything going, dear? Did you come to a decision about what you were worrying about?'

I know she is referring to what we spoke about in her garden yesterday and the whole "trust your instincts" thing, but I feel like she has a right to know because she was helpful enough to offer her advice yesterday when she didn't have to.

'Yeah, I had a long think about things and a good chat with Sean,' I say, deciding not to mention that our 'chat' turned into something a little more physical. 'And we've decided to stay.'

Eileen smiles. 'That's lovely, dear. We would have missed you. And your baking, of course.'

I laugh before giving her a wave and heading back to my home, smiling all the way as I go. It was only a small and simple gesture to hand out buns to my neighbours, but I hope it has done some good as well as shown that Sean and I are here to not only stay but be a valuable part of this community. Maybe Jackson's troublemaking comes from a confidence that we will leave and he won't have to deal with us, so maybe he will stop now that he sees we are not put off by it. And maybe Chris and Abi's flirting comes from a belief that if anything did happen between us then we would be the ones to leave the street, not them, just like James and Sarah did. But we're not going anywhere. Sean has decided that, and as I close my front door and head back into my beautiful kitchen that smells of baked buns, I am glad that he was able to change my mind on the matter.

This is our home.

And nothing is going to come between us and that.

42

SEAN

I'm feeling satisfied right now, and it has nothing to do with all the leftover buns I have gorged myself on since I got home from work. Instead, my good feelings are down to the fact that I was able to talk my wife out of the drastic idea of moving house as a response to all the things that have been going on with us lately. Leaving this street was the last thing I wanted to do, and it was surely the last thing our bank manager would have wanted us to do too because we would definitely have lost money overall if we had moved house again so soon after buying. I know this place isn't perfect, but like I said to Katie the other night, we came into this home with the intention of not only being here for a long time but also starting a family in it too, and that is the plan we are now going to stick with.

My wife is out of the house attending an art class at the local college, and I'm looking forward to an evening of having the place to myself. I dropped her off earlier, and I'll be picking her up again in a couple of hours, but there's plenty of chill-out time to be had before then. But before I can sprawl out on the sofa and find some live sport to watch, I need to head out to the car to retrieve my briefcase that I left in there by accident when I got home earlier. I could leave it out there overnight, but it has important documents inside it, and I wouldn't like to run the risk of this being the one night when somebody breaks into my vehicle and takes the contents. You never know, and certainly not on a street like this, so I'm definitely not going to tempt fate.

I open my front door and head for the car, but I pause when I see that Albert is coming down the driveway towards me.

'Oh, hello,' he says as he gives me a wave while still approaching.

I give him a warm greeting back, but internally, I'm feeling deflated. So much for a quiet night on my own. What does this old chap want, and how long is it going to take?

'I was wondering if you had a minute to come next door? I have something to show you,' Albert asks, and my chances of my peaceful night alone are dwindling by the second.

'Erm, I guess. Is everything okay?'

'I think it's better if I just show you,' Albert says rather mysteriously, and he turns and heads back up the driveway.

I let out a sigh as I put my car keys back in my pocket and forget about retrieving my briefcase for the moment, instead following my neighbour onto his driveway. I'm expecting him to take me into his house, but he doesn't. Instead, he leads me down the side of his property and into the back garden before we walk across his pristine lawn and down to the shed at the bottom by the back fence.

This might be a good time to ask Albert for some tips on grass maintenance, but it appears that he has something more pressing on his mind, so I say nothing as he unlocks his shed and opens the door. It's obvious that the plan is for both of us to go inside, and I'm wondering how we can both fit because I know my shed is barely big enough to accommodate a lawnmower, never mind grown men, but then I see that this shed is nothing like my own. It's bigger for a start, and not only that but it has been internally modified so that it is less of a shed and more of a man cave.

'Welcome to my den,' Albert says, but there's no hint of bragging about it. It's just spoken in a very matter of fact way, which leads me to think that what he is about to show me might be a little more serious than just a beer fridge or a signed football photo.

'Wow, I didn't know you had a den,' I say as I step inside and look around at the cosy cabin. It's pretty basic for a man cave, but then again, most men are pretty basic too. There's an armchair beside a bookcase full of books as well as a couple of framed photos of Albert and

Eileen along with a young man who I'm not sure I recognise.

'That's my son, George,' Albert tells me when he sees me looking at the photo. 'He lives Down Under.'

'Oh right. Cool.'

I shift my attention away from the photos to the bookcase, but there are not many titles on there that would appeal to me. Other than looking at the chair, I'm not sure what else Albert could be showing me in here. But then he goes over to the bookcase and picks up what looks like a wallet that people would use to keep photographs in before the digital age came around and people just took photos on their phones. But Albert is of a different generation, and as he opens the wallet and takes out several photos, I guess that he still does things the old fashioned way.

'Maybe it's none of my business,' he says as he looks at me before handing me the photos. 'But from an old chap to a young one, I wanted to let you know in case something was going on. You're at work all day, so you wouldn't know otherwise.'

I have no idea what he is talking about, and I'm just about to ask him when he passes me the photos and I look down at the first one. Straight away, I see Katie and Chris.

'What is this?' I ask as I go through the other photos, but I see they are mostly more of

305

the same. Various images of my wife and the man from Number Three. Sometimes on my doorstep, sometimes on his and one of her going into his house.

'This is what's been happening while you've been at your office,' Albert tells me. 'Katie and Chris have been spending a lot of time together.'

'But there's nothing going on.'

'I hope so.'

'What do you mean?'

I look up from the photos after I have finished going through them as Albert eases himself into the armchair by the bookcase.

'You know all about the couple who lived in your house before you, right?' Albert says, and I nod my head.

'James and Sarah?'

'That's right. Well, when they were living on this street, it was Sarah who went to work in an office while James was around more in the day. Anyway, over time, I started to notice him visiting Number Three quite a lot and often, Abi would visit his house too. I would see them out of my window as they have to cross past my house to get to the other ones.'

'Okay. And?'

'Well, this went on for some time, and I didn't do anything or say anything to anybody, not even Eileen. But maybe that was a mistake

306

because they were obviously having an affair, and in the end, their marriage was ruined.'

'Why are you telling me this?'

'Because I don't want to make the same mistake again. Maybe if I'd said something sooner then James and Sarah might not have split up and ended up moving. But I didn't, and things went the way that they did. I vowed to myself that if I ever had suspicions again then I would let the other party know. Like I said, Sarah was at work all day just like you are, so how would you know if something was going on?'

'You think something is going on between Chris and my wife?'

'I don't know. All I do know is that I've seen them crossing over to each other's houses a fair bit since you moved in, and that's why I have started to document it. I'll leave it up to you to decide what you do with that information.'

'Let me get this straight. You think my wife is having an affair?'

'I didn't say that. I'm just trying to be a friend, from one married man to another.'

I look back down at the photos again and see Katie and Chris smiling, but it's the one where she is going into his house that I find myself looking at the most. But maybe these can be explained. At least I hope they can when I mention them to my wife later.

'Wait a minute. Didn't Sarah have an affair with Chris too?' I ask, referring back to the previous couple who lived in my house.

'Apparently so,' Albert replies.

'So why are you making out like it was just James and Abi who did wrong?'

'I'm not. I'm just saying that I didn't know about Chris and Sarah, but I had my suspicions about Abi and James, and I wish I'd done something about it sooner. It probably wouldn't have been enough to save their marriage, but who knows?'

I decide I've had enough of looking at the photos, so I hand them back to Albert and turn to leave.

'I hope I haven't intruded,' the old man says before I can leave. 'But I'd like to think that someone would tell me if my wife was getting close to another man while I was out all day.'

I pause in the doorway of the den and think about Albert's last remark. Then I step outside onto the grass and head for home, no longer thinking about the man in the shed behind me and instead thinking about my wife, who I will be picking up from her art class later this evening.

When I do, I am going to have some questions for her.

43

KATIE

I gather up my paintbrushes and my notepad as the art class comes to an end, and the other students begin to make their way to the exits. It's nine PM, so I imagine everybody is keen to get home and I'm no different, but that doesn't mean that this wasn't a fun experience. It's been a while since I attended a class like this one, and I enjoyed it. The teacher was helpful, the lesson was interesting, and the work I produced on my canvas has given me plenty to think about for my future work. Even though I am now a full-time artist, that doesn't mean that I should ever stop trying to learn, and that is exactly why I enrolled in this class tonight. I came to learn and learn I did. But now I'm ready to go home and relax.

Walking through the college reception and saying goodbye to a couple of the other students as I go, I push my way through the glass doors that lead out into the car park and scan the rows of vehicles for any sign of Sean. I spot him parked at the end of the nearest row, so I hurry towards the car, excited to see my husband and tell him all about what I have just learned. But when I get in the car, I can immediately sense that something is not right.

First of all, Sean doesn't ask me how my class was. Instead, he just waits until I have put my seatbelt on before driving out of the car park and taking us back onto the main road.

'How was your evening?' I ask him when it becomes clear that he is not going to ask me about mine.

'Interesting,' he replies, which is a rather mysterious answer.

'What do you mean?'

'I mean that it was interesting. I learnt a few things like I'm sure you did.'

'What are you talking about?'

'I'm talking about the little chat I had with Albert.'

I'm aware that Sean is driving a little aggressively, going a little over the speed limit and passing through a light that had just turned red, which is very unlike him. He seems to be in a rush to get home, or rather, he is too distracted to concentrate on his driving.

'What did you talk about?' I ask as I glance at his hands gripping the steering wheel tightly.

'He showed me some photos.'

'Of what?'

'They were of you.'

'Me? What are you talking about?'

'They were photos of you. And they were photos of Chris too.'

I stare at my husband, trying to make some sense of what he is telling me, but I can't, and it's not helping that he is looking at the road ahead because I can't see the full range of emotions on his face.

'Sean, what do you mean they were photos of me and Chris?'

'I mean that's exactly what they were. Photos of the two of you together. At our house, at his house. Apparently, you've been going back and forth quite a bit while I've been at work.'

'What? Who said this? Albert?'

'Yeah, but he didn't have to because the pictures proved it.'

'I don't know what you're getting at. So what? I've been to Chris's a few times, and he's been to ours. You know that. Most of the time I was taking him something, or he was bringing something over for us. The painting. The exhibition ticket. The damn hedge trimmer, remember?'

'Albert seems to think it's been happening a little too often to not be suspicious.'

'How would he know? Has he been spying on me?'

'He didn't have to. His house is right in between ours and Chris's, so he can see you both walking past every day.'

'It's not been every day!'

'Well, there were a lot of photos!'

'That doesn't mean anything!'

I can't believe what's happening, but this was the last thing I was expecting when I got into the car tonight. I thought Sean and I were in a better place now and had put all these silly anxieties about our neighbours to bed, but I guess not.

'You really think I'm having an affair with him?' I ask, but Sean fails to either nod or shake his head which might be for the best because if he had nodded then I probably would have been so angry that I would have grabbed the wheel and forced him over to the side of the road.

'Answer me!' I cry, and Sean finally looks at me, taking his eyes off the road for the first time since I got in the car beside him. But it's only for a second, and when he does, I see the sorrow in his eyes.

'I don't know what to think,' he confesses. 'But why else would Albert show me those photos if he didn't think he was helping me?'

'Because he's a busybody with nothing better to do. Can't you see that? Eileen is the same! They're lovely people, but they've stuck their nose in so many times they're only making things worse now.'

Sean turns back to the road as I throw my hands up in exasperation.

'Tell me this. If I was having an affair with my neighbour then why would I be the one who suggested moving?' I ask him, and I feel like I might have him there.

'I don't know. Because you were terrified of the truth coming out and wanted to move before it did?'

I can't believe my husband's response. Is he joking?

'You can't seriously think that?' I ask. 'I suggested we move to help our marriage, not because I was doing something to jeopardise it!'

'It makes sense now,' Sean goes on. 'You had your fun, but you knew it was a mistake, and you knew that the truth would come out in the end, just like it did with James and Sarah. That's why you wanted us to move. You thought you would get away with it if we just left.'

I'm incredulous, and I also need to have a break from this insane conversation.

'Stop the car!' I cry, feeling as though I need to get out and get some fresh air.

'No, we're almost home,' Sean replies, but I don't care.

'I said stop the car! I'm not sitting here next to you if you think I'm the kind of person who would have an affair!'

Sean looks at me but still keeps driving, and that's when I reach over and tug on the steering wheel, trying to get him to move to the side of the road.

'Jesus! What are you doing?' he cries as he wrestles control of the wheel back from me and steadies the vehicle, but I shout at him again until he slows down and pulls over to the side of the kerb.

I open my door as soon as we have come to a stop and take off my seatbelt, feeling as though I'm suffocating with every second that I spend in this enclosed space.

'What are you doing?' Sean asks me as I get out.

'I'm walking home. I can't stay in this car with you!'

'Don't be silly. Come on, get back in.'

'No!' I cry before I slam the door.

I start walking in the direction of our street, but Sean winds down the window and drives slowly alongside me.

'Get back in the car, Katie,' he orders me, but I don't even look at him. I just fold my arms across my chest and keep walking down the dark pavement.

'I'm going to drive off,' he warns me, but I still refuse to engage with him.

'Fine!' he says. 'I'll take this little tantrum as proof that you've been rumbled and you're not happy about it!'

With that, Sean hits the accelerator pedal and speeds off, leaving me alone on this quiet street. I'm furious at him for leaving me but not half as furious as I am at him accusing me of being unfaithful.

As I watch the lights on the back of his car disappear around the corner, I know that he is definitely not coming back for me. I really am walking home. Fine, I don't care. I'd rather be on my own right now, and the way I'm feeling, I'm not even sure I want to see Sean when I do make it back to the house. Not if he thinks so badly of me. And not if we're only going to have another argument when I get there.

44

SEAN

I'm absolutely seething as I park my car on my driveway and release my strong grip on the steering wheel. Then I look at the empty passenger seat and feel a little guilty that Katie is out on the streets instead of sitting here beside me. But that feeling of guilt soon evaporates when I remember that not only was it her idea to get out of the car but that she didn't do a very good job of convincing me that I had nothing to worry about with those photos. The fact that I realised her wanting to move house might have just been a way of covering up her indiscretion has only made me feel even worse, and as I get out of the car, I feel like I'm on the warpath and need more answers. But I can't get them from my wife because she isn't here right now. Therefore, there is only one other place I can go for them.

Number Three.

I slam my car door before storming across the street, my fists clenched as my eyes burn a hole into the front door that I am preparing to bang on. When I reach it, I hammer my fists against it until I get an answer from

316

within. But it's not Chris who opens the door, it's Abi, and she looks shocked when she sees how distressed I am.

'What's wrong?' she asks me.

'Where's Chris?' I say, looking past her and into her home in case her husband is nearby.

'He's gone out for a run. Why?'

'I need to speak to him.'

'Okay, but he's not here.'

'Damn it!'

I turn away from the door and plan to head home, where I will keep watch from the window until I see Chris return from his jog. But before I can go, Abi calls after me.

'Is it anything I can help with?'

I turn back to look at her in her doorway, and she looks genuinely compassionate, even if she doesn't know the full extent of my situation. It's at that moment that I realise that the thing I am worrying about also affects her too.

'I just really need to speak to Chris. It's about Katie,' I tell her.

'What about her?'

'It might just be better if I speak to him.'

'No, you can speak to me. What about Chris and Katie?'

I regret not just walking away a few seconds ago because now Abi is going to be just as unsure about things as I am.

'I think something has been going on between them,' I tell her. 'They've been going to each other's houses while we've both been out.'

'What?'

'I asked Katie about it just now and she stormed off out of the car. She denies it obviously, but she wanted us to move house, and it's starting to make sense why now.'

Abi looks just as confused as I feel, but then her expression becomes one of anger.

'He promised me he would never do anything like this again.'

I get that she is referring to his past and Sarah, and even though she has a past of her own with James, I can see why this new betrayal would sting.

I feel bad for myself, but I feel bad for her too, and that's why I return to the door to check that she is okay.

'I need a drink,' she tells me before going back into her house, but she leaves the door open, and I assume that's because she doesn't mind if I stay.

I see her disappear into her kitchen before I hear the sound of glasses being taken from a cupboard. Then she pops her head back around the kitchen door and tells me that I am welcome to wait here until Chris returns if I would like to.

It's either this or going back to my empty house and waiting on my own, and why should us two be left alone when it's Katie and Chris who have caused this mess? That's why I enter the house and close the front door before joining Abi in the kitchen, where she hands me a glass of wine.

'We'll get to the bottom of this as soon as he gets back,' Abi tells me, and I nod my head before following her into the living room and taking a seat beside her on the sofa.

I do my best not to get caught looking at the photos of Abi and her husband on the mantelpiece because that could make this awkward situation even worse, and instead just stare into my wine glass and shake my head.

'You know, Katie used to worry about me and you,' I say to Abi as she takes a sip. 'Maybe she was tricking me into thinking I was the only one capable of doing something I shouldn't.'

'Don't think like that.'

'I don't know what to think.'

I take a long sip of my wine and look back to Abi beside me.

'Of course I liked you. Katie was right to be a little jealous. But I would never have done anything to hurt her. But now I just feel foolish for doing the right thing while she has been doing this.'

'It's not your fault. Whatever's happened, it isn't your fault.'

'Isn't it?'

'No, of course not. Take it from somebody who knows what it's like to make a mistake. The only person to blame is the person who made that mistake. Not the partner.'

'I suppose.'

'It's the truth. What I did with James was my mistake, just like what Chris did with Sarah was his mistake. If anything has happened with Chris and Katie then it's on them, not us.'

I nod my head and take another sip of wine, feeling its calming effect already starting to work on me.

'Thanks for this,' I say. 'It's much better than drinking alone.'

'No problem. We're friends, right?'

She smiles at me, and I can't help but smile back. Abi always has a way of making me feel good around her, much like Katie had the same way.

'You're a great guy, and whatever happens, you'll get through this,' Abi says, and now our eye contact isn't breaking. Our faces are quite close, and it wouldn't take much to bring them closer.

And that's when I let my confused emotions get the better of me and go in for a kiss.

'What are you doing?' Abi cries as she pulls away from me and gets up off the sofa.

'I'm sorry. I don't know,' I reply rather pathetically.

'Get out.'

'Wait, Abi, I-'

'Just go before Chris gets back.'

'But I need to speak to him.'

'You should have thought about that before you tried to kiss me.'

'I'm sorry! I'm all mixed up with everything that's going on.'

'So am I, but that doesn't mean you can do that.'

'I know. It was a mistake, I'm sorry.'

I don't know what I was thinking, and I get up off the sofa to try and apologise some more. But Abi isn't having any of it, and she tells me to leave again, so I guess I have no choice.

I hear her front door slam behind me as soon as I have stepped outside, and then I make the short walk back to my house feeling like the biggest idiot in the world. I shouldn't have done that, and I've probably ruined my friendship with Abi now. I guess I misread the signs. She really was just being nice to me and not wanting anything more. Thank God too, because what if she had kissed me back?

I reach my front door and wish Katie was inside. But she isn't, and I'm not sure when she will be back. I take out my phone and try to call her but there's no answer. I hope she's okay, but I'm aware that she is out on the street alone after dark. I should never have driven off, no matter how mad I was at her.

That's why I get back into my car and decide to try and find her.

45

I'm five minutes from my street now, but my feet aren't exactly rushing across this pavement as I go. That's because I'm not excited to get home. Why would I be? All that is waiting for me there is a husband who thinks I've betrayed him, so forgive me if I don't feel thrilled at the prospect of walking through my front door.

I know that the most direct route back to my house is by following this main road all the way up the hill, but I need a little more time than that, so I turn down a side street and decide to make a small loop of the area to allow myself more of a chance to collect my thoughts. As I do, I have the idea that perhaps my first port of call when I get back to my cul-de-sac shouldn't be to my own house. Rather, it should be to Number Two where I can hopefully speak to Albert and ask him why he felt the need to not only photograph Chris and I whenever we spoke, but also pass that information onto my husband as if I was doing something wrong.

I know Sean views what Albert has done as one man looking out for another, and I'm sure his heart was in the right place, but his actions

323

are definitely misguided. My marriage has nothing to do with anybody else, so who knows why Albert felt the need to stick his nose into it. But then I wonder if I brought this on myself by seeking advice from Eileen recently. She had to have shared what I told her with her husband because most couples share everything, and maybe that's why this has happened now. Eileen knew that Sean and I were having problems, passed that on to Albert, and he has put two and two together and come up with six. That's the only reason I can think of for this mess spiralling out of control.

I keep on walking, but it's getting chilly, and I hadn't exactly dressed for an evening stroll when I left to go to art class earlier, so I decide to stop wasting time and walk back the way I should be going. The sooner I bite the bullet and get home, the sooner this silly situation can be resolved. My plan is to go and speak to Albert first and let him know that he has made a mistake. Then I will go and speak to Sean and tell him that he either trusts me or he doesn't.

If he doesn't then I guess we are finished.

The thought of that brings a tear to my eye, but I wipe it away quickly and quicken my pace, determined to get back before I talk myself out of my determined mindset and end up adopting a weaker one instead.

I reach the sign for our cul-de-sac but spotting it fails to give me any of the warm, pleasant feelings one might usually get when they return to the place where they live. Instead, being on this street makes my stomach churn, and I think back to when I suggested to Sean that we move. That was what my instincts told me, and like Eileen said when she gave me her advice, instincts should always be trusted.

Walking up the road, I pass Number One as I go, and I notice that the curtains are still open in the living room, allowing me to have an unobstructed view right inside to see where Ian and Jackson are sitting on the sofa watching television. They don't see me, and I look away quickly in case they glance up, but at least it looks like they are having a more peaceful night than I am.

Next up is my house, which I'm planning to skip in order to go and speak to Albert, but I stop when I notice that Sean's car isn't on the drive. He should have been back by now after he drove off and left me on the street, but he's not. Where could he be?

I look around as if I'm magically going to see his car somewhere else on here, but there's no sign of it, so I can only imagine where he might be now. Driving around aimlessly, perhaps? Or maybe he's gone and checked himself into a hotel after feeling like he's too mad at me to sleep in the same house? Whatever he is doing, I remind myself that I have done nothing wrong and keep my belief that the truth will come out in the end.

It's as I am standing on my driveway wondering where my husband might be when I lose my confidence in going around to Number Two and having a go at Albert for what he has done. Maybe it's because he is elderly, or maybe it's because I'm just too soft for my own good, but I decide that I will speak to him in the morning. But I'm aware that the reason for my change of mind might also be because I've realised that my husband is not in the house now like I thought he would be, so suddenly, the prospect of going inside doesn't seem quite as daunting.

I walk to the front door but then curse out loud when I realise that I didn't bring a house key out with me this evening. I didn't see the need to because Sean was collecting me, but that was before we ended up going our separate ways.

Damn it. I'm locked out.

Looking back down the dark street at the main road at the end, I wonder how long Sean is going to be, and I suppose I better call him to find out. But then I suddenly remember that we have left a spare key underneath one of the bins that we store in the back garden, and I realise I will be able to get inside without my husband's help after all.

Opening the gate and walking down the side of the house, I almost fail to notice the dark shape at the bottom of the garden until it moves.

I let out a loud scream as I realise that somebody else is in this back garden with me, and that's all it takes for them to rush for the hedges. But as they go, they pass through a patch of moonlight on the grass, and I see their grey, hooded jacket beneath their face, which is covered by a balaclava.

'Hey!' I cry, figuring this must be the person that has been tormenting us for weeks, but they are gone almost as quickly as I saw them, disappearing through the broken fence at the back of the garden and leaving me standing alone, afraid and in shock.

I don't know who that was, but I do know one thing. It wasn't Jackson. I just saw him sitting on the sofa with his dad next door, so there's no way he could have got around here so fast. That means the teenager isn't the one who has been causing the trouble around here after all.

So who is it?

46

SEAN

I've been driving around for almost half an hour now, but I haven't been able to find Katie out on the streets. Either she's home already or something's happened to her, and I just have to pray that it's the former. We might be at war at the minute, but I still want her to be okay. Pulling over to the side of the road, I decide to try her mobile phone one more time before I complete the short drive back home. But when I take my phone out of my pocket, I see that I have five missed calls from my wife. Damn it, I must have accidentally flicked the switch on the side of my device to set it to silent.

Calling Katie back with a knot of anxiety in my stomach in case she was calling me because she was in trouble, I hope she will pick up and at least let me know that she is okay. But she doesn't answer, and that does nothing to ease my concerns.

Pulling away from the side of the road, I drive back home as fast as I can within the speed limits, hoping that I just missed spotting Katie when I was driving around and that she is already back before me. When I reach our driveway, I see a light on inside the house, and that makes me feel a little better because it must be her. She's home, so at least she's safe. Now there's just the small matter of dealing with all the problems we have.

I enter the house, unsure of what I'm going to say to my wife or what she might have planned to say to me, but I wasn't expecting to find her sitting at the kitchen table writing cards.

'There you are,' I say as I approach the table. 'I was driving around looking for you.'

'I used the spare key to get in,' she tells me without looking up from the table where she is continuing to write cards.

'What are you doing?'

'I'm writing invitations.'

'For what?'

'A barbecue.'

'What barbecue?'

'The one we're going to host this weekend.'

'What are you talking about?'

Katie keeps writing as I sit down at the table opposite her, and she only stops when I reach out and take hold of the pen in her hand so she can't keep ignoring me.

Finally, she looks up and stops what she is doing, and that's when I see the determined look in her eyes.

'I'm inviting all of our neighbours to a barbecue, and it's important that they all come.'

'You're doing what?'

'You heard.'

'I heard, but it doesn't make any sense. Why would you do something like that? We've got things to talk about, and do you really think I want to be in the same place as Chris, never mind Ian and Jackson?'

'You're going to have to put on your big boy pants and suck it up because they are all going to be here, and it's important that they are.'

'Why?'

'You'll see.'

Katie goes back to writing again, and I watch her working for a moment, all the while wondering if my wife's strange behaviour now is just her brain's way of trying to come to terms with being caught out with Chris earlier.

'We need to talk,' I tell her. 'I want the truth.'

'So do I,' she replies. 'That's why I'm doing this.'

That makes absolutely no sense to me either, and I bang the table in frustration. That seems to be enough to get Katie to realise that she needs to give me a little more information than that, so she stops writing again and looks at me.

'I have not cheated on you, and I will prove it,' Katie says. 'I also want you to know that Jackson was not the person who has been sneaking into our back garden all this time.'

'What? How do you know that?'

'Because there was somebody in our back garden tonight when I got home, and it definitely wasn't him because he was sitting on the sofa with his dad at the time.'

'There was somebody in our garden tonight?'

'Yes, but I'm fine. They ran off. But it wasn't Jackson.'

'You're sure?'

'Positive.'

I look around at the handwritten cards on the table, and Katie takes that as her cue to enlighten me on what she plans to do with them.

'I'm going to put these through the letterboxes of our neighbours' homes tonight, and I've made it clear that I need everybody to attend. Then when they're here, we might finally start to get some answers.'

'I don't get it.'

'You will do. Just trust me.'

I feel like I've heard that sentence a lot since we moved into this house, and it seems that I have to put my faith in trust again. I'm not sure it's got me very far before, but after what I attempted with Abi tonight, I feel like I might owe it to my wife, providing she has been as faithful to me as she insists she has been.

'Okay, fine,' I say, shrugging my shoulders. 'I trust you and whatever crazy plan you have concocted.'

'Good,' Katie says with a smile, and it's not the smile of a person who has something to hide or of a person who is worried about her relationship. Instead, it seems like the smile of a person who is in control and confident about what is going to happen next.

'Will you tell me what you're planning?' I ask her as she finishes putting the cards into envelopes and seals them all.

'You'll see,' she says before licking the last envelope and dropping it onto the pile with the others that are now ready to be delivered. 'Just make sure you've got that barbecue ready to go on Saturday.'

47

KATIE

I pour the salad out of its bag and into the large bowl before drizzling the dressing all over it and then place it onto the side with the rest of the food that will be served over the next hour or so. Before I move onto the next task, I glance out of the kitchen window, and I see that Sean is in position in front of the barbecue, although I'm not sure his food prep is going quite as well as mine. There seems to be an awful lot of smoke coming from the barbecue, and he's having a hard time seeing the sausages that are sizzling away on top of it. Bless him, he's never been the best chef and struggles even with a barbecue, which some might say is traditionally the man's domain. But he's trying his best, and that's all I can ask for.

The doorbell rings a few seconds later, and that tells me that our first guests have arrived, so I take off my apron and head out of the kitchen, but not before sticking my head out of the back door to let Sean know that the party is about to begin. When I open the front door, I see Ian and Jackson standing on our doorstep, neither of them looking particularly thrilled to be here but having both made an effort anyway. Ian is holding a four-pack of lager, and Jackson seems to be holding the same until his father assures me that the teenager's drinks are non-alcoholic as I welcome them and allow them inside.

I thank them for coming as I lead them through the house and out into the back garden where my husband is still battling a huge plume of black smoke from the barbecue, and Ian gives a chuckle when he sees him.

'I think you needed to clean it better before you started,' he tells Sean, and my husband initially looks a little annoyed at the piece of advice before he sees me mouthing to him to be polite and just lets out an awkward laugh instead.

'Take a seat, guys, I'll get you both a glass,' I say to the guests as I gesture towards a couple of the camping chairs that we have set out on the lawn.

'It's fine. We'll just drink out of the cans,' Ian tells me as he nods for his son to sit down, and I smile at them before heading back into the house.

Once I'm back in the kitchen, I make a quick check on the time and see that it has just gone two o'clock, which was the time I specified the barbecue was going to begin in my invitations. There are still four more guests to arrive, but I'm sure they will be here any minute now, and sure enough, it's not long until the doorbell goes again.

This time it's the turn of Albert and Eileen to step inside, and I thank them for the lovely dishes that they have brought around to accompany the food we are going to have today. Eileen tells me that she has made both a normal lasagne and a vegetarian one, and that's because she worried there be might a non-meat eater coming today, and barbecues tend not to be much fun for them. But Albert scoffs at that and tells me he is very much looking forward to tucking into a few burgers and sausages this afternoon, and I laugh as I take them into the kitchen where I give Eileen the chance to leave her handbag inside the house before we go out. She removes it from her shoulder as I place the lasagne dishes down, and then I lead the couple out into the garden and let them start making small talk with the others.

Everything is going well so far as I start making a cup of tea for Albert because apparently, it's far too early in the day for him to start drinking yet. But his wife doesn't seem to share the same opinion because she has asked me for a whiskey which I am now pouring her from out of Sean's stash.

I return to the garden to hand over the drinks, and when I do, the conversation is as sparse and awkward as I suspected it would be in these early proceedings.

I approach my husband over on the smoky side of the garden and ask him how it's going.

'Fine,' he replies as he pokes and prods a couple of the sausages on the grill.

'Don't forget to talk to everybody,' I tell him with a wry smile, and he rolls his eyes before taking a swig from the bottle of beer that I furnished him with earlier.

'Can't you just wake me up when this is over?' he says to me, but I ignore his comment and give him a kiss before the sound of the doorbell goes again.

My husband instantly looks tense, and that's because he knows who it is at the door. It will be the couple from Number Three, and as much as he's not enjoying having Ian and Jackson here after their previous altercations, I know he's feeling even more awkward about having Chris and Abi in the house.

'It's going to be okay,' I tell him before leaving the barbecue and going inside to answer the door.

I take a deep breath before opening it because of who is on the other side, but I need to push through this and get it over with, so I turn the handle and then put a smile on my face as I welcome Chris and Abi to the barbecue.

Chris seems as pleased to see me as he usually is, but Abi seems a little off with me. But I don't let that distract me from what I have planned today, so I lead them through the house, accept the bottle of wine they have brought and then tell them to head out into the garden and take a seat because the food should be just about ready now.

They do as they are told, and I watch from the kitchen window as they say hi to the other guests before I see Sean give an awkward nod towards Chris while Abi just takes a seat and says nothing to anybody.

Everybody is here, and this is what I was hoping for.

Now it's time to get to work.

48

SEAN

Well, this is just as uncomfortable as I thought it would be. I'm cooking for all of my neighbours, including the man who almost pressed charges against me for assault and trespassing, as well as the man I suspected of having an affair with my wife. And to top it all off, the woman who I almost kissed in a stupid moment of weakness is here too, and not only that, but she is now chatting with Katie. Talk about a complicated social gathering in the garden. My nerves feel as if they are as overcooked as these sausages on the grill in front of me. But despite my misgivings about this whole situation, my wife keeps urging me to trust her, so I guess that's what I must do. But I can't wait for this barbecue to be over. Maybe then some of this will start to make sense.

'These sausages are lovely,' Eileen says from her seat behind me. 'Compliments to the chef.'

'Thank you,' I say, and I wave my cooking tongs in the polite old lady's direction before doing my best not to burn the next batch. I think she's just being kind because I definitely burnt those sausages, but I'll take any compliments about my cooking any time, whether they are genuine or fake.

I've been standing at the barbecue ever since our guests started arriving, and I'm planning on spending as long as I can here because it's giving me a great opportunity to avoid sitting with them and making small talk. I know Katie won't be impressed by my distinct lack of social skills so far, but this event was her idea, not mine, so I feel like I'm entitled to do whatever I can to get through it. Having my back to everybody is a good tactic to make this whole thing easier, as is the beer that I have to hand at the side of the barbecue too. But I realise I'm going to have to turn around and face everybody again when Jackson calls my name.

'Hey, Sean,' he says, and I turn around to see him chewing a hot dog as he speaks. 'Your grass is looking better now.'

I stare at the teenager, and I can't tell if he is being sarcastic or not because I can never tell with him. All I can do is nod my head and say thanks before telling him that I've tried putting some new fertiliser on it, and it seems to be responding a little better than the last one I tried.

Turning back to the barbecue, I think about how Katie was adamant that Jackson was not the person who has been sneaking into our garden, which would mean that he was not to blame for the broken plant pots, the broken window and the damaged camera, as well as my plant pot that ended up in next door's garden, and that Ian was not able to explain when I asked him. My wife hasn't told me who else could have caused all of that trouble, just that it isn't the teenager who lives next door, but until I get evidence of it being somebody else then I will remain sceptical. Of course, if it is somebody other than Jackson then it would mean that all the drama I caused next door when I was hauled away by the police was a silly mistake on my part, so it seems I will have a certain amount of pride to swallow if it does turn out to be somebody else. But until then I am remaining on my guard around the teenager, and indeed his father.

'This wine is lovely,' I hear my wife say, and I look over my shoulder to see that Chris has picked up the bottle he brought and is now showing her something on the label. Meanwhile, Abi is sitting quietly beside her husband, running her fork through the salad on her plate, and it doesn't look as if she has much of an appetite. I'll take that as more of a sign of her awkwardness at being here with me after I tried and failed to kiss her than the fact that my cooking is bad. But I make sure I turn around and look back at the barbecue before she can look up at me.

I have no idea if she told Chris about what almost happened between us, but I have to assume not because he hasn't come around to my house and had a go at me about it. I'm grateful for that because it means that Katie still doesn't know about it, and I'm hoping that she never will. But I am curious as to how Chris explained himself to his wife when she would have asked him what was happening with Katie after I went to their house that night and made my claims about Chris and Katie's potential affair. Did Abi bring it up with him? Did they argue? Did he have an explanation? If so, I presume he has pleaded his innocence and begged for trust just like Katie did with me. But that's still an awful lot of unanswered questions, and the longer this barbecue goes on, the more I'm beginning to wonder what it is exactly that my wife has planned.

It seems that I am going to be left to wonder some more because it's only a few minutes later when Katie gets up from her seat and walks over to me before telling me that she has to go inside for a little while and that I am to make sure our guests are entertained until she gets back.

'You can't leave me on my own,' I urge her under my breath.

'I'll be right back. You'll be fine,' she tells me, but I'm not as convinced of that as she is. But she's already walking away before I can say anything else to her without everybody hearing me, so I'm left standing with the tongs in my hand, the crispy sausages below me and our six neighbours looking at me and waiting for their host to initiate the next conversation.

'So,' I say, picking up my beer and racking my brains for something that we can all talk about for the next few minutes until my wife returns. 'What do we think about this good weather we're having?'

49

KATIE

I creep up the stairs as quietly as I can, even though I know that I have the house to myself. I can hear the voices in the garden where the barbecue is still in full swing, and I feel pleased that my husband has managed to keep the conversation going somehow amongst our guests, because the last thing I need is for people to get bored and start leaving early.

They can't leave until I have done what I need to do, so I better be quick about it.

Reaching the top of the stairs, I look along the landing at the three doors up here. They are all closed, so I am just going to have to work through them one by one until I hopefully find what I am looking for. Opening door number one, I see that this is the bathroom, and that tells me that this house has exactly the same layout as my own. I try to tell myself that the familiar layout can set me at ease and almost make me think that I am just walking around upstairs in my own place, but I'm not in my own place, so it isn't that simple.

Looking around the bathroom, I don't see anything of interest because all there is here are the usual fittings that one would expect in a room like this. I wasn't expecting to find what I was looking for in here anyway, so I move on to door number two.

I expect this to be the master bedroom because that's what would be behind the door in my house, and sure enough it is. I see the double bed, a couple of bedside tables and a large wardrobe, but there are no discarded items of clothing on display, unlike my own bedroom, which could definitely do with a tidy up. Hurrying over to the wardrobe, I fling the doors open and look inside, my eyes scanning the rack of dresses, shirts and coats that hang down from the rail. I rummage through them all with my hands and make sure to check behind, below and above the clothes too, but I still don't see what I am looking for, so I close the wardrobe and move on to the bedside tables.

Opening the drawers on the tables, I rummage through piles of underwear, thinking how I would hate it if somebody was going through my intimate things like this, but not allowing myself to feel guilty because that might make me stop, and I have come too far for that now. But a search of the bedside tables yields no fruit either, and I'm just about to leave the room and move onto the last door when I decide to check under the bed.

Dropping to my hands and knees, I lift the edge of the duvet up and peer under the bed, and I see several suitcases under here, presumably stored out of the way until the homeowners need them to go on holiday. I run my hand across them all to make sure they are empty, and they seem to be, so I let out a sigh and get back to my feet before making sure the duvet is left hanging exactly as it was before I moved it.

Leaving the master bedroom, I head for the third and final door up here, and I already know this will be the spare bedroom because it's the same in my place. For me, it's the spot where I do my artwork, but I don't know what the residents of this house tend to use it for, so I'm intrigued to find out.

Opening the door, I look inside, and it instantly feels as if I've been put into a capsule and sent back in time. Everything here looks like it's straight out of the seventies and eighties, and it almost feels like one of those ghost towns where the residents just left one day and the evidence of their former lives remained behind, trapped in time forever.

Walking into the room, I take a moment to look at some of the posters on the wall as well as some of the trophies on the shelves and the photos on the dressing table. But as interesting as this all is, I still haven't found what I am looking for, so I need to stop getting distracted and focus on the task at hand.

Opening up the wardrobe in here, I see that there isn't much hanging on the rails and that most of the clothes seem to be folded neatly in a pile at the bottom of the unit. I almost didn't bother to check through them, but something makes me pause at the last second, and I decide to go through the clothes just in case.

I don't know what it was, but maybe you could call it instinct.

Whatever it was, I'm glad it worked because no sooner have I checked under the first item of clothing at the bottom of the wardrobe then I find the first thing I am looking for.

It's a grey coat.

And underneath that is the really damning piece of evidence I needed to find.

It's a balaclava.

50

SEAN

I keep checking the back door to the house for any sign of my wife returning, but so far, there has been none. I don't know where she has got to, but I can feel myself getting more irritated at her by the minute because she has left me with all the guests at this barbecue that it was her idea to organise.

I've done my best to keep the conversation going, but if I'm honest, my heart isn't really in it, and I think some of the other people here have started to realise that. Jackson is looking at his father like he wants to leave, Albert and Eileen are munching solemnly on some burgers and Chris and Abi have barely said a word to each other in the last five minutes, let alone to me or anyone else. This barbecue is in danger of dying quickly, and I don't think that's what Katie wants because apparently, this was all part of some kind of plan of hers. But whatever it is, I have to say that it doesn't seem to have worked. That is until I suddenly see the back door open, and my wife re-enters the garden with something in her hand.

Our guests look up from their food when they hear Katie arriving back, and like me, I'm sure they are all wondering why the hell she is carrying a grey coat and a balaclava in her hands. First of all, I'd like to know where she got the balaclava from because it's not the kind of thing people carry around with them and second of all, I'd like to know what she thinks she is going to do with it. But before anybody can say anything, Katie throws the balaclava and coat down onto the grass, right at the feet of two of our guests.

'It's been you all this time,' she says with venom in her voice. 'You've been sneaking into our garden, and you've been spreading lies and rumours about our neighbours so that we would get ourselves into trouble. The only question I have for you is why? Why would you do all of this to us?'

I stare at my wife with my mouth wide open, in stunned disbelief at her little performance, and I'm not the only one who looks shocked. Ian and Jackson are shocked, Chris and Abi are shocked, and most of all, Albert and Eileen are shocked, but that could be because the old couple are the ones who Katie has just directed her tirade at.

Everybody turns to look at Albert and Eileen to see what their response is going to be, and I'll admit that I'm as intrigued as anybody. Does Katie really think that these two are the ones behind everything that has been going on since we moved in?

'I'm sorry, are we playing some kind of a game?' Eileen asks as Albert leans forward in his seat and picks the balaclava up off the grass.

'You know what I'm talking about,' Katie continues. 'This is the balaclava and coat your husband was wearing when he was in my garden the other night. I found it in your spare bedroom!'

'You've been in our house?' Albert asks, looking up from the supposed pieces of evidence to my wife's angry face.

'Yes, that's why I invited you all around. I needed to get you out of the house so I could look for that. And I found it!'

'How did you get in our house?' Eileen asks me as Albert continues to look at the coat and balaclava as if they are some foreign objects that he has no explanation for.

'I took the key from your handbag just after you arrived,' Katie replies with a smug grin on her face, and Eileen doesn't seem thrilled about that, as one would imagine.

Albert and Eileen share a puzzled look with each other, and that gives the rest of the confused bystanders a chance to interrupt.

'What the hell is going on?' Abi asks first, beating me to that exact question by a millisecond.

349

'What's going on is that for some reason, Albert and Eileen have been trying to ruin mine and my husband's lives with their lies!'

'I really don't know what you're talking about, dear,' Eileen tries, but it's obvious that it is going to take a lot more than that to satisfy my raging wife now.

'Yeah, you're not the only one,' Ian pipes up, and for the first time since this little drama began, everybody looks away from Albert and Eileen and towards my wife for some kind of a proper explanation.

'When we first moved in here, Albert and Eileen paid us a visit,' she begins, and I think back to the night they came to our house not long after we had finished unpacking our things. 'They were welcoming us onto the street, but they also told us they had a few things they needed to warn us about.'

'What things?' Chris asks, and I feel like that might be a chance for me to jump in and help my wife because at least I can answer that question. But I still have no idea where Katie is going with this.

'They told us that Jackson was trouble and that he had a history of sneaking onto other people's properties and causing damage,' I say, and I see Ian and Jackson both raise their eyebrows in exactly the same fashion, looking very much like the father and son duo that they are. 'And they told us that Chris and Abi would look to seduce us and that we should stay away from them at all costs.'

Now it's the turn of Chris and Abi to raise their eyebrows, but Katie doesn't miss a beat and stays on the offensive.

'That's right. You told us those things,' she says to the old couple. 'You made us think that things were happening when they weren't, and made us jump to conclusions that were wrong. Jackson wasn't in our garden, and Chris and Abi weren't trying to seduce us. They were just being friendly! But you made us think the worst about these people, and because of that, it brought out the worst in us!'

'That's quite a story,' Eileen says, and she turns to her husband with a shake of the head. 'I think it's time we were going.'

'Fine! Leave if you want to!' Katie cries. 'But I'm calling the police, and I'm going to have them look into you two because you're seriously screwed up!'

'How dare you talk to us like that,' Albert suddenly snaps, and he gets up out of his seat a lot quicker than when he originally sat down in it. Are his usual weary, slow movements all an act? Is he actually a lot nimbler than he was letting on? He must be if he was the one in our garden and not Jackson.

'How dare you try and drive a wedge between me and my husband!' Katie fires back as Eileen stands up too and reaches out to her husband to get him to come with her. But Albert doesn't move, and he looks like he has something to get off his chest.

'Stop being so self-absorbed,' Albert tells my wife with disdain in his voice. 'This was never about you two. It was about this house. You were just in the way.'

'What the hell does that mean?' I ask him.

'It means this house should never have been built. We petitioned against it, and we did what we could, but we lost, and this street has never been the same since.'

'You're mad at us for somebody else building this house?'

'Yes, I'm mad at you. And the previous owners! And the owners before that! Because none of you should have been here! This was a beautiful space that me and my wife got to look at every day until the builders moved in and spoilt it for us!'

I look around at both my wife and everybody else sitting in their seats with their food going cold on their plates, but everybody seems just as baffled as I am.

'You made up all these lies because you wanted us to hate being here and move out? Is that it?' I ask.

'Albert, we really should be going,' Eileen says, and she tries to take her husband's hand again, but he doesn't budge.

'Yeah, that's it,' Albert admits, looking me straight in the eye. 'And you two were so gullible that you believed us. Just like James and Sarah did and just like Greg did before that.'

'What do you mean by that?' Katie asks. 'You did this with the others.'

'Yes, we did, and they bought it all too, hook, line and sinker,' Albert says, and he almost seems proud of himself. 'Greg went and got himself a restraining order, James and Sarah had an affair and broke up, and we got our way because they all moved out. Then it was your turn.'

'What the hell have you done?' Ian says as he gets to his feet and steps towards Albert, making the older man take a small step backwards. 'You spread rumours about my son, so people thought he was trouble? That's why we've had so many problems over the years?'

Albert says nothing, so we all take that as a yes. Then it's the turn of Chris to stand up and start piecing his involvement in this together.

'Why would you tell people that me and Abi would try and seduce them?' he asks.

'Because it would instantly mean that everything you did to them from that point on would seem like flirting, and that would lead to

353

them having all sorts of different thoughts that they would never have had if they thought you were just being friendly.'

'So that's why James and Sarah ended up getting close to us,' Abi says with disgust on her face. 'They thought we liked them too, and it led to all of us making a mistake and cheating on our partners?'

'That was all your fault, but yes, we helped start the ball rolling,' Albert replies.

'What do you stand to gain from all of this?' Katie asks, and that's probably the best question so far because as crazy as all of this is, I still haven't been able to figure that one out.

'Albert, come on, we need to go,' Eileen tries again, and she goes to leave, but Jackson stands up and blocks her path, and she doesn't fancy her chances of forcing her way past an angry teenage boy.

'No, it's okay. They have a right to know,' Albert says, and he steps beside his wife to show that he is ready and willing to protect her from Jackson or anybody else who is angry with her. 'Since this fourth house was built, we've been making it our job to try and get people to find a reason to leave again. We've been hoping that eventually the house will get such a bad reputation after all the quick sales that nobody will want it, and it will one day be torn down by the same useless council who agreed to build it.'

'You did all of this to get us to move out?' I ask, and Albert nods.

'Why the hell didn't you just move if you couldn't stand this new house spoiling your view?' Abi asks, and Eileen suddenly feels compelled to answer that one.

'Why should we move? We've been here for over forty years! We raised our son here! We're not the problem, this house is!'

Albert takes his wife's hand as she wipes away a tear with the other one, and it's obvious now just how much emotion is tied up in all of this for them. But I don't think that's quite going to garner them any sympathy from their hostile audience, and Katie just proves it a few seconds later.

'I want you out of this house, and I want you off this street as soon as possible, or I swear to God I'll kill you,' my wife says, and I'd be impressed with her threat if I wasn't so afraid of it too.

Albert finally takes that as his cue to leave, and he leads his wife away while Katie escorts them out, presumably to make sure they don't mess with anything else in the house before they're gone.

While the conniving old couple are being shown out, the rest of us who live on this street stare at each other in silent shock and wonder what the hell happens next. I guess we'll all have to sit down and discuss it properly before making a decision. Before we do, I turn back to the barbecue to see that the sausages that were cooking on there are now burnt to a crisp. But somehow, I think that's the least of our problems.

51

KATIE

Five months have passed since that dramatic day in our back garden when we had all our neighbours around for a barbecue. A lot has happened in that time, but the most important thing to occur is that a 'SOLD' notice has just been fixed to the 'For Sale' sign outside Number Two. Albert and Eileen have done what we requested of them and sold their house, and now they are finally leaving this street for good.

After the scheming elderly couple left the barbecue that day, Sean and I spoke with the rest of our neighbours about everything that had happened. There were apologies and even a few tears as we all worked our way through our history on this street and realised that so much of what had happened had been set in motion by the thoughts that Albert and Eileen had put in our heads. Ian and Jackson had never understood why their next-door neighbours would get angry with them and threaten violence, just like Chris and Abi had never known the full scope of why those who lived at Number Two A always seemed to become enamoured with them and risk their relationships. We knew then that Greg,

James and Sarah had just been victims of a cold and calculated game and that Sean and I were very close to falling foul of it too. If I hadn't gone into the back garden for the spare key that night so quickly after seeing Jackson at home then I might never have started to figure it all out. But I did, and that's how I saw the grey coat worn by the intruder. It was the same grey coat that I had seen hanging on a hook in the hallway of Eileen's home when I had gone round to visit her. Then all I had to do was trace back all the problems we had to the night Albert and Eileen came to our house and gave us their 'friendly' warnings, and I realised who the real problem was on this street.

It's funny that we spent all the time we lived here worrying about those at Number One and Number Three when it was the old, sweet couple at Number Two who were really the threat. Sean and I battled feelings of jealousy and lust when it came to Chris and Abi after being told that they would most likely be trying to seduce us, and Sean lost his temper and almost ended up with a criminal record after being led to believe that Jackson was the intruder in the garden. But all along it was Albert who was in our garden, and he even later admitted to being the one who had damaged our lawn so that it would never grow properly when we went around to speak to them later that night. He confessed that he had been so blinded with his hatred of our house that he was willing to do anything, big or small, to make it an awful place to live so that over time, nobody would want to live there anymore, and it might be knocked down again. It was a crazy plan, ambitious but flawed because he and his wife could never have known for sure that it would work in the long run. But they were certainly willing to try, and being retired, they had plenty of time on their hands to do it.

When Sean and I went round to Albert and Eileen's after the barbecue, we weren't just going for more answers. We went there to give them an ultimatum.

"Leave the street, or we would go to the police."

Albert initially put up a fight and said that we lacked evidence, but Sean was in no mood to argue and told the man that even if the police failed to get them, the other neighbours would. He said that as a collective, everyone else on this street would make Albert and Eileen's lives so miserable for the rest of their days that they would wish they had never moved there, and that seemed to do the job in convincing them that maybe it was time to sell up and buy in a different part of town.

It might have seemed a little harsh to force an old couple out of the home that they had not only raised a child in but spent most of their adult lives in themselves, but I only had to think of how close Sean and I came to breaking up after what they instigated, as well as the fact that it came too late for James and Sarah, who divorced, and Greg who carries a stain on his record forever. But it's not just those of us who lived at Number Two A that suffered. The other neighbours did too, and it's hard not to believe that both Chris and Abi, and Ian and Jackson have had their lives altered and affected by what Albert and Eileen did.

Would Chris and Abi ever have betrayed each other if James and Sarah hadn't believed they were a couple of adventurous lovers and got too close to them for comfort? Maybe but then again, maybe not, and it's a fine line between two couples staying faithful to each other and one of them getting a divorce and selling their house. And what about Ian and Jackson, two poor people who had to put up with neighbours banging on their door and accusing them of all sorts? They could easily have reacted badly to that and ended up in trouble with the police themselves, although it's not much consolation that Greg took the punishment for accusing Jackson of doing something that Albert actually did.

Now the truth has come to light, things are much better between us and our other neighbours. Sean and I see Chris and Abi on a regular basis, no longer living in fear that we are being secretly seduced by them, and Sean and

Ian have also been known to enjoy a beer together from time to time now. Even Jackson is a little more friendly with us, although he's still a teenager, so there is a limit to how friendly he is with anyone. But all in all, we get along with each other now that we aren't dealing with all those horrible pre-conceived notions that Albert and Eileen fed us on day one.

In the end, everybody on this street felt it was the right thing to do to ask Albert and Eileen to leave, and reluctantly, they agreed. Now they have gone, and that means everybody else's troubles should be at an end. It also means that we are going to get a new neighbour or two. Forgive me if I'm not overly excited about that idea, but I've had enough of neighbours for a while. But I'll try not to let that colour my mood towards whoever is taking over the occupation of the house next door.

Sean and I don't know who the new buyer is, just like Chris, Abi, Ian and Jackson don't know either, but we don't care. Whoever it is, they can't be any worse than the previous owners, that's for sure.

EPILOGUE

I've almost finished unpacking my things into my new home when I hear the knock at the front door. I'm not sure who it is but if I had to guess, I'd say it might be one of my new neighbours popping round to welcome me onto the street. Sure enough, when I open the door, I see two smiling faces standing before me. It's a man and a woman and they tell me their names are Sean and Katie and that they live at Number Two A, which is the house right next door to me.

I shake their hands and thank them for their welcome before giving them my name, which I tell them is Martin, and letting them know that it will just be me occupying this house. That's right. No wife, no kids.

Just me.

Katie rather flatteringly calls me an eligible bachelor and Sean jokes that he's jealous of me which gets him a playful punch from his wife, and I laugh along at all the hilarity with the good grace and humour of a new neighbour who just wants to fit in to his next area and make friends.

Sean and Katie ask me if I have met any of the other neighbours yet and I say that I have not, but that I am very much looking forward to doing so, which is true in a way. Then they wish me good luck in settling in and let me know that I should feel free to call around at theirs anytime if I ever need anything, even if it's just a cup of tea and a chat.

They seem like a lovely couple, and I thank them again before waving them off and closing my front door. Then I return to the last remaining box that needs unpacking and carry it upstairs into the spare bedroom where I will take out the contents and put them on display. It feels strange being back in this room again after so many years, but it's almost exactly as I remember it and that's because the previous owners have left this room in the same condition that it's been in forever.

It's those previous owners who are on my mind now as I open the box and take out the photo frame inside which shows the pair of them smiling into the camera. Then I put the frame on the dressing table in here, beside all the photos of me from my childhood and below all my posters and trophies that have been here since I originally called this house my home over forty years ago.

With the last box unpacked, all there is left to do then is take out my mobile phone and make a call. When it connects, it's Eileen who answers it.

'Hi Mum,' I say. 'I'm in.'

'Wonderful dear,' she says to me down the line before calling for her husband to tell him the good news too. Then I tell her that I have already met Katie and Sean and that they were more than gracious in welcoming me to the street. But my mother tells me to be careful around them and that they are not as stupid as they look, and I know to heed that warning because they were responsible for the downfall of my parents on this street, and I can't let them do the same thing to me.

I tell Mum that I will be round to her new house for roast dinner this Sunday and that I'll take Dad to his new local pub for a couple of pints afterwards, before I say goodbye and hang up the phone. Then I walk over to the window and look out onto the cul-de-sac and a wry smile curls up the edges of my lips.

Having moved back all the way from Australia to be here, it's been quite the lifestyle change, but I'd do anything for my mum and dad, and that's why I agreed to their idea about me buying their old home. They were forced to sell it by the other residents on this street, but none of them has to know who they really sold it to. My parents have kept the house in the family, as it should be, and that means I can keep their plan alive.

I am introducing myself as Martin to disguise the fact that my real name is George, but it's my surname that is the most important thing to keep a secret. It's the same as Albert and Eileen's, of course, and it will give me away should anybody on this street discover it. So I'll just have to make sure that they don't.

As I stand at the window, I feel like this doesn't compare to Australia.

It's actually better.

That because it's good to be home.

And it's certainly going to be good to mess with my new neighbours.

Download My Free Book

If you would like to receive a FREE copy of my psychological thriller 'Just One Second' then you can find the book at my website www.danielhurstbooks.com

LETTER FROM THE AUTHOR

Thank you for reading *The Neighbours* and I hope you had as much fun delving into the lives of Katie, Sean and the rest of the residents of the cul-de-sac as I had creating them. I love to write, and I hope my story gave you a little entertainment and escapism from the realities of the world.

Without readers like you, I wouldn't be living my dream as a full-time author, so thank you for picking up this book and thank you for any review you may choose to leave for it afterwards. Reviews really are the most powerful way of getting attention for my books as they help bring in new readers. If you have enjoyed this book then I would be extremely grateful if you could spend a couple of minutes leaving an honest review on Amazon or Goodreads (it can be as short as you like).

Thank you and I hope you enjoy your next read.

Daniel

Also By Daniel Hurst

TIL DEATH DO US PART

What if your husband was your worst enemy?

Megan thinks that she has the perfect husband and the perfect life. Craig works all day so that she doesn't have to, leaving her free to relax in their beautiful and secluded country home. But when she starts to long for friends and purpose again, Megan applies for a job in London, much to her husband's disappointment. She thinks he is upset because she is unhappy. But she has no idea.

When Megan secretly attends an interview and meets a recruiter for a drink, Craig decides it is time to act. Locking her away in their home, Megan realises that her husband never had her best interests at heart. Worse, they didn't meet by accident. Craig has been planning it all from the start.

As Megan is kept shut away from the world with only somebody else's diary for company, she starts to uncover the lies, the secrets, and the fact that she isn't actually Craig's first wife after all...

OUT NOW

THE WOMAN AT THE DOOR

It was a perfect Saturday night. *Until she knocked on the door...*

Rebecca and Sam are happily married and enjoying a typical Saturday night until a knock at the door changes everything. There's a woman outside, and she has something to say. Something that will change the happy couple's relationship forever...

With their marriage thrown into turmoil, Rebecca no longer knows who to trust, while Sam is determined to find out who that woman was and why she came to their house. But the problem is that he doesn't know who she is and why she has targeted them.

Desperate to save his marriage, Sam is willing to do anything to find the truth, even if it means breaking the law. But as time goes by and things only seem to get worse, it looks like he could lose Rebecca forever.

Nobody knows the woman at the door. *But she knows you.*

OUT NOW

THE TUTOR

What if you invited danger into your home?

Amy is a loving wife and mother, to her husband Nick, and her two children, Michael and Bella. It's that dedication to her family that causes her to seek help for her teenage son when it becomes apparent that he is going to fail his end of school exams.

Enlisting the help of a professional tutor, Amy is certain that she is doing the best thing for her son, and indeed, her family. But when she discovers that there is more to this tutor than meets the eye, it is already too late.

With the rest of her family enamoured by the tutor, Amy is the only one who can see that there is something not quite right about her. But as the tutor becomes more involved in Amy's family, it's not just the present that is threatened. Secrets from the past are exposed too, and by the time everything is out in the open, Amy isn't just worried about her son and his exams anymore. She is worried for the survival of her entire family.

OUT NOW

371

RUN AWAY WITH ME

What if your partner was wanted by the police?

Laura is feeling content with her life. She is married, she has a good home, and she is due to give birth to her first child any day now. But her perfect world is shattered when her husband comes home flustered and afraid. He's made a terrible mistake. He's done a bad thing. *And now the police are going to be looking for him.*

There's only one way out of this. He wants to run. *But he won't go without his wife…*

Laura knows it is wrong. She knows they should stay and face the music. But she doesn't want to lose her man. She can't raise this baby alone. *So she agrees to go with him.* But life on the run is stressful and unpredictable and as time goes by, Laura worries she has made a terrible mistake. They should never have ran. But it's too late for that now. Her life is ruined. The only question is: *how will it end?*

OUT NOW

THE ROLE MODEL

She raised her. Now she must help her…

Heather is a single mum who has always done what's best for her daughter, Chloe. From childhood up to the age of seventeen, Chloe has been no trouble. That is until one night when she calls her mother with some shocking news.

There's been an accident. *And now there's a dead body…*

As always, Heather puts her daughter's safety before all else, but this might be one time when she goes too far. Instead of calling the emergency services, Heather hides the body, saving her daughter from police interviews and public outcry.

But as she well knows, everything she does has an impact on her child's behaviour, and as time goes on and the pair struggle to keep their sordid secret hidden, Heather begins to think that she hasn't been such a good mum after all. *In fact, she might have been the worst role model ever…*

OUT NOW

THE BROKEN VOWS

He broke his word to her. Now she wants revenge…

Alison is happily married to Graham, or at least she is until she finds out that he has been cheating on her. Graham has broken the vows he made on his wedding day. How could he do it? It takes Alison a while to figure it out, but at least she has time on her side. *Only that is where she is wrong.*

A devastating diagnosis means the clock is ticking down on her life now and if she wants revenge on her cheating partner then she is going to have to act fast. Alison does just that, implementing a dangerous and deadly plan, and it's one that will have far reaching consequences for several people, including her clueless husband.

Hell hath no fury like a woman scorned…

OUT NOW

INFLUENCE

Would you kill for a million followers?

Emily Bennett dreams of being a social media influencer, just like her idols, Mason Manor & Ivy Lane. But shortly after Ivy's untimely death she is contacted by a secretive businessman who offers her the chance at the fame and fortune she so desperately craves.

While Emily initially gets to experience the things she has always wanted, it soon becomes clear that her new employer had sinister motives for approaching her and it isn't long before she discovers that the life of her dreams comes with the kind of conditions that are the stuff of nightmares.

Social media isn't life or death.

It's more important than that.

OUT NOW

THE 20 MINUTE SERIES

20 Chapters. 20 Characters. 20 intertwining stories.

An original psychological thriller series showing how we are all more connected to each other than we think.

What readers are saying:

"If you like people watching then you will love these books!"

"The psychological insight was fascinating, the stories were absorbing and the characters were 3D. I absolutely loved it."

"The books in this series are an incredibly easy read, you become invested in the lives of the characters so easily and I am eager to know more and more. Roll on the next book."

THE 20 MINUTES SERIES (in order)

20 MINUTES ON THE TUBE
20 MINUTES LATER
20 MINUTES IN THE PARK
20 MINUTES ON HOLIDAY
20 MINUTES BY THE THAMES
20 MINUTES AT HALLOWEEN
20 MINUTES AROUND THE BONFIRE
20 MINUTES BEFORE CHRISTMAS
20 MINUTES OF VALENTINE'S DAY
20 MINUTES TO CHANGE A LIFE
20 MINUTES IN LAS VEGAS
20 MINUTES IN THE DESERT
20 MINUTES ON THE ROAD

About The Author

Daniel Hurst lives in the North West of England with his wife, Harriet, and considers himself extremely fortunate to be able to write stories every day for his readers.

You can visit him at his online home www.danielhurstbooks.com

You can connect with Daniel on Facebook at www.facebook.com/danielhurstbooks or on Instagram at www.instagram.com/danielhurstbooks

He is always happy to receive emails from readers at daniel@danielhurstbooks.com and replies to every single one.

Thank you for reading.

Daniel